# Lori Hayes

## *High Tide*

A Crystal Coast Novel

Published in the United States by Seaquine Publishing

ISBN: 978-0-9993988-3-8

## DEDICATION

I want to thank Marilyn Acker for moving to the coast and for introducing me to the most amazing place on earth, including the wild horses of Shackleford Banks. With her support and encouragement, I became a writer.

# Other books by Lori Hayes

High Tide

Coffee Break

## Also writing as Lisa Morgan

Christmas Horse

Troubled Hearts

Mystery Horse

Running Wild

Trail Trouble

# *ACKNOWLEDGMENTS*

I want to thank Carolyn Mason and Anita Kimball from the Foundation for Shackleford Horses for answering all my questions, and for sharing your interesting stories. Thank you for your endless service in helping the wild horses.

I also want to thank equine veterinarian extraordinaire, Dr. John Seal, for answering my many questions while writing this book. Any mistakes are clearly my own.

And last but not least, I want to thank Marilyn and Ronald Keizer for all their long hours editing this book. I also want to thank Ronald for being a patient packhorse so I could explore the island and photograph the horses.

# CHAPTER ONE

The weathered stallion jerked his head from the island sea grass and glared at Claire Kincaid. His snort rang through the air, the intensity of his warning jolting through her body. Chills ran down her arms. He wanted her to retreat but her feet refused to move.

He sat back on his haunches, a daunting rear that suspended in place for a long moment. As if to emphasize his point, he struck out with his front leg in a slow and deliberate motion.

With a camera slung around her neck, Claire thrust her folded arms upward to protect her head from the stallion's beating hooves. Surprised when nothing happened, she peeked from a small cavity between her elbow and hand. Her heart raced faster. He was pawing the sand, ready to attack. Claire's slight frame would be no match against eight-hundred pounds of wild horse.

Quickly, she scanned the area for his herd and realized she had walked between the stallion and one of his mares, a big mistake. Not wanting to agitate him further, Claire commanded her feet to move. Carefully she backed away and relaxed her body in an attempt to mollify the stallion. She tilted her head downward and studied him through loose wisps of her black hair.

Even though she'd backed away, his body was still tense. Claire assumed a more submissive position by turning sideways. If the stallion perceived her as harmless, he might even allow her to follow the herd tonight. She could use the horses' keen sense of hearing and smell to protect herself against the unknown. The last passenger ferry of the day had inexplicably departed twenty minutes earlier than scheduled, leaving her stranded on the desolate North Carolina barrier island.

The stallion stopped pawing and stood motionless, no longer ready to attack but still on high alert. She waited patiently, using her peripheral vision to monitor his body language. At last, he relaxed his body and turned away, but not enough to permit her to move closer.

Claire was counting on the predictability of herd behavior. Indirectly, she watched the stallion but he seemed in no hurry to grant her permission to move closer.

She'd have to be patient. Despite her predicament, she allowed herself to inhale slow, deep breaths of the fresh sea air. A faint fishy smell danced on the breeze. The tang of sea salt dotted her chapped lips, tasting oddly reassuring. The island held familiarity, as if she'd returned home after years away.

Somehow, she knew deep in her bones that her father, a man she barely remembered, had been to this windswept island before, and recently. She needed to find Robert Kincaid, to fill that empty place in her heart marked "family."

The stallion's casual movement caught her attention. He turned his back to her and lowered his head to eat a clump of grass. The subtle communication offered Claire acceptance and admittance to the herd's perimeter. She picked up her daypack from the sand and edged closer.

To her delight, the herd seemed to ignore her. She watched as a faded brown mare pawed the beach in search of drinking water, a sharp reminder that Claire had packed only enough water for a day trip. She should have brought more to eat and drink, but then

2

again, she'd never entertained the idea of spending the night out here.

Claire took a few pictures as the mare drank from the hole. The thought of sipping the brackish liquid repulsed her. Claire swallowed hard, her throat dry and parched. What would she do when she ran out of water?

Competing for attention, Claire's stomach growled. With only a partially eaten granola bar left in her pack, she resisted the urge to devour it. Suddenly she felt vulnerable, fear taking over. She was out here alone, abandoned, with barely enough food or water to last the next couple of hours.

She fought off the fit of rising panic. Perhaps her new employee, Shirley Gaines, would realize Claire hadn't returned to the photography studio and inform the National Park Service. Shirley always left the studio at five o'clock, though, and most likely locked up without realizing Claire hadn't returned. Unfortunately, no one but Shirley knew her whereabouts.

Maybe one of the other shop owners would notice Claire's darkened apartment above the store. She usually had a lamp burning until the late hours of night while she cropped or framed her favorite photos. She doubted, however, anyone knew a newcomer's routine. Most likely, she'd have to make it through tonight until the ferry arrived first thing in the morning.

Eventually the horses drifted toward a small cluster of scrub oaks at the base of a tall dune, and Claire followed. She loved the way the flat-topped trees looked. The salty breeze naturally pruned the branches, giving the trees the appearance of leaning away from the ocean. An abundance of manure piles layered the ground underneath the gnarled limbs.

The stallion stopped dead in his tracks. He stared off into the near distance at a tall, brawny man about Claire's age.

Claire stilled. She had no way to escape from the island, and a man was out here roaming the dunes. Did he have a boat, or had the ferry left him behind, too? Was he dangerous?

She slowly approached the gnarled tree and stood behind the narrow trunk to watch him. Maybe he was a fisherman and his buddies were hanging out close by. They might have set up camp on the beach, with plans to indulge in a night full of cheap beer and exaggerated stories about the day's catch. She shuddered at the idea of them reeling in a lone, stranded female.

Her heart began to pound, her breath shortening with each successive thought. She might be in serious danger.

In addition to the man's large size, she spied green coveralls, a blue windbreaker, and a green ball cap. He also walked slightly bowlegged, as if he'd just dismounted from a horse. He seemed athletic, and if she had to defend herself, he would be impossible to fight off. The image of a vulnerable, female dolphin ensnared in a fisherman's net flashed through her mind.

Was she overreacting? Under different circumstances she might even find him attractive. If she explained her situation to him, maybe he'd offer a ride back to the mainland. If not, he'd be aware of her vulnerability and the fact that she'd forgotten her cell phone at home as usual. She sucked in her breath, the risk too big to take.

The man continued to walk without noticing her, and Claire didn't dare move. Once he disappeared around a dune, she released a heavy sigh. "Wow, what a close call." The stallion looked up, curious, but then continued to graze.

She leaned against the tree trunk and strained her memory to recall tomorrow's ferry schedule. She remembered the glossy brochure that she'd picked up earlier at the ticket booth and pulled it from her pack. Her heart sank when she read that during off-season, the private boat only ran if the owner had enough customers. The brochure listed ten-thirty as the tentative departure time from the island. With an ominous man wandering the island, the first pick-up time felt like an eternity away, if the ferry even showed up.

In an attempt to distract herself temporarily, she kneeled and turned her focus onto the horses. The setting sun highlighted everything it touched, including the horses' top lines and manes, with a fiery-orange hue. A brand-new colt with a dark golden coat and a flaxen mane and tail nursed from his mother. Behind the pair, a pregnant brown-colored mare stood awkwardly and watched Claire. She looked ready to deliver any minute. The birth would make a nice succession of photos, but wild horses didn't deliver their foals with humans around. Claire made a mental note to return in a day or so to check her progress.

The pregnant mare stared at Claire's camera. Her black, fire-tipped forelock and mane blew in the breeze and one eye poked out from underneath. "Your hair looks about like mine when I wake up in the morning." Claire laughed and the mare watched her with interest as she clicked a couple of photos.

Her own black mane fell from her ponytail and whipped against her face in the freshening breeze. She hoped the stronger wind didn't indicate inclement weather approaching. That was the last thing she needed.

Claire studied the sky.

Black thunderheads were gathering out at sea, and an intense storm did indeed threaten to hit the island. She caught a whiff of a light scent of rain that laced the breeze. Not good. She ran her hands across her arms to keep warm against the chilling air. Once the sun disappeared below the horizon, the temperature would rapidly dip. Claire untied a brown fleece sweatshirt from her waist and pulled it over her head.

For solace, she rubbed the contours of the pewter mustang necklace her father had given her when she was young. Then she thought about his wise foreman, Black Eagle.

*What would Black Eagle do?* Would he leave the horses behind to find shelter? No way. He would stay with the horses. Once, during a visit to an island similar to this one, he had said, *Claire, the horses have survived for over three hundred years. They know where to find water and shelter.*

They could also detect wild animals, and snakes, and … fishermen.

Claire glanced around and wondered where the horses would find cover if the storm hit. She squinted to sharpen her vision in the fast-approaching dusk and surveyed the immediate area. It offered nothing other than a few black, looming scrub oaks, a dark layer of sand, and the tall silhouettes of several dunes. Then to her relief, she saw a dense maritime forest not too far away.

The breeze picked up, and in unison the horses stopped eating and made their way toward the forest. She tried to follow them as they wove through the inland dunes, but the late evening grew darker by the minute. Horses had better eyesight in the dark than humans did, and she struggled to see and to stay near the herd.

When Claire's foot caught in a clump of grass, she tripped and hit the ground hard, pain shooting through her ankle. She lay there, sprawled on the hard sand, and began to shiver.

\*\*\*

After a long day's work, Jeff Rhoades entered the Salty Mug. He glanced around for a private spot to sit, but all the scarred wooden tables were full. He just wanted to enjoy a thick, juicy hamburger and then go home, but half the town seemed to be dining out at this late hour. When he spotted his brother at the bar, he reluctantly gave up his desire for privacy and chose a tall stool beside him.

"Hey, Tom. Why aren't you with Sally and the kids?" Jeff pulled off his green ball cap and ran his fingers through his stubby brown hair. His dad had taught him never to eat a meal wearing a hat, and even as an adult, he still respected his father's rule.

"I had to work late, so they went to her mom's for dinner." Tom pushed his empty plate aside and pulled out his credit card. "I've been meaning to talk with you anyway."

When Donovan, the long-time bartender, approached, Jeff ordered the usual before turning his attention to his brother. Whatever he wanted to discuss must be serious, because that's the only time Tom wanted to converse about anything.

"What's up?"

Tom cleared his throat. "Lynette." He hesitated for a moment. "Are you sure you're doing the right thing?"

Jeff clenched his jaw at the mention of Lynette Cooper, the town's most successful real estate agent. "Heck no. Is anyone ever sure?" Jeff chuckled, trying to make light of the pointed conversation. When the bartender approached with a soda in hand, Jeff appreciated the distraction. He reached for the glass, thanked the bartender, and took a long drink to allow himself a moment to think.

Lynette wanted a commitment. Jeff suspected her motivation had to do with his father being the largest landowner in the area, and his mother's wealth from the steel distribution company she'd owned. Of course, he couldn't prove his suspicion.

Jeff almost accepted the trade-off. He wanted a wife and a family more than anything. Besides, he loved Lynette and she was a local. He couldn't risk being with someone who wasn't from the area because he belonged here in Big Cat. It meant a lot to him to protect the Islander Ponies and his heritage on the island. He couldn't marry someone else and risk his future wife wanting to return to the city. He'd already been through that with his ex-girlfriend Dana.

"Maybe you've mistaken love for familiarity?" Tom suggested. "That would be understandable considering your history together."

"Maybe." Jeff thought about what Tom said. He'd practically grown up with Lynette, so he considered his brother's observation plausible. They had things in common, mostly memories, and maybe someday she'd even learn to respect the horses.

"I can't say our relationship is overflowing with passion," Jeff admitted, "but I've known Lynette a long time." He looked down, remembering the turmoil he felt when Dana left. He was playing life safe now. "Anyway, romance doesn't last. It has a way of lighting up fast and bright, burning deep enough to leave permanent scars before it fizzles out."

"If you're talking about Dana, she never fit in here. Maybe you need to let go of the past."

Jeff didn't answer.

"If you're hesitating, that's a warning sign," Tom said.

"Possibly, but I know what I'm doing." Jeff had pondered some of the same concerns. "I admire Lynette's go-getter tenacity. People respect her, except for my family, and she's beautiful. I'm sure it's normal to second-guess a big decision like this."

"I disagree."

Again, lack of passion meant she couldn't scorch his heart.

Rather than accept his brother's painful observation, Jeff said, "Mom and Pam need to concern themselves with their own lives. This conversation smells of their interference." He loved his mom and sister, but they had annoying qualities.

"Point taken," Tom said. "We just wonder how long you'll be happy with a plastic princess with the personality of a jackhammer."

Jeff flinched at the harsh words. "That jackhammer personality is what makes her a successful businesswoman."

"True. But she's rather self-centered," Tom said.

Jeff's stubborn streak kicked in. Where did his family get off trying to interfere with his life? He just wanted to eat his dinner in peace and leave.

"Does Lynette want kids?" Tom asked.

Another pointed question.

As of yet, they weren't even sleeping together; she'd insisted on integrity. But Jeff understood why she wanted to wait until their wedding night. Lynette played by society's rules.

"Sure, she wants kids eventually," Jeff said with more conviction than he felt.

"Think about what I said. If you aren't convinced about the relationship, get out while you can. Three weeks isn't a lot of time to be having second thoughts."

"I'm not a quitter, Tom. And I won't let someone else run my life, especially Mom and Pam."

"Fine." Tom frowned and stood. "For my conscience, I needed to have this conversation before you did something stupid."

The bartender slid Jeff's dinner in front of him.

"Later." Tom strode toward the door and left the restaurant without another word.

Peace, finally.

Despite the unpleasant conversation, Jeff's stomach rumbled. He'd worked up such an appetite today that he hadn't bothered to change out of his work clothes, other than shedding his green coveralls before entering the restaurant. He picked up his thick burger with anticipation, and just as he took a large bite, Steve Jones, one of his best rangers, sank onto the stool next to him.

"Jeff, we have a problem."

# CHAPTER TWO

Sprawled on the hard sand, Claire commanded herself to get up. But her ankle throbbed and she didn't think she could stand.

The horses were gaining distance, forming a darkened shadow ahead. If she didn't pick herself up and continue on, she would lose sight of them for sure.

She needed to move now, before the storm hit.

Claire rocked onto all fours, groaned from the pain pulsating around her ankle, and slowly stood. When she tentatively stepped forward, a hot surge shot up her leg. She squealed into the dark night.

The wind increased, blowing sand into her face, the granules stinging her cheeks like tiny shards of glass. She sheltered her eyes with her hands, and barely able to make out where she stepped, she limped her way through the deep sand. Finally, as she neared the edge of the forest, cold rain droplets fell from the sky and splattered on her skin.

When the horses slowed to enter the dark thicket one by one, Claire caught up with them. The trees were so dense they seemed impossible to penetrate, but the horses knew exactly where to walk. She barely made out a narrow path winding through the undergrowth and trees.

But before Claire stepped into the forest, she pulled a bottle from the side pouch of her pack. She needed water, and the rain gods blessed her. She untwisted the lid and placed the bottle behind a large stump to block it from the wind. Then she grabbed the thick ferry brochure from her pack to make a funnel. Any water she could collect, she'd be thankful for later. She removed her beloved camera from its plastic Ziploc and hoped it would remain dry in her water-resistant daypack. She opened the flimsy baggie to collect more rain.

The last of the horses entered the thicket, so she needed to hurry. She stood with a groan and reluctantly hobbled behind them into the woods. The forest grew darker, far too scary to enter alone. She didn't want to lose the horses but didn't want to lose track of her precious water bottle, either. To her relief, the herd stopped a short distance ahead.

The rain pounded in sheets behind her, but because of the abundant trees, only an occasional drop landed on her. The musty smell of wet, decayed vegetation on the forest floor enveloped her in the darkness. She felt alone, so much alone out here. As she stepped over a fallen log, a patch of Spanish moss brushed across her face and she gasped.

*I'm okay. It was only moss.*

Up ahead the horses huddled closely together. Claire wondered if they wanted protection from the rain, or from wild animals. Or worse yet, from a man who needed shelter, too. Claire's skin prickled at the thought. She couldn't hear anything except the storm. And in the darkness, she could barely see—someone could be nearby, waiting to attack, and she'd never know. Then she remembered Black Eagle's mantra, "Trust the horses." They wouldn't be standing here calmly if danger were near.

A flash of lightning lit up the path, and then a clap of thunder cracked overhead. The storm moved right on top of them. Another shot of light illuminated the dense woods, which looked undisturbed by human hands. When the thunder finally rolled off into the distance and the rain slowed, the horses left the cover of the forest. Claire stepped off the path and onto the wet, soggy sand.

Thirsty, she walked to the stump but stopped abruptly. The now empty bottle, lying on its side a good distance away, glared at her as if angry she'd left it behind. Thanks to her brilliant idea, she no longer had any drinking water left. Her mouth felt like cotton, and her body begged for liquid. She picked up the baggie and drank what small amount she'd collected, but it only made her thirstier. Frustrated, she shoved everything into the pack's side pouch and forged ahead.

Still limping somewhat, she followed the horses through a maze of dunes. Off in the distance the sky started to clear and the moon promised to be full. The horses eventually stopped and a few of them dropped onto the sand to rest. They apparently intended to spend the night here, or at least the next several chilly hours.

With the outside layer of her clothes damp, the night promised to be long and cold. She *almost* hoped the fisherman lurked nearby.

***

Jeff didn't want to hear about Steve Jones's problem. Not now. He wanted to devour his sandwich and then retire for the night. Jeff chewed quickly while he motioned for the ranger to continue talking. Maybe if he hurried his employee along, he'd be able to eat in peace sooner.

"There's a woman stranded on Pony Island." Steve leaned closer and lowered his voice. "Evidently she missed the last ferry and no one realized it until now."

Jeff paused, then swallowed a bite of hamburger. This couldn't be happening. He took a large gulp of soda and looked at Steve. "How'd that happen? Who's the woman?"

"She's new in town. The name's Claire Kincaid. She went over there to take pictures for her new photography studio on Front Street." Steve snatched a French fry from Jeff's plate. When Jeff didn't complain, he grabbed another one and shoved it in his mouth. "Shirley works for her, and when Claire didn't show up on time, her employee went to the ferry service. They'd already closed for the day, so she called us."

"Maybe the woman came back on the ferry and went somewhere else." Jeff pulled his plate away as Steve tried to steal another fry. "What proof do you have that she's still on the island?"

Steve frowned. "I have no solid proof, but it seems likely."

Jeff glanced at the time. "If she's there, we need to get going. She's probably wet and cold after that brutal thunderstorm." He took another large bite of his burger and then stood. He couldn't quite squelch his irritation at having to forfeit his dinner to rescue a woman who should have had sense enough to catch the last ferry.

"The crew is waiting," Steve said, now standing.

Jeff chewed vigorously and nodded. With his mouth half full he said, "I have warm clothes and extra supplies in my truck." He wiped his hands on a napkin, tossed a ten-dollar bill on the bar, and said, "Let's go."

Within the hour, four men hopped out of a skiff and onto the beach. "Let's split up," Jeff commanded. "She could be anywhere, but if she's smart, she's probably close to the ferry dock or the maritime forest. If you spot her, inform me right away."

"She might be lost," Steve defended the woman, adding to Jeff's irritation. "It's night and since she's new to the area, she probably doesn't know the island."

"True," Jeff said, trying to keep his voice level. "We'll cover a larger area to begin with." Jeff pointed his flashlight toward the general vicinity of the ferry dock. "Okay, here's the plan. Melvin, you survey the dock region and the western portion of the dunes. Steve, I want you to search around the maritime forest and the main trail that runs through it. Dick, look around the marsh pond and the surrounding dunes, and I'll search the point and the dunes straight ahead. If we don't find her over here, we'll take the boat around to the northeast side." With that, they departed.

Jeff looked up at the full moon. The stars were out en masse, like thousands of diamonds strewn atop a black velvet blanket. Thankfully, no hint of the earlier thunderstorm remained, and the bright moonlight made it easy enough to see without a flashlight. He loved the peaceful island at night, so rugged and wild.

He glanced up and down the beach on the Sound side. The woman had most likely found shelter in the dunes and used them as protection from the constant breeze and the blowing sand. The dunes covered a vast area, and the island stretched close to nine miles long and less than a mile wide. He hoped they found her within a reasonable amount of time because, if he allowed himself to push aside his irritation for the moment, he'd bet she was miserable.

He visualized the island. The dunes to his left were bigger and offered more wind protection, but they were almost desert-like, without trees for shelter until you reached the maritime forest. The dunes to his right were significantly smaller and offered almost no protection from the wind. However, the dunes straight ahead were larger and did provide at least some protection, with their scattered clusters of trees and shrubs that she could use for shelter. That was also Magic's territory. The stallion could be a bit temperamental with humans, so he hoped she hadn't had a run-in with him.

He'd check out Magic's territory first to eliminate his concern about the woman tangling with the wild herd. Certainly, she'd have enough common sense to stay away from the horses, but then again, he'd seen too many enamored tourists walk too close, without a clue about the danger.

He hiked over and around one tall dune after another, and when he eventually rounded a smaller one, he stopped dead in his tracks. Magic was lying down while two guard horses stood watch over the herd. Off to the right, a plastic tarp hung over a low tree branch, stretched out in the shape of a tent. He'd most likely found the woman, and a smart one at that. Some beachgoer had probably left behind his trash, and she'd used it as protection from the elements.

Without thinking first or radioing his crew as he'd commanded them earlier, he approached the tent. "Ma'am?" When no one answered, he called out again.

Jeff tried to pull open the flaps of the tarp but a puckered section held tight. He tugged again and a woman's hair accessory fell to the ground and freed the makeshift door. "Ma'am?" He pulled the tent flap back and peered inside.

The woman sat on the ground, atop the excess plastic with a portion of the tarp draped over her legs. When she turned to grab a small log with the clear intention of pummeling him if he stepped closer, she revealed a most exotic profile that almost stole his breath. Her distinct forehead sloped into a slightly long but sexy nose, and the moonlight accentuated her high cheekbones. She turned and stared at him, her dark, possibly brown eyes widening. Despite her wild look, or maybe because of it, an intense protective instinct stirred inside him. Messy black hair hung down her backside, and olive-looking skin, that he imagined to be soft as a foal's coat, enhanced her attractive femininity. He resisted the urge to pick her up and comfort her.

"I'm Jeff." He barely recognized his own husky voice. He pulled off his blue windbreaker and offered it to her. He could spare the jacket since his trusty green coveralls were plenty warm. To his surprise, instead of accepting the jacket, the woman launched the log at his head. He ducked just in time. She picked up another log that she'd used to spread the tent apart, and the right side of the tarp collapsed inward.

"Get away from me or you'll be sorry," she warned.

He instantly backed up and lifted his hands in surrender. "I'm not trying to hurt you." When she didn't lower the log, he continued. "I'm a park ranger. Shirley reported you missing." He should've mentioned that first.

Her expression softened. "You're a ranger?"

Jeff nodded but stayed back, outside the door. "I'm Jeff Rhoades. I'm the head ranger that works out here with the horses. I'm also a wildlife biologist." He flicked on the powerful flashlight and it flooded the tent with a warm glow. Their gaze met for a prolonged second.

Claire noticed the badge pinned to his khaki shirt that proved him a ranger.

Against her better judgment, she lowered the log slowly.

"Why were you wearing a blue windbreaker instead of a green park ranger one?" she asked, looking at the jacket in his hand. He no longer held it out to her.

"I'm supposed to wear green but I like the blue one better. Why are you out here alone, following the horses?" he asked.

His gruff voice, contrasted with the beauty and the peaceful ambience of the island, surprised her. He seemed slightly annoyed, as if she had inconvenienced him. She probably had.

"I missed the ferry; sorry about that." She tried to stand to minimize the height disadvantage, but when her head hit the tent roof, she ended up hunching over.

She wished he wasn't so attractive. It bothered her to admire his tall and muscular body when she was out here alone, vulnerable. No doubt he was the same man she'd noticed walking through the dunes earlier this evening.

"But why follow the horses? They're dangerous. Wild."

As if she hadn't known the horses were wild. What did he take her for, a tourist? Then she reasoned he didn't know her history.

"I'm a photographer from Big Cat." Claire forgot and stood straighter, bumping her head on the tree branch supporting the tent. So much for trying to appear more confident than she felt. "I've studied horses all my life, so I know how to respect their space." For some irritating reason she desired his approval and wanted to convince him that she understood equine behavior.

"You're from the city." His voice held a slight, bitter edge. He looked down and stared at his weathered boot before he met her gaze again. From the powerful beam of the flashlight, she noticed his eyes were possibly the color of the sea. She knew instinctively that those eyes turned stormy when he grew angry, and she noted the comfort they offered now despite his gruff exterior. She looked away before she lost the ability to speak clearly.

"Charlotte, actually. I moved here last week." She noticed his shoulders visibly stiffened. "I'm renting the building next to Stephanie's Books."

Her experience dictated that she shouldn't trust him, but judging from his eyes, he seemed safe enough. Her mother would say that men couldn't be trusted, ever. However, Black Eagle—the one man Claire trusted completely—had always said, "You can see a person's soul through their eyes. Follow your instincts, Claire, no matter what people say. If his eyes are hard, he can't be trusted. If they are soft and kind, he is friendly." Her instincts said he was trustworthy.

"Why would a city girl move to Big Cat alone?"

"I needed an island fix. A hero fix, too," Claire quipped. "I thought I'd get lost out here and need rescuing."

He made some kind of noise from his throat. "Don't you own a cell phone?"

"Of course I do."

"Why didn't you call for help?" His voice held a hint of humor and he appeared to resist a smile. He cleared his throat.

"I left it at home." Claire looked away and felt her cheeks grow warm. Uncomfortable with him staring at her, she angled her body away. The man screamed of danger, but not in a physical way. A good-looking stranger, one she found herself attracted to, posed a threat to the well-constructed barrier that she hid behind. A dull ache spread through her.

Claire felt Jeff's scrutiny. She probably looked like quite a sight, a mess to behold after all the wind and rain.

"You haven't answered why you were following the horses."

She turned back to see him check the time on his phone, again giving her the feeling she'd kept him from something important.

"My father owned a ranch and I rode before I walked." She chose first to lend herself credibility before answering his question. "His foreman was Native American—Black Eagle was his name—and he taught me about horses and herd behavior. I enjoy photographing them and that's why I'm out here. When the ferry showed up early and left me behind, I decided I was safer with the horses than on my own."

He frowned. "The ferry picks up passengers exactly on the bottom of the hour, especially the last run of the day." He rubbed the bottom of his chin as if he were thinking. "They keep a passenger list. If you didn't show up on time, they'd call the Park Service to find you. Besides, they'd never leave anyone stranded out here."

"Well, they did. I'm out here, aren't I?" It bothered her that he questioned her explanation. Automatically, he'd assumed that being left behind was her fault instead of the ferry owner's. How frustrating.

"Still, the horses are dangerous. Not a good idea to follow a herd you don't know well."

"If the horses are so dangerous, then why are *you* traipsing around out here at night, all alone?" She considered the question fair.

He grew silent for a moment and then laughed a good-natured, belly-roar laugh. "You have spunk. Did Black Eagle teach that to you, too?"

"No. Are you poking fun at me?" She couldn't help but laugh with him.

"I'd never make fun of a stray woman on an island." He stepped toward her with his jacket and wrapped it around her shoulders. An awkward moment passed between them and neither moved until he finally stepped away. "I need to radio my rangers to let him know I found you."

Claire donned her daypack while Jeff pulled the plastic tarp down from the tree. She glanced over at the mare and foal in the moonlight, and then at the pregnant one, silently bidding them goodbye. She'd already grown fond of them.

On the hike back to the boat, he shoved the tarp into a trashcan. "You're limping. What happened to you?"

His compassion surprised her. She was usually the observant one who noticed when something was wrong or off-kilter, not the recipient of such concern. "I fell over a clump of grass in the dark. It's nothing. I think I sprained my ankle, and it should be fine after I rest it tonight."

She felt him staring at her again. With her current state of appearance, she probably gave new meaning to the term "nature girl."

"You're one tough woman."

He wrapped his strong, warm arm around her before she could argue. "Hold onto me." When she hesitated, he said, "Put your arm around my waist so you can walk."

She didn't move. He smelled sexy, of fresh air and brine, and wild like one of his horses.

He cocked his head in challenge. "Otherwise I'll have to carry you."

Unnerved, she slid a shaky arm around him.

Maybe this was what it was like to trust a man. Her ankle throbbed even more.

# CHAPTER THREE

Claire pushed her cereal bowl away as she finished reading the last line of an article in this morning's newspaper. Apparently an elderly gentleman, who was now residing in a nursing home, had just reunited with his long-lost daughter after fifty years.

Thanks to the Internet, the woman had seen an article about the man's painful journey with cancer. Once the woman mentally removed years of wrinkles, she realized she was staring at a picture of her biological father. She'd been searching for him for years. Sadly, her aging father thought he had no family left, until she walked through the front door of the nursing home. The article referred to their reunion as bittersweet—bitter because he was suffering from lung cancer and sweet because they'd finally reunited. Claire hoped he lived long enough for father and daughter to reestablish their relationship.

Regret coursed through Claire over all the years she'd lost with her own father.

She fingered her neck to rub the treasured pewter necklace he'd given her, which was a leftover, soothing habit from childhood that served her well.

Her heart rate skidded to a halt. Her neck was bare! She gasped and felt her neck again in desperate search for the necklace. She'd never once taken it off since the day her father had latched it around her neck. Where was it?

She ran into her bedroom. In a daze she threw back the bedding and searched the linens. No necklace. She crouched to the floor and searched under the bed.

Still no necklace. She leaned back against the wall, trying to relax her mind so she could think sensibly. When had she touched it last? She remembered back to yesterday, to when the ferry had left her stranded. She'd definitely worn the necklace then.

*Make a plan, Claire.*

She'd go back to the island and retrace her steps, and with any luck, she'd find the necklace lying in the sand. Most likely it wouldn't be that easy, but losing the necklace wasn't an option. She had no choice but to return today, even if it meant she'd have to ride the unreliable ferry again. But this time she'd be prepared.

First, she needed to pack ample food and water. She stood on wobbly legs and walked back into the kitchen. Encouraged by her new plan, she stared into her perfectly organized pantry.

To an outside observer, she probably looked a bit anal-retentive, what with the cans neatly arranged in alphabetical order on the shelves. Her mother, who had owned a restaurant in Charlotte, had drilled into Claire's head the importance of an orderly kitchen. Claire sometimes wondered what it would feel like to be a little less tidy. She challenged her analytical nature and reached in to move one can out of place.

There, a perfect start to what her cheating ex-boyfriend referred to as her lack of spontaneity. Who knows, maybe Phillip Edwards had a point.

Claire made a stack of peanut butter and jelly sandwiches and stuffed them, along with six bottles of water, into her daypack. Certainly, she'd packed enough this time.

Next she needed extra clothes, so she returned to her bedroom. In an effort to gauge the weather, she opened the blinds.

To her surprise, a man dressed in green eclipsed the usual view of the ferry dock and the river across the street, along with the nearby channel leading to the ocean.

Jeff Rhoades stood next to a Ford pickup truck, parked close to the ferryboat pavilion. He held open the extended cab door for a brown Labrador retriever to hop out of the backseat and join him. Anxiety knotted Claire's stomach. She knew exactly what Jeff planned and had to stop him.

She strapped on a pair of sandals and ran down the steps from her apartment to the alley. In almost record time, she darted around the front of the building and across the street. Thankfully, Jeff had stopped to talk to a bent-over, elderly gentleman dressed in a suit. By the time she almost reached him, he finished with his conversation and began to stride toward the ticket booth labeled *Pony Island Excursions*.

"Jeff!" He stopped and she caught up with him. "You aren't planning to confront the ferry owner, are you?" The dog sniffed her hand and demanded Claire pet him. She gladly obliged. His fur was slick; perhaps Jeff had just given him a bath.

"They can't leave you stranded out there. That's inexcusable." He stared at her with an electrifying intensity, as if he were looking straight into her battered soul. Then, to her relief, he shifted his unnerving gaze to the dog. "Frank isn't usually friendly to strangers."

She shrugged, pretending nonchalance. "He must know I like dogs." Claire scratched the pleading canine behind the ears before she looked up at Jeff again. "You're right, the ferry shouldn't leave people behind, but everything turned out fine. I'd rather not create a scene."

He set his jaw. "They're responsible for the people they drop off. The owner never called the ranger station for help, probably because he had no clue he left you out there." He took a step forward. "The public relies on their service."

*The public.* A small part of her had secretly hoped he intended to protect *her*, and for an instant, the need for a friend battled the desire for independence. She fought to hide her disappointment. Jeff's confrontation with the ferry owner had nothing to do with friendship. He wanted to protect the "public" by preventing the ferry from abandoning others. His objective was important, noble even, but she'd mistaken his motivation.

He stepped toward the ticket booth. With resolve, she grabbed hold of his arm. The warmth, the intimacy, the touch surprised her. "I can handle this … the ferry owner, I mean."

He looked down at her with what seemed to be a hint of respect. "I'm sure you can, but there's something you don't understand. The new owner is a constant problem and breaks most of our rules. I've wanted a bigger reason to come down on him, and this is it."

When she remained quiet, he spoke with purpose. "It's about righting a wrong, Claire. The man has an obligation to people and he failed."

She nodded. He was right; the owner had shirked his responsibility. She understood his reasoning, even if it dented her pride. Why was it bothersome that he considered her the public?

Jeff started to walk again and Claire hurried alongside him, determined to reach the ticket booth at the same time. When they approached the stand, a hardworking, redheaded woman with short hair backed away to summon the owner. She must have known Jeff didn't want a ticket.

The owner appeared from a small office attached to the booth. "What can I do for you, Jeff?" The rugged man stepped forward and eyed Claire curiously, grinning. His eager smile revealed a mouthful of brown-stained teeth, and his bloodshot eyes roamed over Claire's body. The despicable man had some nerve.

Maybe Jeff wanted to protect her from the slime ball after all. Then a thought popped into her mind: Why allow Jeff the pleasure?

She moved ahead of him and stared at the nasty little man, who grinned wider at her approach. "I was stranded last night on

Pony Island," she said in the most professional voice she could manage. "The ferry arrived early and left me behind."

"Honey, I didn't forget no one." He spat a stream of tobacco juice close to her sandal.

"Well, you've forgotten your manners. And the name isn't 'Honey,' it's Claire." She tried to force her voice to be steady and calm. Jeff had said the owner kept a list of everyone who went out to the island. "I want to see your passenger log for yesterday." She wanted to know if someone had scratched her name off as a returning passenger, or if any notes might indicate what had happened.

"I don't need to show you anything."

She reached her limit of being polite. "Then maybe," she said with authority, "you'd prefer I call the *Crystal Coast Observer*. I'm sure a reporter would be interested in my story, especially since tourist season is around the corner." The man's eyes widened. Was he afraid of bad publicity? Good. He deserved to sweat a little.

Jeff raised his eyebrows and cracked a small smile. "How'd she get left out there?"

"Beats me, but I didn't forget no one."

Jeff lowered his voice. "I suggest you track your passengers more closely. Leaving someone on the island is serious; the Park Service can revoke your ferry license."

The man narrowed his eyes. "And you take this as a warnin'," he barked. "Stay out of my business and we'll all be happy." He whirled around and headed back inside the pavilion.

"Do you really plan to call the paper?" Jeff patted his thigh to call Frank to his side after the dog finished marking the ticket booth.

"Nah, but maybe he'll think I'm serious." She smiled, unable to hide her mischievous thoughts as they walked together toward the quiet street. In another month, the shops and restaurants would be crowded with vacationers.

"Remind me not to make you mad." He studied her with interest as they strolled along. "Actually, we make a good team."

24

"We do?" A team? Nobody had ever told her that, much less a virtual stranger. Unsure of why she rather liked the idea, she frowned. "And to think, I just lost my ride back out to the island."

He stared at her in disbelief. "You planned to use his ferry again?"

"Of course," she said in earnest. "I need to fill my studio with photos before the tourist season begins." *And more important, I need to find my necklace.* She stopped walking when he reached out and lightly touched her elbow. The light contact almost felt like a caress.

"I have to work out there today anyway. I'll give you a ride," he offered. His bright eyes met hers directly, as if he wanted her to accept his offer.

She looked out at the fog that hovered over the water, despite the clear weather on the mainland. "Do we have to wait for the weather to improve?"

"No. The fog's already lifted some." He looked at the time on his cell phone. "I have to drop Frank off at my brother's house first. What if we meet at the dock behind the *Salty Mug* in a half hour?" He pointed to the restaurant next to the ferry booth.

Claire heard her mother's scolding words echo through her mind. "Men have expectations of women who ask for favors, Claire."

***

While Claire waited for Jeff at the dock, the redheaded woman from the nearby ferry booth jogged toward her. She reached Claire with an even breath despite her sprint. "Claire? Is that your name?"

Claire nodded and noticed the woman had the muscled tone of a long-distance runner. "I'm sorry, but I don't know your name." What did the redheaded beauty want? The possibilities were endless and stirred Claire's curiosity.

"I'm Virginia Stallings, but please call me Jenni." She reached out to shake Claire's hand. "I'm sorry Bob was so rude to you. He's owned the ferry since last fall and hasn't learned proper customer service yet. He's about to get a crash course, though, with tourist season coming up."

"He needs a decade, not a season to teach him," Claire said with humor.

Thankfully, Jenni took her comment as intended and laughed. "Look, it's not my business," she said. A serious expression wrinkled her freckled face. "But I like to help people. I heard you're searching for your dad. I might have some useful information."

Strange, but she didn't remember telling anyone about her personal quest to find her father. Surprised that someone knew about her hidden agenda, Claire paused a moment to absorb the news. When she could speak again, she said, "Really? I've found no hint of him, even though I've been told he lives here." A boat hummed off in the distance but she didn't turn to look. Her thoughts remained focused on Jenni and any possible clues about her father.

"There's a mysterious man that often visits Pony Island." Jenni glanced at the approaching boat. "I don't know him; he keeps to himself, but he's always on the island whenever there's a crisis with the horses. That's not often, but people have seen him at other times, too. I bet Jeff knows him."

"How do you think he's tied in with my father?"

"He lives on the outskirts of Big Cat. He's kind of a horse whisperer. People say that you have that wisdom, too."

Claire hid her brief shock. "I guess so. I never thought of my style as whispering, but maybe it is. Who told you about my method?"

"You've obviously never lived in a small town before." Jenni feigned a smile. "News spreads faster than a disease around here."

What an analogy. "Do you know what the man looks like? Tall, short, anything?" The boat pulled up and hummed behind Claire.

"I don't know, but the information seemed significant enough to mention. I have another suggestion, too." Jenni waved at whoever waited in the boat, probably Jeff. "Lynette Cooper's father is president of Coastal Barrier Bank here in town. He knows everybody in this area. You could ask him if he knows your father."

Why was Jenni so eager to help? "Thanks," Claire said. She heard Jeff call her name from the awaiting boat. "I need to run. I appreciate the tip."

"Good luck." Jenni flashed a curious grin and watched as Claire climbed into the boat with Jeff.

"What was that all about?" Jeff asked after they motored away.

"Nothing really." She needed time to ponder the new information. Could the horse whisperer and her father be one and the same?

***

Intrigued, Claire watched as Jeff navigated the skiff with ease through the swirling mist and increasingly shallow water. The estuary resembled a complex labyrinth made up of deserted islands, golden marsh, and fog that spiraled off the water and parted to allow the boat to motor through.

If only she could be honest with him and explain the real reason she wanted to come back to the island today. She silently argued that he most likely walked the island every day, that a second pair of eyes looking for her necklace would increase the chance of finding it. Unfortunately, her mother's words echoed through her mind again. Claire had already allowed him to help her enough, and her mom was probably right—men expected women to repay favors.

She stared over the bow of the boat. "How do you find your way through this maze?"

"Experience, really. Plus I use equipment." He didn't look at her, but instead remained focused on his task. "I love being on my boat in the fog."

Normally, she loved foggy weather, too, but today it presented a problem. It would make finding her necklace more difficult.

Jeff motored into a small cove. When the bottom of the boat scraped against the sandy floor of the Sound, the impact rocked her forward, then backward.

He killed the engine and jumped out of the skiff, into the shallow water. With sexy force, he tugged the boat onto the bank. "Here." He extended a muscled arm and reached over the bow to help her climb from the boat.

Hesitantly she placed her hand into Jeff's calloused palm. He radiated warmth and strength.

"Do you want to join me while I work?" he asked, seemingly oblivious to the heat their touch generated before he dropped the contact. "Once the fog lifts, you might get some interesting photos of the different harems."

His invitation tempted her, but an uneasy feeling of vulnerability overcame her. She had to resist her attraction to him, resist his generosity. Relationships hurt too much. She fingered the vacant spot on her neck. If she wanted to find her necklace, she'd have to go her separate way.

Without explanation, she said, "Thanks, but I have a few places I want to explore." The words came out too soft and tender. "Can we meet up when I'm done?"

"Sure," he said. "Call me when you're finished and I'll let you know where I am." He pointed to her bulging pocket. "You did bring your cell phone this time, didn't you?"

"Absolutely."

"Let me have it." When she handed him the phone, he programmed in his number. "How's your ankle today?"

She hadn't thought about it before now. "It seems fine." She wiggled her foot around to demonstrate full range of motion. "I'm not sure how long I'll be. Are you in a hurry?" It could take hours to find the necklace, and that was if she were lucky.

"Take your time," Jeff said. "I have plenty of work to do. Here's a map of the island." He dug his hand deep into his pocket, pulled out a neatly folded map, and opened it for her to study. "I'll be south of the ferry dock to start," he explained, and pointed to a hand-drawn dock with a crudely sketched boat next to it. "Then I'll head around the small dunes by the ocean. After that, I'll work my way back to the dock and head north past the marsh pond."

She hadn't been north yet and still needed pictures of the horses in the pond. Her business sense dictated she needed to devote at least a little bit of time to photography while she was here on the island.

"Why don't we meet at the marsh pond then?" she asked.

"Sounds good. Call me when you're finished exploring, and please don't get lost again." He pointed to the map, to a shaded circle near the forest labeled marsh pond. "It's tricky to find."

She also noticed a scribbled tree and a tiny cross just north of the pond. Old cemeteries fascinated her, and they made interesting photographs, which she suspected would sell well.

Claire shoved the map into her pocket and watched Jeff walk off. An annoying flutter danced in her belly. She didn't want a man right now, didn't need to get involved with a local, but if she did
….

***

Jeff had left Claire quite a while ago, and thoughts of her still swirled around in his mind. She was an interesting one, and something about her intrigued him. Most women he knew were too prissy to step foot on the island to begin with. For Claire to return so soon after the ferry had left her stranded was just short of remarkable. He couldn't believe she'd actually planned to use that poor excuse for a ferry service again. That thought kicked in a surprising urge to protect her.

Jeff also found Claire to be a challenge, and unfortunately, he thrived on challenges.

Claire reminded him of someone. She definitely held some similarities to his sister, Pam. They were both nuts about horses, and animals in general, if Frank's immediate affection for Claire was any indication. Nothing seemed to intimidate either woman. Then he realized the similarity wasn't to his sister but to his mother.

His mother had once flourished when she ran the family-owned steel distribution business that his brother Tom owned now. She handled any crisis with confidence and ease, and she had earned the respect of most people in town. Like his mom, Claire seemed devoted to her business. She was, after all, out here in the fog, demonstrating dedication to fill her studio with pictures of the beloved wild horses.

Jeff spotted the herd grazing up ahead. Gerome, a young stallion, had three mares in his harem. Last year he had been a bachelor, but somewhere along the line he had stolen two younger mares and one older one. Gerome's ambitions, which were undoubtedly to increase the size of his harem and to reproduce as much as possible, were about to be somewhat thwarted. Jeff had Gerome's older mare on the list for birth control administration.

This part of his job required patience. He had to approach the horses slowly, which offered plenty of time to think. Unfortunately, his thoughts returned to the new photographer in town. Why was she here? Newcomers usually didn't move to Big Cat unless they knew someone in town, or unless they relocated because their spouse wanted to move back home.

She'd cause a stir with the men for sure, because single, attractive women in Big Cat were scarce. She'd also be a threat to the women's tight-knit community, because of her looks, her intelligence, and the business rivalry among the female shop owners.

Lynette would most likely be her archenemy, even though she was Claire's landlady. He'd bet money on it. As soon as Claire became successful, Lynette would feel threatened. She owned a large portion of the buildings on Front Street since her daddy, a wealthy banker, supported Lynette's financial endeavors. Of course Lynette wanted her tenants to be successful since they rented her buildings, but he doubted she'd want an outsider to compete against her popularity.

Jeff climbed the sand dune nearest the mare and waited. Eventually, when the herd seemed unbothered by his presence, he shot the birth control dart into her rump. Afterward, he packed up his equipment to search for Samson's herd. Samson, a large, well-established stallion, had at least ten mares in his harem. A few years ago Samson had had a run-in with an aggressive tourist who harassed his herd. The clueless man had actually tried to lasso the stallion. As a result, Samson mistrusted humans even more than normal, and that meant Jeff had to exercise extra patience when he approached the harem.

Forty-five minutes later, Jeff edged close enough to sit atop another dune. After he administered the birth control, a deep voice from behind him said, "Jeff."

He turned around to face a Native American man and shook his head in wonderment. "It took a while before the horses let me up here. How'd you approach so fast without them running away?"

The man grinned. "Because I'm a horse whisperer."

# CHAPTER FOUR

Along the sandy beach of the Sound, Claire followed several sets of wet hoof prints, headed in the general direction of the marsh pond. Lost in thought, she barely heard a noise rustle behind her. When she heard the snap of driftwood, she spun around. Nothing followed her except the heavy feeling of someone watching. She studied the nearby dunes for any evidence of somebody trailing behind, but saw no one.

Claire continued to walk, her senses on high alert. *Jeff*, she thought, *I'll call Jeff.*

She dialed her phone with shaking hands. Unfortunately, the call went straight into voice mail. Despite her effort to remain calm, at the beep she left a stilted message. "Jeff … hey, this is Claire. I think there's somebody … Oh, never mind. You must be busy." She hesitated and glanced around. "I'm finished … so I can meet you at the marsh pond if you're close by. I should be there in twenty minutes or so. Um … see you soon." She clicked the phone off and scanned the dunes again. At least she hoped Jeff showed up soon because she didn't want to be alone. She had to admit, the sound of his recorded voice had somewhat helped to ease her mind.

Sadly, that's where her trust ended. She couldn't help but raise an emotional barrier, like a wall built to guard a castle. What was wrong with her, that she couldn't trust a man to help?

*I didn't even tell him about my necklace*, she thought, *and now I want him to protect me.* She wanted security and out of habit, she touched her bare neck.

Loneliness overcame her. The necklace held a connection to her past and was solid proof that her father existed. Lately, she needed all the proof she could get because believing in memories grew harder and harder as the days passed. Sadly, she'd had no luck finding the necklace. She'd retraced her steps from last night the best she could, but without success. Most of her footprints from yesterday were gone thanks to the thunderstorm, and with the fog this morning, it made the task even harder.

As difficult as it might be to ask Jeff for help, if she wanted the necklace back, she probably needed to enlist his assistance.

She sighed at the irony. Odd how just last night he had frightened her, when she thought him a predator, and now she almost welcomed his company—more than she cared to admit. Jeff meant safety. An annoying tingle of warmth pulsated through her and Claire willed the feeling away.

She looked around again and no longer felt someone nearby watching her. Whoever had been observing her was now gone.

Still, she wanted to reach the marsh pond and Jeff as quickly as possible. She quickened her step, but up ahead the horses' hoof prints seemed to disappear into a long rivulet caused by tidewater. Claire squinted to sharpen her vision but couldn't discern if the water was passable for her. She pulled out the map and studied the scribbled drawing. With no rivulet indicated, it became obvious the hand-drawn map lacked accuracy.

*Trust the horses* rang in her head again, but an internal alarm clanged louder. She slid off her daypack, removed her camera from its baggie, and looked through the viewfinder. The fog had lifted enough now to use the camera's zoom lens as a telescope.

Indeed the horses had walked that way, but she definitely saw water, through which the horses had apparently waded across. She surveyed the area for another option, and realized the only alternative was a trek through the mudflat on her immediate right, recently exposed by the receding tide. She repacked her camera and stepped hesitantly into the mushy, mud-like sand. Her foot sank several inches. No wonder the horses hadn't walked this way. The resistance of the muck caused a dull ache in her bum ankle. At the risk of further injury, she continued to cross the soggy mudflat.

When she'd given Jeff an estimated time to meet at the marsh pond, she hadn't factored in navigating wet, sticky sand. At this rate, the marsh pond might take longer to reach than she had anticipated. Would Jeff wait for her? Would he be concerned if she didn't show up on time? Focusing on where she placed her feet, Claire picked her way through the deep gunk and around a large tidewater pool.

Thank goodness she hadn't walked this way last night in the dark.

At least a half hour later she finally cleared a bend and set foot on dry land again. The terrain, now heavily wooded on one side and aqua water on the other, reminded her of a remote island in the Caribbean. Straggly fallen trees lined the beach like piles of pirate skeletons washed ashore.

According the map, the marsh pond should be inland along the edge of the large forest. Claire headed for the woods, and sure enough, the horses had come this way.

She followed the hoof prints away from the beach and onto a path when her cell phone rang. "Claire, I got your message." Jeff's deep voice resonated with concern. "Are you okay? You sounded upset."

"I'm fine." At least now that her destination was within sight, and, to be honest, that he was on the phone. He didn't need to know she'd been worried about her safety and had turned to him for support. "Sorry, I didn't mean to alarm you."

"Glad you're okay. Where are you?"

"I just reached the marsh pond."

"Great, then you can go with me to find my last two harems for the day."

"When will you be here?"

"I have to say goodbye to an old friend first. I won't be long."

What did he mean by an old friend? Before she could ask, he ended the call. Jeff's mysterious side intrigued her. She couldn't help but wonder if his friend was the horse whisperer.

And maybe her father? So far, everyone she'd asked claimed not to know Robert Kincaid, but someone in Big Cat had to know him.

Hurtful words from the past haunted her. "Claire, face reality. Chasing fantasies is a waste of time," her mother's long-term boyfriend had often said. "Besides, your father never loved you."

How would he know anyway? Claire set out to prove him wrong.

She walked past the marsh pond and the familiar herd she'd followed yesterday. The pregnant mare hadn't delivered her foal yet, the poor miserable girl. The other mare, the one with the colt, ignored her baby as she waded through the water. Priceless. Claire climbed a dune, one of the biggest she'd seen yet, and snapped a sequence of pictures of the horses knee-deep in the pond with the golden reeds in the background.

The scenic view of the long narrow island, combined with the horses and the promise of an afternoon spent with a certain wildlife biologist, made the trek through the mudflat worthwhile. Claire let the thought evaporate in the light breeze.

*Take more pictures, Claire. Concentrate on filling the photography studio before tourist season begins.*

Always curious about the environment around her, Claire gazed off into the distance. As if to accentuate the mystique of the still-foggy water, a commercial container ship appeared on the ocean side. It looked like a ghost ship, barely visible. She clicked more pictures and hoped the camera had the capability to pick up the faraway vessel. For some reason, she knew Jeff would like the picture. After all, he'd mentioned that he loved to steer his boat through the fog. She'd make certain to print a copy for him.

Claire lowered the camera, distracted by the sense of Jeff's presence. Sure enough, she looked down from the dune and saw him approach the pond. She seemed to have a spiritual connection to him already, one similar to her natural bond to the wild horses. How was that possible after having known him such a short time?

He hadn't spotted her yet. As he neared the sand dune, she slowly raised the camera. She wanted a picture of him before he noticed her. The cowboy-like man with a bowlegged gait walked with his brow furrowed as though lost in thought. She admired how his muscles filled out his shirt, and how he carried himself in a most self-assured way. His masculine build against the background of the water, sand, and horses made him look like a model in an advertisement for expensive cologne.

The camera clicked a couple of times before the noise caught Jeff's attention. She hadn't thought he'd notice the sound, but he evidently had a keen sense of hearing. He looked up and stared right at her. Busted.

She quickly stowed the camera away and pretended not to notice him. Maybe if she ignored his reaction, he'd think she had photographed the horses instead.

No such luck. He scurried up the dune with athletic ease and pointed toward her bag. "So you want a picture of me. That's the most flattering compliment I've gotten in a long while."

"Arrogant, aren't we? Maybe you weren't my subject at all." She zipped her daypack and pulled it onto her back while she avoided his eyes. She never lied well.

"Yeah, right. I saw the camera pointed at me." He flashed a smile.

"And you're a ham." She flashed the same smile back at him.

He wiped the grin from his face and cleared his throat. "Are you ready to head north?"

"Yes," she said and started down the steep dune ahead of him. Claire hadn't travelled far before her ankle gave out and her feet slid from underneath her. She landed hard on her bottom.

He didn't quite hide the tender streak that danced in his eyes. "Let me help you up." He reached out and offered his hand.

Her mind briefly stopped processing all logical thought. Before she could think of reasons to refuse his help, she grabbed his hand and held onto it until they reached the base of the dune.

As soon as they reached the bottom, she tried to disguise the slight hitch in her step.

"By the way," she said, "I don't even know what you do out here as a ranger." Last night she'd been so cold, she hadn't thought to ask about what his job entailed. Again, this morning, she'd been too concerned about the confrontation with the ferry owner, and her mission to find her necklace, to inquire about Jeff's duties.

"I administer birth control to mares for one thing."

She stopped and stared at him. "Birth control?" Her voice raised an octave.

He halted beside her, too close for comfort.

"Yeah," he said teasingly. "Does that bother you?"

She planted her feet in place and fought the urge to back away. "No, but I thought the horses were supposed to be wild."

His face seemed to brighten at her curiosity. "They are, but we manage them so they don't overpopulate the island. If that happened, there wouldn't be enough food or water to sustain them." His words held such enthusiasm as he shared his knowledge. "We limit the population to around a hundred and twenty. When the foals are weaned at about two years old, we take some of them off the island and put them up for adoption."

"Isn't age two awfully old to wean a foal?" she asked. "We always weaned our babies at five or six months."

"That's how horses do it when left to their own devices. Once the mare gets pregnant again and the second baby arrives, the mother forces the older one away. I thought you studied wild horse behavior?"

She shook her head. "I studied domestic herd behavior on my father's ranch. I remember occasional visits to watch the wild horses on an island, though."

"See that golden-colored colt, the one that's nursing?" He pointed to the colt Claire had emotionally attached herself to over the past two days. When she nodded, Jeff said, "When he's older, he'll be adopted."

Her eyes widened. She stepped away and managed to put a casual, comfortable distance between them. "Really? I've taken a bunch of pictures of him. He's a cutie."

Jeff nodded. "His name is Dante. A group of students studies the horses, and they name the foals after the mare's lineage. His mother's name is Danielle; therefore, his name had to start with a D."

"What's the stallion's name?"

"Magic."

"That fits him. He has a majestic appearance."

"He does. If your father owns a ranch, how did you end up in Charlotte?" His voice held a definite edge again when he mentioned the city.

"I moved when I was nine."

"Why do I detect there's more to the story than you're sharing?" he asked. The last horse had finished drinking, and the herd lined up single file to walk along the beaten path.

Before Claire could answer, the stallion flared his nostrils and snorted. About a hundred feet away, another stallion stood off to the side with his harem while they waited their turn for a drink.

"The stallions have a pecking order, too," Jeff explained, "and the herds take turns at the pond in order of dominance.

When Magic approached the other stallion, both reared up for show. Then, in an animated trot intended to prove their strength and power, they strutted alongside each other. They spun and reared up again, and with aggressive force, struck out at each other. Neither stallion made contact with the other.

Always amazed at how possessive the males could be of their mares, Claire watched in fascination instead of grabbing for her camera. If neither steed backed down, they'd fight until one of them suffered injury or death. The other stallion, apparently uninterested in stealing a mare today, retreated and the tiff ended.

The stallions' behavior, at least in her mind, seemed so typically male to want an assembly of adoring females. Certainly, Phillip Edwards, her ex-boyfriend, fell into that category since she'd found him in bed with her neighbor.

It seemed that while a woman dated a man, she had to give up her precious freedom. She envisioned marriage would be even worse and didn't understand how independence and men were supposed to blend. Well, no more. She'd recovered from the pain and found her freedom. Never again would she make the same mistakes.

Claire pulled her attention back to the horses in time to hear Jeff's words.

"Let's not get too close to either herd. We need to head that way." He pointed to a worn path that twisted around a clump of trees. When they were safely away from the horses, he pursued their previous conversation. "So why did you move when you were nine?"

She froze in place, but he continued to walk. Despite her usual reluctance to share much in the way of personal information, she felt compelled to tell him the truth. She needed to unload the burden. Maybe the temporary crack in her armor had to do with the vulnerability she felt since she'd lost her necklace.

"Because my mother woke me up late one night and said we were leaving."

He stopped walking and listened intently.

"She waited until my father and Black Eagle had left to save a cow caught in a barbed wire fence. She wrapped a blanket around me, and we drove off with a few bags in the backseat. We didn't stop until we reached Charlotte. I haven't seen my father since."

"What? How could she steal you from your bed?"

"She didn't steal me. She's my mother." Claire clenched her teeth. "Of course you'd automatically take my father's side. What makes you think it was my mother's fault?"

"Why would she take off in the middle of the night after your father left the house?"

"I don't know, but I'm sure she had a good reason."

"Why don't you ask her?"

"Because she died of ovarian cancer." Claire swallowed hard. "That's why I want to find my father. He's all I have left."

Her mother's death sank into the empty space between them, like a sunken ship lying on the bottom of the ocean.

Finally, since she remained frozen in place, Jeff reached forward and tentatively wiped a tear from her cheek. "I'm sorry, Claire. That must be really rough."

"It's okay." Uncomfortable with the intimate moment, she pushed his concern aside. "Do you by chance know Robert Kincaid?"

He shook his head. "Is he your father?"

"Yes. Before my mom died, she told me he lived in Big Cat."

"I can ask around. Paula Kraft would be our best bet. She's the large animal veterinarian here. Maybe she knows him since he owned horses."

"It's worth a try. Nobody else I've asked seems to have heard of him."

"We'll find him, Claire."

Why did he say "we"? Did he plan to help her? A mixture of emotions surfaced—first excitement, because she had an ally, and then dread, for fear she'd be indebted to him.

"What's your mother's name?" he asked. "That might be important information."

"Virginia Kincaid. She was Italian, if that helps."

"Virginia doesn't sound like an Italian name. Is that where you get your dark hair and olive skin?"

"I guess so. I never questioned her name before." Uncomfortable at having shared enough personal information for the time being, she turned the spotlight away from herself. "What about you? Do you have a big family?"

"I have more family than I want sometimes." He hesitated, and she could tell he regretted his comment. "I shouldn't have said that. Sorry."

His comment hurt but she wouldn't admit that to him. "It's okay. How could that be? I mean, how could you regret family? What a problem to have."

"Family can be a problem, all right. They love to butt into your life all the time. Heck, even when you breathe they offer an opinion about it. But I can't imagine life without them."

"Hold onto that thought the next time they make you mad," Claire said. Their eyes met and this time she didn't turn away. The electricity between them stirred her insides.

"After you meet them, we'll see if you hand out the same advice."

She blinked. He wanted her to meet his family?

# CHAPTER FIVE

"Are you limping again?" Jeff asked when Claire hopped sideways to avoid the incoming tide. A zigzagged trail of tiny footprints dotted the hard wet sand behind her.

She fell into step next to him. "It's not a big deal. I walked through a mudflat earlier, and it aggravated my ankle a little, that's all."

He watched as she looked up at the seagulls that squealed overhead. Something about her brought out the tender feelings inside him, ones that he preferred to keep hidden. Then she giggled with joy as the seagulls flew in circle, scavenging for remnants of food on the beach. He loved seeing her lighthearted side.

It was difficult, but he resisted the overwhelming urge to reach for her hand. He reminded himself that his thoughts were inappropriate. He had other plans for the future that didn't include her—plain and simple—plans that made sense when he had originally made them. He wasn't sure why he allowed Claire to distract him, but he found his attraction to her disturbing.

She tossed her hand up as if to shoo away a fly. "My ankle's fine, really." She misunderstood why he was staring at her, obviously thinking he didn't believe her about her ankle.

"Do you want me to wrap it?" He asked because he cared, but really, he prayed she said no. It was best to avoid the intimacy of holding her foot across his lap while he slowly bound her ankle. Just the thought made his mouth parch.

"No, thanks. As I said, I'm fine." She turned away, her cheeks a bright shade of red.

Unfortunately, he liked her shy side.

Too bad he liked her resilient side too. "I'd say you're passionate about horses if you're willing to tromp around the island with a sprained ankle." Not to mention that she'd spent a good portion of last night out here with a bum ankle, without much in the way of warm clothes or shelter. Most women resented his horses and refused to step foot on the shores of the island.

She definitely proved to be tougher than she looked. Not that he wanted to think about the way she looked, with that straight, dark hair, so long and thick. A man could dream of running his hands through it, but not him, definitely not him.

She turned back to face him. "I'd say passion is something we have in common then."

Their eyes met and held for a long moment.

He abruptly changed the subject. "I have two herds to find and then we'll be finished." He reminded himself that he just met her, and not to be fooled by the comfortable camaraderie between them.

When she stepped ahead of him he noticed the limp again. He sighed and grabbed for her hand. "Let me help give your ankle support." To Jeff's surprise, his voice sounded gruffer than he'd intended. He needed to stop the constant stream of thoughts about her, but now that he held her hand, it proved next to impossible.

Eventually they passed a fallen log on the outskirts of the large maritime forest. Even though he worked on the island almost daily, he never took the beauty for granted. "This is a great place for a picnic," he said as he pointed to the downed tree. "Have you eaten lunch yet?"

"I've snacked some but haven't actually sat down to eat." She fingered her bare neck and looked sad.

He decided not to ask, not to probe into her private matters.

Claire glanced up at him and seemed troubled. "Last night ... I lost a pewter mustang necklace that my father gave me. I retraced my steps but couldn't find it." She hesitated and stared out at the water. "I know it's a long shot, but if you happen to see it, would you let me know?"

What was he supposed to say? That seemed an impossible task, to find a necklace in miles of deep sand.

"It's a pewter horse on a silver chain. He gave it to me for my birthday a week before we left home for good."

Jeff swallowed hard. How could he refuse? Her father, who seemed innocent, had given her a birthday gift right before her mother had taken off for Charlotte with Claire in tow.

"Sure, I'll look out for it," Jeff said. Claire had suffered enough pain and loss without this added to the mix. Not only did he intend to look for her necklace, he decided to find her father. Every child deserved to know her dad.

But why did Jeff feel the need to help Claire? That puzzled him. He had his own problems. He knew all too well that once he began to search for her father, he wouldn't stop until he finished what he'd started. Maybe offering to help her would distract him from his growing doubt about his relationship with Lynette.

He tried to ignore his disturbing thoughts, but when they sat on the short log together to eat their lunch, trying not to touch each other, his overly alert mind focused on every move she made.

In a small attempt to distract his wandering mind, Jeff eyed the abundance of sandwiches spilling out of her pack; she was certainly prepared. "I haven't had a peanut butter and jelly sandwich since I was a kid," he said. "Want to exchange one for some trail mix?" He dangled a baggie of raisins, almonds, and cashews in front of her face to tempt her. "I made the mix myself."

To his surprise, she snatched the plastic bag out of his grasp and in return, tossed a sandwich onto his lap. Then she dipped her slender fingers into the baggie and scooped a handful of trail mix into her mouth.

She closed her eyes, a pleasant murmur escaping from her throat while she chewed. Unable to stop staring at her lips, he froze when she reopened her eyes and caught him watching her mouth. Thankfully, she ignored the awkward moment.

"I'm impressed with your culinary skills," she said with humor laced in her voice.

Culinary skills? Hardly.

She picked up her water bottle and drank a long gulp. When she finished, she nestled the bottle into the sand by her feet.

"We need to get going and find those mares." He wiggled his eyebrows. "Before it's too late, if you know what I mean."

"We wouldn't want any unplanned foals, now, would we?" She giggled. "Okay, I'm ready." She shoved another handful of trail mix into her mouth and handed the baggie back to him.

"Keep it if you want."

She chewed and swallowed. "Thanks. Don't mind if I do." Claire slid the baggie into her pocket before she reached down and retrieved the water bottle at her feet. "I actually ran out of water last night, and I'm not about to run out today. I packed six bottles."

"You could always drink from the marsh pond if you run out." He winked at her. Playing with her was fun.

"Believe me, last night I almost drank from a hole one of the mares dug. I had this bright idea to stick a ferry brochure in my bottle to funnel rainwater. Too bad that didn't work. The wind knocked it over."

"Very resourceful." Not only was she a looker, she loved horses, and she was intelligent—a dangerous combination. "It's not a good idea to drink standing water, anyway. You have to watch out for bacteria. The horses find it tasty, though." He buckled his daypack around his waist again and retightened the shoulder straps.

They hiked for close to twenty minutes before they sighted another harem off in the distance. Once they were closer, Jeff said,

"Okay, let's approach from over there." He pointed to a small dune to the right of them, about a hundred feet away. "I need to get closer."

They travelled parallel to the horses. He carried on with his business as if the horses weren't there. As usual, he never made eye contact with them, nor did he even glance in their direction.

When they'd reached the base of the dune and climbed to the top, he sat down to give the impression he planned to rest. This wasn't the case, but more the image he wanted to portray so the horses wouldn't flee. He glanced back at Claire, who mirrored his actions, and she appeared relaxed and casual. She even knew to avert her eyes from the herd. She definitely understood horses.

Jeff looked up at the cloudless blue sky, down at the sea oats that blew in the breeze, and at the white-colored sand that they'd just traversed. Yes, he could spend his entire life right here on the island, just as his ancestors had done.

He removed his daypack, unzipped it almost silently, and then paused. When the horses remained in place, Jeff pulled out the dart gun. Before long, he aimed at one of the mare's haunches and shot her with the dart.

The mare raised her head in protest and glared at them. Jeff stared at his boot and pretended to dust off sand. His demeanor remained calm and he occupied himself for at least five minutes while he fiddled with his shoelace, a blade of sea grass, and the buckle on his pack. When the mare ignored him again, he raised the dart gun, aimed at a different mare, and then returned the gun to his bag.

He smiled at Claire. "Mission accomplished. You can take photos now if you want."

"Where did you shoot the darts?"

"Into their rumps. It doesn't hurt other than a sting."

The mare that had glared at them earlier returned to munching the sea grass and seemed oblivious to the intruders who had invaded her biological system.

Claire angled her camera at the grazing stallion, and Jeff imaged she included the picturesque beach, a tangle of scrub oaks, and the tall sea oats behind him.

"What a colorful shot," she said, and then turned to snap a photo of him.

"Hey, stop that."

"If you don't like it, why are you smiling?"

Okay, she got him on that one.

He actually wished he knew more about photography. "You know, I'd like to see the pictures sometime."

"Absolutely. Maybe I'll display the one of you in the bay window of my studio." She laughed.

"That should scare half the town away." He scrunched up his face in horror and then chuckled. "If you take a day trip to the northeast side, you can see the lighthouse on Cannon Island." He leaned back on his elbows and watched her. "That's Dancer's territory, and you can get great pictures of his herd with the lighthouse in the background."

"I'll do that. Thanks."

He looked at his watch. "We need to keep moving." Jeff stood and offered his hand to help her. He had to admit that occasionally, being too polite to women got him into trouble. Women often took advantage of him. He couldn't help it, though. His daddy and granddaddy had pounded it into his brain as a child to treat women with respect. One time he'd made the mistake of asking, "What if the woman doesn't deserve it?" He'd gotten a whipping he'd never forget.

She looked away from him and appeared shy, but took his hand anyway until she stood. Then she dropped it "Where is the next herd?"

"Northwest of here." He pointed off into the distance. "Goliath's land is beyond that farthest dune. Each herd hangs out in certain areas of the island. The stallions have worked out whose territory is whose."

She snapped her pack into place and brushed a thin layer of sand off her jeans. "Okay, I'm ready."

Jeff glanced at her. He had believed once before that a woman could affect a man and lead him to places he'd never been, but that had been a farce. His ex-girlfriend had packed up and moved back to the city, Charlotte actually, just as Claire would do. He'd give her six months tops, and then she'd run back to the noise, traffic, and stoplights. He'd be stupid to make that mistake again, to believe an outsider could love it Down East and stay around. In another three weeks he'd never have to worry about Claire, or any other woman, moving away again.

# CHAPTER SIX

Claire sensed her life changing, but she had no idea why. Pony Island made her feel connected, as if she belonged here, as if her past had joined her future. The most logical explanation seemed to be the horses, but another reason could be Jeff. Perhaps it was a combination of both. Horses were like a well-developed root system that had started in her early childhood. Her love for horses seemed as natural as breathing. And Jeff, he was in his element around the Islander Ponies.

She watched as he navigated the rough terrain with ease. He definitely knew the island well. When they approached another rivulet that cut inland, he looked back and said, "You'll have to follow me closely. A shallow ledge runs under the water here. If you deviate by even a couple of feet, you'll fall in."

She shot him a thumbs-up and stayed close. With the murky water, it seemed almost impossible to know where to step, but Jeff had obviously done this many times. She wondered how often he'd gotten drenched before he'd finally learned to pick his way through the water. When she couldn't stand the curiosity any longer, she asked, "How do you know where to cross without falling in?"

He flashed a cocky grin. "See that old tree stump?" He pointed behind her.

She risked her balance and turned to look back. She saw a wide stump perched on the sandy bank. "I see it."

"Now look ahead. See that tree?"

She glanced at the only tree near the rivulet. "Yes."

"If you step in the water where the trunk is, and line up with the tree, you'll never fall off the ledge."

"How did you figure that out?" His ingenuity amazed her.

Jeff's laugh drifted back to her as they splashed through the water. "I learned the hard way," he said. "The first time I crossed, I followed the herd, but I wasn't directly behind them. Sure enough, they crossed without any problem but I fell in. I couldn't figure out why it was knee deep for them but over my head. That's when I found the ledge. You have to trust the horses."

A gasp caught in her throat at the familiar phrase. She continued behind Jeff in silence, thinking about Black Eagle.

"The horses have beaten paths they travel," he said.

She recalled something Black Eagle had told her, when she'd questioned him about the trampled paths in their horses' overgrown paddocks on the ranch. He'd said, "The trails offer familiarity and safety. Horses are prey animals, and they use the trails to escape predators. Domestic horses still have that instinct, and they use the survival technique, no matter if they're in a field or a paddock." The same logic applied to navigating the cloudy water. The shallow ledge made it easier to cross, and it provided a natural defense against less wily enemies, which would fall into the deeper water and allow the horses a chance to escape.

Claire climbed from the slimy bank of the creek and held back a wince. Her ankle throbbed more now. She could have done without the added resistance of the water, after her trek through the mudflat earlier. The easy choice would be to accept Jeff's offer to wrap her foot, but she resisted that idea again. A believer in the power of positive thinking, she always tried, whenever possible, to forge on without complaint.

To distract herself, Claire stared at Jeff's backside and realized that in addition to his physical attributes, his personality appealed to her as well. He appeared to be the perfect man for her, horses and all, but she understood all too well that perfect men didn't exist. He was still a man, still capable of abandonment and unfair expectations.

Besides, she most definitely wasn't interested in another relationship, not at this time in her life. A better choice would be to stick with her original plan to develop a solid business. That way she could focus on an independent life, one that included horses and photography, and maybe a few friends. She could consider Jeff a friend. Things were much simpler that way.

He broke into her thoughts. "This part of the island is on higher ground. There used to be an old fishing village over there." He pointed to a clearing, now void of any indication of prior habitation. "The trees and dunes helped protect the village from the wind."

"People used to live here?" She guessed that explained the graveyard she'd seen on the map. As much as she had come to love the island already, she wouldn't want to live here.

"Oh, yes. Some of them were my ancestors. In fact, I think of the horses as the last remnants of my heritage on the island."

No wonder he'd been so protective of them that first night.

Jeff pointed to a cluster of trees where a huge oak marked the entrance to a small, grassy clearing. Grave markers poked out of the sand.

"Eventually the hurricanes drove the villagers off the island and onto the mainland," he said.

"I don't blame them. I'd leave, too."

He shot her a scornful expression, as if he judged her as a person who liked to bail when things got tough. From the frown on his face, he seemed lost in a bad memory. Had someone broken his heart and left him behind?

She shrugged off his disapproval. "Do you mind making time for me to take pictures of the gravestones?" She found history to be interesting in general, but North Carolina history held unique appeal. She thought about her father again.

"Not at all." He walked around a large, collective mound of manure and led the way to the graves.

The dilapidated gravestones would indeed make unique photographs. She recalled the small family graveyard on her father's property. He used to love to tell stories about the people buried there, tales that his family had passed down for generations. From the standpoint of Claire's photography studio, these pictures might be a success. She'd bet the tourists had no idea the graveyard existed beyond the beaches they sunbathed on. For that matter, maybe the locals didn't know the graves existed, either, or if they did, she'd guess most hadn't seen them. She zoomed in to capture the writing on the individual gravestones, and zoomed out to include a panoramic view of the cemetery. Yes, Claire loved to photograph history.

The horses were history, too.

"Why do they call them horses instead of ponies?" she asked while she snapped more pictures. Until she'd moved to Big Cat, she had mistakenly called them ponies because of their small size.

He chuckled. "That can be a heated topic. Folks around here get upset if you call them ponies; DNA testing has proved they're actually horses. Locals sometimes call them 'Islander Ponies.' Sometimes tourists hear that and shorten the name to ponies, but the locals frown upon that."

"Why do you think they're so small?" Claire asked, interested in the horses' history. She loved his passion for the animals.

"A diet that consists mostly of Spartina grass might stunt their growth."

"Malnutrition instead of genetics?" She leaned closer to him, fascinated by his knowledge.

"Maybe, but Spanish horses are smaller to begin with," he explained without moving away. His eyes danced, possibly with delight at her interest. "The Islander Ponies date back to when the Spanish galleons sailed through our waters. Some of the ships carried horses when they sank, and the horses are believed to have swum ashore to the barrier islands."

That brought up an interesting idea. "Why don't the horses swim off the island then?"

His gaze sharpened. "Why should they? They have what they need to survive right here: food, water, land. They're *committed* to the island."

What an odd comment. She had the distinct impression he felt she wasn't committed to either the area or to her new business. Why did he care?

He stepped away and added a few feet of space between them. "There is the harem I'm looking for." He pointed to a horse's back end, barely visible around a dune. "Let's walk to the right, over to that dune, and climb it so we're above the herd."

Claire followed Jeff as she had done before. Thankfully, he walked slowly in an effort not to scare the horses. Her ankle still hurt, but at this pace, she could easily keep up with him. But by the time they reached the top of the dune, she welcomed the reprieve.

She really needed to elevate her foot with a bag full of icy goodness. Unfortunately, she'd have to wait for that luxury until she returned home. Besides, she was having too much fun spending the afternoon with Jeff to think about leaving.

When they settled on the dune, Jeff pulled the darts from his pack. Eventually, after the herd accepted their presence and appeared to ignore them, he aimed the dart gun at a brown-colored mare. A moment later, Claire saw her flinch. The horse pinned her ears and glared at a mare that stood next to her, as if to say, "Hey, why'd you do that?" Then she bit her friend on the rump in retaliation.

Claire couldn't restrain a giggle. Jeff glanced back at her and winked; a smile brightened his face. He had such straight white teeth, and those eyes … She forced her attention back to the horses and away from the man who knelt in front of her.

He shot two more darts and surprised Claire when he sat down instead of repacking his equipment. "So what happened after you moved to Charlotte?"

Before she could answer, a lump formed in her throat. She swallowed hard, trying to force it to go away. Until now, she had preferred not to dredge up the painful details of her past, but sharing her life with Jeff felt safe. "For a while ... we stayed in a cheap motel." She grew silent and Jeff didn't push her to answer. "My mom finally landed a job as a waitress, and we upgraded to an apartment. She worked during the day while I went to school. At some point, she became manager and we bought a little white house close to her work.

"Over the years I asked her about my father, why we moved, and if I could contact him, but she always refused to talk about him." Claire paused to take a deep breath. "I tried to call him but he must have changed his number to an unlisted one. I tried to write him. I suspect my mom intercepted the letters and threw them away. At some point, she ripped out his information from my little address book, even though she denied it. My memory eventually faded. Later, once I had access to the Internet, I searched for him, but I never found a trace. My mother died without any explanation, other than her final confession that my father lived in Big Cat." A tear slid down Claire's cheek. "And she said ... he loved me and always had."

He stared at her for a moment. "Come here." He pulled Claire closer and put his arm around her. "I'm so sorry."

"You didn't know." His strong arms warmed her like a safe cocoon. Strange that Jeff's comfort reminded her of her father's foreman instead of her dad. But she had no memory of Black Eagle ever hugging her. Interesting, now that she thought about it, most of her vivid, childhood memories were of Black Eagle, not of her own father. Maybe he'd been too busy working the farm to play with her. Confusion crept through her mind. No one had elicited the level of comfort and security that she'd just experienced from Jeff. The insight seemed significant, but no matter how hard she tried to sharpen the focus of her youthful memories, they refused clarity.

"What's your father's name again?"

"Robert Kincaid." She wiped another tear away and straightened her shoulders. What was she thinking? Jeff must think her a fool to expose her vulnerabilities to a virtual stranger.

"Have you asked around to see if anyone knows him?"

"Yes, at least the few people I've met." She choked down another sob. She refused to flat out cry, not now, not in front of him.

"I might be able to help you. I know a lot of people on the coast."

"I appreciate the offer." She pulled away to regain control of her emotions. "Jenni mentioned a man, a horse whisperer, who hangs out on the island and helps when there's a crisis. Do you know him?"

"No one really knows him, but sure, I know who you're talking about. His name is Jim."

"Oh." She looked down at the ground.

"Why the long face?"

She hesitated before answering. "I hoped he was my father. I know ... that sounds silly."

"Not at all. I wish the answer to your problem was that easy."

She grew quiet. How naive to hope that a strange man who liked horses could be her father. Jeff probably thought her childish at the very least.

He seemed to notice Claire's discomfort and his expression grew serious. His now quiet mood and his new focus on repacking his equipment only proved her thoughts foolish. "Are you ready to go home?" he asked.

No. She wasn't ready to leave Pony Island yet or Jeff, but her time with him had to end at some point.

"Listen," he said and patted her shoulder. "Your father is out there somewhere, so don't get discouraged. There has to be a trace of him, and we'll find it."

***

The return trip to the mainland didn't last nearly long enough. Before she realized it, he had pulled the boat into a private slip. They weren't at a dock she recognized. "Where are we?" she asked. A pelican flew from a piling, and several seagulls scurried away along the oyster-littered shore.

"In Morrisboro," he said. "The Park Service keeps boats here because it's closer to the ranger station and to Pony Island. Besides, Big Cat is smaller and waterfront land is more expensive there."

"What's with the name Big Cat?" she asked. "That's an unusual name for a town."

He climbed out of the boat and onto the dock. He held out his hand for her. "Years ago, somebody spotted a cougar crossing Front Street." At her surprised, he grinned. "Yeah. A cougar, around here. The papers reported that a big cat ran around these parts, and the name Big Cat stuck. When they incorporated the area, nobody questioned what to name the town."

"I'm glad I didn't see a cougar last night while I was alone on the island," she exclaimed. "I knew I had a reason to be worried about wild animals."

"I doubt the story is even true. Don't give it a second thought. By the way, do you mind if we stop by my brother's house to get my dog?" he asked. He sounded almost reluctant. "Frank comes with me everywhere except the island."

"Why don't you bring him there?"

"He needs to stay on a leash, and it's cumbersome to work while I'm holding onto him."

"The first time I went over there," Claire said, "a man had a dog with him. As soon as he hit the beach, he let the dog off the leash. I didn't realize there was a leash law, but since it's a park, that makes sense."

His face hardened. "The Park Service enforces the leash law and we issue fines, but some people don't listen. It's a problem, but so far nothing serious has happened."

"People only care about themselves."

"I disagree. There are lots of good people out there. I do believe in humanity for the most part."

She wished she shared his outlook about humankind; she truly did. Her faith in people had vanished the night her mother had left her father behind without any explanation. She'd always hoped her father would find her, and when he didn't, she'd suffered a great deal of disappointment. She didn't want to be cynical, but perhaps distrust defined her character. What a sad thought, but she was never one to mince words, even to herself.

Unable to align with Jeff's optimistic viewpoint, she answered his question instead. "Sure, I'd love to pick up Frank."

He looked relieved. "Good. Most women who ride in my truck complain because I let him tag along in the backseat. The poor guy is well behaved. He doesn't even lick you if he's told 'No.'"

"I don't know what kind of women you hang around with, but I love dogs. Aren't they supposed to be man's best friend?"

"Exactly. Man is the operative word, not woman."

"I'd love to have a dog. We used to have several on the ranch before my mom and I left. But once we moved to Charlotte, my mom refused to own another pet. I guess it was selfish for me to ask. We could barely afford our own food much less feed a dog. I'd get one now, except that wouldn't work with my landlady. It's in my lease that I can't have animals."

She couldn't read Jeff's expression, which had gone rigid. He opened the door of his awaiting truck and reached out his hand to help Claire climb into the passenger side. She told herself that his gesture was nothing more than Southern charm, but she loved it anyway. The men she usually dated never opened the door for women. She cherished the pleasure.

When he drove down a long gravel driveway, Frank came running from around a bend, barking with delight. The dog kept pace with the truck until Jeff parked in front of a shed, a thin cloud of dust surrounding them despite the prior thunderstorm. The land seemed to dry out fast on the coast, maybe from the dusty and sandy soil. Jeff had barely opened his door when Frank, now coated in a light layer of dirt, greeted him with a slobbery tongue.

"Hey, boy." Jeff climbed from the truck, patted Frank on the head, and to Claire's surprise, walked around and opened her door once again. She had expected him to pick up Frank and then drive her home immediately, but the unplanned visit with his family would probably do her good. She needed to get out and meet people.

"Do you mind if we stay a bit?"

She shook her head, secretly glad for the company, and climbed from the truck. "Hi there, Frank." She reached down to scratch the eager dog behind the ears. The first time she'd met him, she'd missed the mischievous spark she now saw in his eyes. He looked to have a large amount of puppy left in him.

Just then, two children ran from the wrap-around porch of a white cottage. A porch swing, abandoned now by the kids, swayed back and forth. When Jeff kneeled down to their level, they launched themselves into his arms. The girl appeared to be about six or seven, and the boy around four.

Jeff looked up at Claire. "This is Buddy, and this is Princess." Jeff laughed as the boy climbed onto the back of his neck.

"That's not my name. I'm Will," the kid declared with defiance.

Jeff looked up at him. "Sorry, pal." Then his eyes met Claire's and their gaze locked. "That's my man, Will, and this is my princess, Kayla." He squeezed the girl, who squealed with delight.

He had children? Claire glanced at his naked finger—no ring. Was he divorced, widowed?

As if to answer her question, a husky but athletic man walked from the house and said, "Kids, don't climb on Uncle Jeffie."

A flood of relief washed through her. Not that she minded kids, she wanted several of her own, but she hadn't entertained the idea he might be married or divorced. "I'm sorry," she laughed, "but you don't look like a Jeffie."

Will's hand slid down over Jeff's eye, and the ranger's lip wrinkled into a pout. At his playful, puckered-up face, she had to laugh again.

"Okay, don't pretend to be sad," she said. "I see now that I was wrong. You look exactly like a Jeffie." She hadn't had so much fun with a man since … since … well, never. She reminded herself, attracted to him or not, she was happy alone, without the obligations and restrictions that a relationship dictated.

Jeff smiled. "Tom, meet Claire. She's Big Cat's new photographer. Her specialty is photographing the Islander Ponies."

Tom raised his eyebrows, as if to ask, "What's the real story, and why did you bring her here?" In a strong but quiet voice, he said, "Nice to meet you, ma'am."

No doubt, based on their charm and similar physique, they had to be brothers. Claire reached forward and shook his hand.

"Big Cat could use a photographer." Apparently shy, Tom looked at the kids instead of Claire. "The only one around here is Ned Cooke over in Mobley, two towns over, and he's close to retiring. The horses are a popular attraction, so I suspect you'll get enough business."

"Claire was out photographing them yesterday," Jeff explained, "and the ferry left her stranded. We got the call after you left the Salty Mug last night."

"The ferry abandoned you?" Tom asked, and frowned.

"Yes," she said.

Tom's frown deepened. "What are you going to do about it, Jeff? This isn't the first time Bob's been a problem."

"Claire took care of him." Jeff winked at her. "He's been warned. I don't plan to take further action unless it happens again."

"It will happen again, or something worse," Claire said. "You can count on it. I don't trust that man."

Both men stared at her until Tom interrupted the silence. "Have you met Lynette yet?"

"She's my landlady."

Tom chuckled. "That will be interesting. Good luck."

Jeff shot Tom a stern look. "Listen, we need to get going. Thanks for watching Frank for me."

Tom nodded and glanced at his watch. "Aren't you going to Mom's?"

Jeff looked at Claire. "Would you like to stay for our Sunday dinner? We usually have roast beef, fried chicken, butter beans, green beans, potatoes; you name it. Oh, and iced tea. The best part is the homemade apple pie."

She met his gaze and dared to hope she could accept his offer.

"I have to warn you, though. My family is kind of overwhelming to a newcomer." Jeff hesitated, and at Tom's nod, he explained his comment. "My cousins show up with their kids, and it gets rather loud."

Loud didn't bother her, but she didn't want to crash his get-together. She also wanted to squelch her growing attraction to him.

"Thanks for the offer, but I'd like to go home," she said without much enthusiasm. She tried to hide her disappointment for not accepting his offer but it was for the best. Maybe she was afraid to get too involved in his life, his family. As usual, she had to analyze everything.

Jeff studied her for a moment. "I promise you'll enjoy the food and the company. It would be a good time to ask around to see if anyone knows your father."

He'd said the magic words.

"You convinced me." She'd have a chance to meet some of the locals and perhaps find out some much-needed information. Her decision, she argued silently, had nothing to do with meeting his large, homey family, nothing to do with feeling lonely.

"Come on, then." Jeff slapped his leg for Frank to follow, and the dog obeyed with the utmost adoration. "We'll be right on time if we drive over there." Jeff opened her door, and then after Claire climbed into the truck, he opened the door to the extended cab. Frank hopped in and sat on a blue-striped towel spread across the backseat.

Jeff disappeared around the rear of the truck and got into the driver's side. "By the way, I live on the far side of the farm, just down that road." He pointed to a dirt track that disappeared behind an old barn. "My grandfather owned all this land, and after he passed away, we subdivided it between my parents, my sister Pam, Tom, and me. I love the farm and living so close to Tom's kids."

"I can't imagine having nieces and nephews and cousins, or even a sibling for that matter."

"We are one big family. It sounds kind of corny, but Mom insists we all get together on Sunday afternoons for an early dinner."

"I didn't know families did that any more. I'm envious." A jolt of longing struck so deeply that it hurt. She looked back at Frank, who now appeared to be sleeping on his towel. Not only did she want relatives, she still wanted a dog.

Moments later, Jeff pulled up in front of an older, two-story house with huge white pillars and a wrap-around porch. Long, narrow windows lined the porch and baskets of brightly colored flowers accentuated the friendly atmosphere. In the summer months, she imagined kids playing under the pecan tree that took up a large portion of the small front yard. Off to the side, an old red barn added to the rural charm.

As soon as they neared the front door, a flood of kids ran from around back. "Jeffie, it's time for dinner," a blonde-haired boy yelled.

"You better save some of that pie for me." Jeff turned to Claire and chuckled. "He ate second helpings last time before I got any." Jeff ruffled the kid's hair and held the door open for the crew.

Jeff made the introductions while people meandered around the buffet table or held back in small clusters. Claire and Jeff both inquired about her father, but unfortunately, no one seemed to know Robert Kincaid.

"Don't be worried about your father," Jeff said. The buffet line advanced and they were almost at the beginning, where the china plates awaited them.

"How can he live in Big Cat and no one has ever heard his name?"

"We're just asking the wrong people. He's out there, and I'll find him." He picked up a blue-patterned plate and handed it to her.

"You mean I'll find him." She noticed he looked hurt by her words. "I appreciate your help, I really do, but I have to do this for myself. I want to see his expression when he first finds out who I am because I need to see that he really loves me."

They made their way through the line before he answered. "I guarantee he loves you. He wasn't the one to leave, Claire."

He motioned for her to sit at the main table. They had just started eating when the screen door slammed shut. Heads turned and a groan escaped from the blonde boy.

Lynette Cooper floated into the dining room. What was Claire's landlady doing here?

"Lynette, glad you could make it," Jeff's mom said with forced friendliness. "We've already started eating. Help yourself to some food."

Lynette flashed a rather fake-looking smile to the large table of people and to the overflow table crammed in the corner. When her glance met Claire's, a frown crossed her perfectly made-up face. Instead of filling a plate with food, she strode over to Jeff, who sat next to Claire.

"Hi, darling." Lynette glanced back and forth between the two of them, and then bent down and planted a long kiss on Jeff's lips. When she finished, she turned from Jeff's reddened face and stared directly at Claire. "I see you met my fiancé."

# CHAPTER SEVEN

Fiancé? Jeff had certainly failed to mention his engagement. A mixture of hurt and anger bubbled to the surface of Claire's confused and overloaded brain. She withdrew and remained quiet, a reaction that had served her well in the past, from the most dangerous situations to the most hurtful.

"Lynette, why don't you get a plate," Jeff said. He scooted closer to Claire to make room for the additional chair that his cousin pushed toward him. Instead, Lynette folded her body against Jeff's and looked at Claire with a calculated smile. She flashed her diamond ring in a way that said Jeff belonged to her.

Then she leaned closer to Claire. "Claire, honey, how are things at the studio?" Lynette's voice, layered with artificial sweetener, made Claire want to gag. Without waiting for an answer, she said, "You know, if you ever need anything, you can call me."

Right. How thoughtful.

Claire sat taller and tried to maintain a confident air. She refused to let her landlady know how she'd just derailed her fantasy about Jeff—a fantasy she hadn't admitted to herself, until now.

"Thanks for the offer," Claire managed to say with a steady voice. "The studio is great." That might be true about the studio, but not about Claire's emotional wellbeing. Tears threatened to overpower her façade. She didn't understand. Jeff had given no indication that he'd been interested in her, but she thought she had detected subtle clues that suggested otherwise. Obviously, she'd been way off base again.

The chatter resumed and people continued to eat their dinner. Uncomfortable with the underlying tension, Claire scooted her chair away from the table. In a low tone, she said, "Jeff, I'd like to leave. Sorry for the inconvenience, but would it be possible for you to take me home now?"

"Sure." He pushed his chair back, but before he could stand, Lynette stopped him.

"Why don't you let me take her? I can eat later." Lynette blinked her eyelashes with delicate and deliberate manipulation.

Why couldn't men see the truth behind such women? It always amazed Claire.

When Jeff hesitated, Lynette spoke again. "Really, I don't mind."

"Claire?" he asked.

"It's fine. Thanks for dinner," Claire said. She thanked Jeff's mother and left the house with Lynette close behind her.

Lynette clicked the unlock button on her shiny blue Mercedes-Benz SLR McLaren Roadster. Claire recognized the model because her mother's egotistical ex-boyfriend had owned one. How fitting. They silently climbed in, neither woman speaking the entire way to Claire's apartment.

Finally, Lynette pulled into the lot behind the studio and stopped the car. "Listen," she said. "I don't know why you were at Jeff's family dinner today, and I don't want to know, but you need to understand something. My wedding date is set three weeks from yesterday, and I expect you to stay away from my fiancé."

Claire stared at her. She really couldn't stand rude and bossy women. "I have no intentions of interfering with your wedding. If you're that insecure about your fiancé, then it seems you both have bigger issues than me." Claire opened the car door, climbed out without another word, and strode toward her studio. She ignored the hammering pulse pounding in the veins on both sides of her neck.

***

Jeff shook his head. How could he be so dim-witted as to allow himself to be attracted to Claire right before his wedding? He didn't need the last-minute confusion it was causing him. But he felt so comfortable with her, so at ease. The last woman who caused those feelings in him was Dana, and that alone set off loud warning bells. He'd bet money that Claire would leave town, too. The fact they were both from Charlotte scared him to death because in the end, she'd run off back to the city, just as Dana had done.

Jeff took a drink of his cola as he sat alone and sulked on a barstool at the Salty Mug. He'd worked this morning, had come back to town to eat an early lunch right down the street from Claire's photography studio. Too bad he planned to go back to work on the island later this afternoon, or, against his better judgment, he might give in to his desires and go see her.

He wondered what she was doing today. Truth be told, he actually missed her.

No matter how hard he tried, she wouldn't leave his thoughts. To his disappointment, all week long she'd managed to avoid him. He'd even gone into the studio to talk with her once, to apologize for whatever had upset her, but she'd asked Shirley to assist him and then left the room. To avoid any questions from Shirley as to why he was there, he bought a framed photograph of Dante nursing in the marsh pond. The photo looked good in his living room, but that wasn't the point. It ticked him off that she was avoiding him.

Jeff liked Claire, had wanted to help her. He'd rescued her from the island, tried to defend her against the creep that owned the ferry, and brought her back out to the island so she wouldn't have to rely on the ferry again. Heck, he'd even pledged to find her father, a commitment he didn't take lightly. So what was the problem? Women were the problem, that's what. They all wanted his help to solve their troubles and wanted to give back nothing. Well, it didn't matter because he had nothing left to give.

When Dana had left him to return to Charlotte three years ago—after she'd handed back his ring mere weeks before their wedding—he had a right to be cautious with women. Dana had claimed to love the quiet coast, but in the end, she needed the buzz of the city. She'd left him for a career and a larger population.

Lynette was another story. She had roped him into an engagement, which made him even more guarded.

He shook his head. Man, his pessimistic attitude stunk right now. He despised the feel-sorry-for-me mindset and needed to pull himself out of his rotten mood.

"Why the long face?" Donovan stood behind the bar and interrupted Jeff's deep thoughts.

Jeff looked up, startled. "Just trying to figure out women."

"You'll be here a long time then. Can I get you dessert while you try to accomplish the impossible?" Donovan ran a wet cloth across the bar. He never stood still for long.

Jeff shook his head. "No thanks." A thought sprang to his mind. He needed some advice from someone qualified to give it. "Donovan, you've been married a long time. What's the key to a successful marriage?"

Donovan's slanted smile revealed too much. "You have to learn that physical beauty goes away in time, and superficial interests can only take you so far. You had better have something deeper in common, something that makes you both excited. In your case, the horses."

The smart advice hit him between the eyes. Lynette didn't see the value in the wild horses or the island. If she had her way, the island would be an over-developed tourist trap, and she'd own a string of rental properties. She measured most things in profits. Her profits. Thankfully, the government protected the horses and their natural habitat.

"Thanks, Donovan. I appreciate your honesty."

"No problem, son. Think about what I said." Donovan saluted in homage to his military years, and shuffled off to help another customer.

Confusion clouded Jeff's mind even more. Females were bizarre creatures. He didn't understand them. Maybe married life, or dating life for that matter, was for someone else.

Perhaps he should let Frank choose his women for him. The dog had a good sense for character and was usually right on. He actually didn't like Lynette. She wanted Frank to live outside, not sleep on the bed with Jeff. He'd give her that much, about the bed, but living outside was out of the question. To Jeff, Frank was a member of the family.

Jeff wanted a simple, happy life, void of relationship conflict. Lately, that's all his life with Lynette seemed to be about, conflict. They argued about the wedding, where Frank lived—inside or outside—about his nieces and nephews who came over all the time, and even Sunday dinners. Lynette would rather work than spend time with family.

And that brought his thoughts back to Claire, who seemed a perfect fit for him, except she wasn't from Big Cat. She wouldn't last here for long. She'd want to leave town as soon as the tourist season ended and earning a living got tough. Sure, Claire seemed to love the horses and his dog, but the city would call her back. It didn't matter that her father supposedly lived around here, and that she had been born in the general vicinity; she'd still leave.

He wished Claire well. If he had any sense, he'd keep his distance from her. That way, when she bailed and left town, he wouldn't feel the all-too-familiar sting of disappointment. He wanted to avoid his complicated issues about relationships and trust, and she unknowingly made him face them head on. He didn't want change; in fact, change would disrupt the safe life he'd created. It might be sad, but he'd accept a loveless marriage with Lynette in order to remain near the horses and his family.

But thoughts of Claire continued to pop into his mind. He needed to get a grip. His wedding date, in two weeks now, hovered over him. He rubbed his eyes with the palm of his hand, but his headache refused to budge. Wasn't an engagement supposed to be a happy time, filled with laughter, choosing flowers and rings together? Instead, Lynette had picked out their rings and had simply informed him that he needed to pay for them.

Jeff wasn't one to back out on plans. He knew all too well the sharp pain that wedged in your heart when your fiancée canceled your wedding at the last minute. Besides, Lynette would provide his basic needs: a wife and eventually a family. He wasn't picky unless he factored in what his heart desired, but she appeared to be the opposite of that.

Before Claire came to town, he'd been content and had plugged along happily, or so he thought. Once he met Claire, his life flipped upside down and he saw a glimpse of what it could be like. He saw weekends on horseback in the Croatan National Forest, tents and campfires, and most important, a lifetime filled with the Islander Ponies. He saw kids galore, who ran and played in his large backyard, kids who jumped off the barn's hayloft into a huge pile of soft hay as he'd done as a child, and pony rides.

He had to stop daydreaming.

"Hi, Jeff." A woman's voice caught him off guard.

He turned to see his cousin Paula, the town's large animal veterinarian, pull out a barstool. He hadn't heard her approach. "Hey, Paula. What brings you here?"

Paula loathed the word "vet" and demanded people call her the town's veterinarian. Since she had earned her clients' gratitude repeatedly, and volunteered her services with the Wild Horse Foundation, people respected her quirk. A definite asset to the horses, she never complained about the long hours spent helping out. She loved horses, especially the Islander Ponies, and specialized in reproductive services. She also happened to be Lynette's best friend.

"I saw your truck out front," she said. "I came by to let you know there's a new foal on the island, born about an hour ago. Floyd Graham, my new assistant, just called me; he'd counted the foals and spotted the newborn, still wet from birth."

"How's the foal doing?"

"I'm not sure. Floyd said it hasn't nursed yet. I'm on my way over there now. I thought you might want to join me."

Jeff's mind immediately shot to Claire. Photographing the new foal would provide quite an opportunity for her. He glanced at his watch and hoped she could leave her studio on a Saturday afternoon. "I have a stop to make first. When do you want to leave the dock?"

"In a half hour. Please, hurry."

***

Claire poured cat food into a dish for the two feral cats that hung around the alley. They usually visited her patio, sectioned off with large pots of pansies planted by a local handyman, once or twice a day. The black cat would come within a few feet of Claire to rub affectionately on the deck chair, but if Claire tried to approach her, she'd scoot away. The gray one, however, remained extremely shy.

"Here you go, kitties." Claire refilled the water dish with fresh water and set it beside the chair. She wanted a farm someday, a handful of cats, maybe a dog or two, and as many horses as possible. Animals represented peacefulness to her, especially cats. They were loyal, unlike men—or people, for that matter—and were safe. They expected nothing from you other than your company, food, and water.

She walked inside the studio and concentrated on hanging framed photos on the wall while Shirley tinkered around and reorganized the print bin. Shirley liked to keep her hands busy and often fiddled with objects or held a mug of tea. She always kept a knitting bag hidden behind the counter to busy her fingers during break time.

Claire didn't mind. Shirley provided a much-needed sense of comfort with her grandmotherly way. Especially this week.

Claire had tried to distract herself from unpleasant thoughts of Jeff and his fiancée. She'd spent long hours at the computer while she uploaded and edited the photographs she'd taken on Pony Island. Several shots excited her, especially the foggy picture of the ship and a couple of Dante. She found her favorite picture to be the one of him trying to nurse while his mother waded in the marsh pond. He had his neck outstretched with his fuzzy nose jutted upward in search of milk while his mother skimmed her muzzle along the water and ignored him. Precious.

Even though she had managed to keep busy, there were many times when Lynette had popped into her mind and had threatened to disrupt Claire's makeshift peace. If she made Lynette mad, the woman could easily ostracize her from Big Cat. Sure, Claire had a lease, so Lynette couldn't kick her out of the studio, but she could make Claire's life stressful. The woman could ruin her reputation, one that she needed to build a profitable business.

On the other hand, if she made nice with Lynette and left Jeff alone, her business had more of a chance to survive.

Claire hammered a nail into the wall and hung one of the prints of Dante. Thoughts of Lynette forced Claire's dire financial situation to the forefront of her mind. She'd already used up most of her inheritance from her mother's life insurance policy and some of the money she had secured from a small loan at the neighboring town's bank. In order to set up a professional studio, Claire had bought equipment, from cameras and lenses to matting and framing supplies. She had also paid a hefty deposit and had a high monthly rent for a store on the popular Front Street. Her survival in Big Cat depended on the success of her photography studio.

It was times like this, when she was really down on life, that she missed her mother most. Life had seemed to stop for almost a year after her mom's death, until Claire decided she needed to scrape up the remnants of her life and mold something creative out of it.

That's when she'd come up with the idea of a photography studio. She had a talent for framing the world in the viewfinder of a camera. She saw angles, variances of color and light, and ways to make the ordinary stand out so people could appreciate natural beauty.

"Claire?"

Surprised, she looked down at Shirley, who was dusting just about every object in her path.

"I heard you talked with Lynette's dad. Are we okay on money?" Shirley avoided eye contact and continued working.

"You don't have to worry about the business, Shirley," Claire said through a nail that dangled from her mouth. She pointed to Shirley with another nail in her hand to accentuate her words. "The studio isn't going anywhere. I went there to ask Mr. Cooper if he knew my father." Secretly, Claire was glad she'd obtained a loan from a bank in Morrisboro, and not from Lynette's dad. Knowing the Coopers a bit better now, Claire wouldn't borrow money from Mr. Cooper if he were the last banker alive.

He had taken advantage of Claire's visit. He'd said, "My daughter owns at least half the buildings on Front Street and several others in the area. It would be wise to keep a low profile." Then he'd narrowed his eyes. "Of course, I understand you are new to town and might not understand how small towns work, but we look out for each other here. It would be easy for someone to encounter difficulties if they start antagonizing people, and I'm sure you wouldn't want that."

Claire had smiled. "Excuse me, sir, but I have no idea what you're talking about."

"I see you either learn slowly, or you like forcing me to state my threat directly." His face turned a deep shade of red when she flashed him another smile. "Fine, we'll play the game your way, this once," he said. "You need to stay away from Jeff and stop following him around Pony Island. My daughter's engaged to him, and if you get in the way, you will find it difficult to continue living in Big Cat. Do I make myself clear?"

"Very." Claire picked a piece of lint from her blouse and let it drop on the floor of his office. "Have a nice day, sir." She walked out of the bank and didn't look back.

"Well, did he know your father?" Shirley asked, breaking Claire's thoughts.

"No." Claire held the nail from her hand to the wall and hammered it a little harder than she intended. When she sighed, the nail in her mouth fell onto the floor and landed by Shirley's foot. "Can you hand that to me?" The accidental diversion worked perfectly, ending the unwanted discussion about her father. Right now she wanted to keep her concerns private. She was beginning to doubt that her father had ever lived in Big Cat.

Unfortunately, she'd had her reoccurring dream again last night. Her dad always stood at the end of a short tunnel, backlit by a stream of bright light. He tried to tell her something, to warn her maybe. Whenever she tried to reach him, she felt as if she had to walk through wet quicksand in a hot desert. On the rare occasion when she accomplished the task, he disappeared right before she touched him.

Claire continued to concentrate on her thoughts while she worked in silence. Too bad Jeff popped back into her mind. She'd sworn she wouldn't involve herself with a man again, yet she had. When she saw Jeff with Lynette's arms wrapped around him, she hadn't expected the strong feelings of hurt to surface out of nowhere. She had no right to be upset about his engagement, had no right to be angry that he hadn't mentioned it. Jeff owed her nothing. But the connection she felt with him, one that had mistakenly made her feel she'd known him for years, confused her.

Shirley walked from the back room, carrying a mug of steaming tea. "Claire, are you okay? You look like you've lost your best friend."

Claire turned to study her gray-headed assistant. Shirley had dabbled in photography and wanted to learn as much as possible. Now that she had partially retired, she discovered a passion for photographing birds. Whenever they had downtime, Claire showed her magazines, explained different techniques, and explained the photography software on the computer.

She liked teaching people and actually had her first class, a basic photography class of six people, scheduled next Thursday. Unfortunately, she couldn't convince Shirley to take the class.

Claire's mind drifted to Jeff and his engagement. What a shame; she actually found herself attracted to him and he was taken.

"Claire?" Shirley asked again.

"Oh, I'm fine. Just busy thinking, which is my worst curse."

"That means it's about a man." Shirley reached up to where Claire stood perched on the small ladder and patted her arm with compassion.

Even though she had met Shirley just over two weeks ago, they had formed an immediate friendship. Shirley's wisdom and perceptiveness amazed Claire. She filled the role of mentor in a way that Claire had never experienced before.

Claire looked away for a fraction of a second and then sighed. "Isn't everything about men? I mean, if you boil life down, isn't that what's left? It's unfortunate really."

"Honey, that's life. God put you on Earth to find a mate, to produce offspring, and to love. You weren't meant to hide away in a studio."

Well, that certainly summed things up.

Just then, the bell above the door tinkled. Claire looked into Jeff's excited face. Her first reaction was joy, pure and exuberant joy, and then the pain surfaced and triggered a protective instinct that she knew too well. "Jeff."

"A pregnant mare had her baby." He grinned like a boy. "We're heading over to the island to check on them. I thought you'd want to come, you know, to take pictures."

Claire glanced at Shirley, who frowned. The woman's wise old eyes held knowledge. She knew Claire wanted a man who was engaged to another woman, and not just any woman. Lynette was the darling of the town.

Then, as if the elder woman changed her mind, she smiled. "Go ahead. I can handle any customers we get. Besides, we could use more foal pictures."

When Claire didn't say anything, Shirley nodded her head in encouragement. She had subtly given Claire permission to follow her heart, her instincts, and her passion—for the horses, of course. Claire thought about refusing; time with Jeff was far too dangerous emotionally. But a sparkle in his eyes, an almost enthusiastic pleading, made her accept.

As Claire walked toward the door, Jeff stopped suddenly. "This picture ..." He fixed his gaze on a print lying on a table, an ordinary picture of the graveyard on Pony Island. "Did you alter this in any way?"

Claire stiffened. "I don't alter my photos."

"I didn't mean to offend you, but there's something unusual about this photograph."

Claire climbed down from the ladder and stepped over to the table to stand beside him. "What do you mean? Everything looks normal to me."

Jeff pointed to a cluster of gravestones. "Those look fine, but look at the one by the woods."

Claire looked closer, and sure enough, a lone headstone stood off to the side, tucked between two trees at the edge of the sand. "Okay, I see the gravestone, but what's so odd about it?"

"That grave isn't there. I mean, I've never seen it before. I know every square inch of that island, especially the gravestones of my ancestors, and that one doesn't exist."

"It looks like it exists to me." Claire crossed her arms defensively. "If you're implying that I altered that picture, you're mistaken. I never, ever, modify my photographs other than to crop them."

"As I said before, I'm not trying to insult you. I can't explain why there's an unknown grave in that picture any more than you can; I'm just telling you it doesn't exist."

"When we go to the island, let's pay the graveyard a visit." Claire gathered her camera equipment and walked into the back room to grab her daypack from underneath the cabinet where she stored the cat food. She packed bottles of water, a store-bought sandwich from the refrigerator, and a couple of apples.

Jeff stared at her with wide eyes from the doorway. He seemed almost spooked, as if he'd seen a ghost instead of an ordinary photograph.

# CHAPTER EIGHT

Tension filled the truck. Claire and Jeff hadn't said two words in the length of time it took to drop off his dog at Tom's house, and to travel the distance to the dock. Unfortunately, all Claire could see when she looked at Jeff was Lynette draped all over him.

Jeff, apparently clueless to the strain between them after all, began to whistle as he parked under a shade tree near the dock. Men. Before he climbed from the truck and opened her door, Claire jumped out. The last thing she needed was for an engaged gentleman to open her door. No thanks.

"Why are you walking so fast?" He caught up with her easily with his long stride.

"I guess I'm excited to see the foal." Avoiding the truth seemed a much safer choice. Her attraction to him, and the pain she felt from his engagement, was a temporary situation. She'd deal with her feelings and eventually accept his choice to marry Lynette.

Claire's step faltered at the sight of a lanky woman standing next to Jeff's boat. Claire had assumed that they were going to the island alone. She wasn't sure why the unexpected company bothered her, other than she had the distinct impression the woman was every bit as surprised as Claire.

"Claire, this is Paula Kraft. Paula, meet Claire Kincaid." Jeff smiled in his usual, charming way. The sun reflected off his teeth and his aqua eyes lit up to match the water behind him. "Paula is our local veterinarian."

"Nice to meet you," Claire said. Ah, the veterinarian he'd previously mentioned. At the first opportunity, she'd ask Paula if she knew her father. Claire held out her hand for a friendly shake.

Jeff bent down to release a line from a cleat on the dock. He tossed the line into the boat, seemingly unaware that Paula hadn't returned Claire's handshake.

Instead of returning Claire's greeting, the other woman concentrated on positioning her Tilley hat, as if the exact placement were of utmost importance. It always amazed Claire how some women could be so rude, yet discreet at the same time. Jeff seemed not to notice.

From the way Paula acted, Claire had to wonder if she was another one of Jeff's admirers. For an engaged man, he sure had a flock of possessive women that circled him.

When Claire hadn't made an effort to climb onto the boat after Paula, Jeff, still on the dock, reached out to offer help. Paula's glare forced Claire's stubborn side to kick in and she graciously accepted Jeff's hand. She tried to ignore Paula's frown and stepped onto the skiff.

Paula cleared her throat, as if to declare center stage. "I'm Lynette's best friend. Have you met her yet?"

She definitely won the blue-ribbon award for rudeness. "Sure. What a nice woman," Claire said. Two could play the game. She refused to engage in the small-minded banter, or to succumb to a submissive position in a pecking order as the horses did. Paula obviously felt threatened by Claire's unexpected presence and wanted to warn her to stay away from Jeff. Well, Paula could just smooth her upturned feathers, because Claire knew all too well that Jeff was unavailable.

Jeff loosened another line, and still holding it in his hand, hopped onto the boat. He started his skiff and with the skill of a lifelong sailor, he navigated out of the choppy slip. The sea gulls squealed and followed the boat. With no offer of food, they soon retreated and flew away.

Claire immediately relaxed. Life on the coast included unique birds, sparkling water, desolate islands, and wild horses. She could definitely get used to living here. And to think, she grew up with the noise and stress of the city. She wanted this lifestyle again, in fact had fantasized about it ever since she'd moved from her father's coastal ranch as a child.

She sensed Paula's scrutiny and turned to find her rigid stare. Why did Paula deem her as such a threat? Evidently, Jeff hadn't informed her that he'd invited Claire to join them, and he hadn't explained her role as photographer.

Communication probably would've helped, but now that she'd experienced this side of Paula's prickly personality, Claire was rather glad that Jeff hadn't mentioned Claire coming along. She imagined Paula on the phone first chance, with a full report to Lynette on Jeff's visitor. Claire realized that challenging Paula wasn't the best way to make friends in a new town. Paula, however, didn't seem to be a friend she'd want anyway.

After a scenic boat ride to the island, Jeff threw out the anchor and jumped into the shallow water of a cove. He pulled the skiff as far as possible onto the shore, aimed the nose of the boat into the breeze, and tossed another anchor onto the beach.

Jeff helped Claire out of the skiff and then turned to offer Paula his hand, but she'd hopped out before he had fully extended his arm.

"I'm glad we don't have to rely on *Pony Island Excursions* today for our ride," Claire said with humor.

"So true." He turned to Paula. "The ferry abandoned Claire out here last week."

"How horrible," Paula feigned empathy. The words sounded concerned enough, but Claire had a direct view of the emotionless expression on her face.

"It wasn't that bad," Claire said in a lighthearted tone. "I got a bunch of great photos of the horses." Claire wanted to be friendly, she really did.

"Oh, so you're the new photographer. Lynette's tenant." Her comment sounded like a pointed accusation.

Paula had jumped at the chance to throw Lynette's name at her again. Her attitude would be almost comical if Claire wasn't the recipient of the snide behavior. "That's right," Claire said. "You should stop by and visit the shop sometime. The studio's open now, and I'm almost finished setting up." She needed to remain friendly and professional to ensure the success of her business.

"Sure. I'll do that," Paula said in a nonchalant tone.

"Let's go, ladies. We're looking for Magic's herd," Jeff said, apparently still oblivious to the undercurrent of tension.

The day could be worse, Claire thought. For one, he could have invited Lynette instead of Paula, but that seemed unlikely. Claire would bet that Lynette avoided the island as much as possible, and most likely avoided Jeff's dog, too. Animals didn't seem to be the woman's strong suit. When Claire had signed the lease, Lynette made sure—a few times actually—that Claire didn't have pets, especially a "nasty old cat."

Jeff led the group around many now familiar sand dunes and eventually pointed to the horses off in the distance.

"We need to be even more careful about how we approach," Paula said in an instructional tone as she looked at Claire. "The stallion will be protective over the newborn and mare."

Claire nodded. She squinted and thought she recognized Dante in the herd, but it could easily be the new foal. She couldn't tell from this far away.

The sun hovered overhead. The heat swirled off the sand in a distinct pattern, and Claire wished she could capture the effect on camera. Before long, she removed her long-sleeve shirt and tied it around her waist. Again, she felt Paula studying her, mainly the cleavage exposed from the low-cut, stretchy blue tank top Claire now revealed.

This time Paula offered her a smile, apparently excited about seeing the new foal. "Come on, let's go!"

When Paula powered ahead of them, Jeff sidled up to Claire. "How's your ankle?"

"Not a problem. It's back to normal—"

"Excuse me" Paula interrupted. "We need to climb that dune over there, but we need to zigzag to get there. I don't want to take a chance of driving the herd away with the newborn."

Jeff agreed and Claire followed their lead. For acting like such a snit earlier, Paula seemed to be knowledgeable and compassionate when it came to the horses.

Once they made it to the top of the dune, Claire spotted the distinct-looking Dante. She had been right earlier, that had been him. Claire scanned the sprawled-out herd for the new foal. Off to the side, a wobbly baby, coffee-colored with a large white star on its forehead and a jet-black mane, attempted to stay righted.

Paula pulled out her binoculars and silently observed the foal. "It's a colt," she eventually said. "He's a cutie, but he seems weaker than normal. I'm wondering if he's nursed yet."

As if to answer Paula's question, the colt fell over and landed hard on the ground.

Claire sat up in alarm. "What's wrong with him? Will he be okay?" She hadn't been around many babies, and what she did remember was vague.

"He's resting," Paula said. "At this age they lack coordination when they get up and down. Of course, I'd prefer to see him nurse right away, but sometimes it takes a couple of hours for the baby to figure it out, even with the mom's guidance." She sighed. "Occasionally, they don't nurse and they get weaker, and if left to their own devices, they die. We'll sit here and watch for a while."

"Die?" Claire asked, her voice shaky. "Can we intervene?"

"No," Paula said. She glanced at Claire with compassion. "They're wild, so we let nature happen the way it's meant to happen."

This side of Paula's personality, the informative veterinarian, Claire actually liked. As long as they didn't battle over Jeff, they got along fine.

The foal lay there, flat on the ground, motionless, except for an occasional flick of his tail. Thank goodness for that little movement, proof to Claire that the foal still lived in spite of Paula's reassurance that the baby was just resting.

"He'll make it," Jeff said with determination, but his voice held a note of distress. "I haven't seen one yet that hasn't. The Islander Ponies are tough."

Claire glanced up at Jeff. Instead of reassurance, she saw alarm in his eyes, raw fear etched with deep concern. She had expected to see the usual calm Jeff, not a frightened man, but she had to admit, his vulnerability touched her.

"What's the baby's name?" Claire asked. She secretly hoped if he had a name, it would personalize him more and therefore make him survive.

"Mario," Jeff said. "This year the theme for names is Italian."

"Come on, Mario, you can do it," Claire whispered.

The silence dragged on until Jeff spoke. "Paula, do you know a man named Robert Kincaid?"

Claire jerked her head up from watching the baby. To her surprise, she'd altogether forgotten that she'd wanted to ask Paula about her father.

Paula set her binoculars on her lap. "That name is familiar. Why do you want to know?"

Claire's heart sped up. "He's my father. He lives somewhere close to Big Cat, and I need to find him. He has horses. My hope is that since you're a vet, you've heard of him."

Paula's spine grew rigid. "I'm a veterinarian, not a vet."

"Okay, veterinarian then." Claire backpedaled, confused as to why Paula had such a strong reaction to the word "vet." "Sorry if I offended you. I just want to find my father." Claire frowned and fought off a surge of conflicting emotions.

"Paula has a thing about being called a vet," Jeff explained. "She had a professor drill that into her. He said it showed a lack of respect."

Claire noticed that Jeff's expression softened. No matter how hard the man tried to deny his attraction, she knew he cared about her. He wore his heart in his eyes, and Claire, against her better judgment, was secretly thrilled.

Thankfully his back faced Paula and she couldn't see the affection evident on his face. Claire had already endured enough tension between the two of them and wanted to avoid validating her suspicions.

"He lives near Big Cat, huh?" Paula asked. "He's not my client, but there's another veterinarian in town. We cover for each other sometimes. Maybe that's why the name is familiar."

Claire's hopes shot upward.

"That doesn't sound right, though," Paula continued. "I know most of the people that live here and in the next town over." Paula's face grew serious, as if to strain her memory. "Closer to Virginia ... I remember someone that helped out a lot with the wild horses up there. That might have been his name. Have you tried some of the towns farther north of here?"

Claire wasn't sure if she should be excited about the lead or not because her mother had specifically said that her father lived in Big Cat. Unwilling to share that private detail with Paula, she turned her head away so the other woman wouldn't see the tears in her eyes.

"No, I haven't searched that area yet," Claire managed to say in an even tone. "This is the only town I've looked in so far."

Jeff leaned forward. "We'll find him, Claire. If he's on the East coast, he's close."

Claire could feel Paula's questioning eyes but didn't glance in her direction. She locked gazes with Jeff, instead. "Thanks."

The foal struggled to stand and diverted their attention. Mario extended his back legs first, and with his front legs still folded, he looked to be praying. Then he managed to coordinate his front legs enough to hold his weight. The baby stood upright and wobbled, and then, when he appeared steady, took a shaky step forward. When he remained upright, he slowly wobbled one step at a time toward his mother, who waited nearby. When he reached her side, he stretched his neck and licked her belly. The mare nosed the baby's haunch to encourage him to nurse on her teat instead.

"At least he's interested in nursing," Paula said. "That's a good sign. Let's hope he figures it out soon before he gets even weaker."

"That means there's hope," Claire said with a nervous twitch in her belly. "Please, baby, nurse."

"Now that the baby is standing again, it's okay to take pictures," Jeff said, giving her the all clear. "We're far enough away that it shouldn't spook them. Just move slowly."

She hadn't wanted to take photographs of the baby before now, but with the possibility of capturing the colt nursing for the first time, she became excited. With an unhurried motion, Claire unzipped her daypack. She carefully removed her camera and lifted it out of its protective baggie without a noise.

She already had the zoom lens attached from her last excursion to the island, the day she'd taken pictures of the old cemetery. The graveyard reminded her of the mysterious headstone that Jeff insisted didn't exist. As long as Mario survived, Claire planned to convince Paula to visit the herd by the graveyard. She wanted to prove to Jeff that she hadn't altered the picture.

Claire fought back a smile. She thought about another picture that she'd taken that day, the close-up of a smiling Jeff on a dune. She'd hidden it upstairs in her apartment. If Shirley saw it, she'd ask too many pointed questions, especially now, after she'd encouraged Claire to join him today. The expression on Jeff's face had said it all. He'd enjoyed their time together just as much as she had.

Claire stuck the lens cap in her pocket and took a picture of the foal, who continued to lick the mare's belly and girth area. Cute, but he needed to suckle a different body part. The mother nudged him again and tried to steer him in the right direction, but the baby didn't understand. Claire readied herself for the magic moment. But there was no such luck.

The baby collapsed and didn't move. Paula, Jeff, and Claire patiently waited. "Is he resting now?" Claire eventually asked.

"I hope so," Paula said. She lifted the binoculars again to her eyes. "He hasn't moved in a while. He's starting to make me nervous." She lowered the binoculars and rested them on her thigh. "I wish he'd move and give us a sign that he's okay."

Claire's gaze met Jeff's concerned eyes. She held eye contact with him for a moment before she turned away, fearful he'd see the pain she felt for Mario in her eyes. Maybe she shouldn't have come; she wouldn't be able to handle it if Mario didn't survive. As if the mare understood their concern, she nosed her baby until he finally moved, and then nosed him again. She also seemed worried.

*Come on, Mario. Get up!*

The mare nosed Mario harder and he stirred. He tried to sit, but collapsed. She nudged him again. He struggled to stand, and on the third attempt, he succeeded. Claire silently cheered for him. Not only was he alive, but he stood and licked his mother's upper back leg.

"That's it, baby. A little more to the right," Jeff said with a thick voice. It sounded as though he was trying to fight back emotion, perhaps even tears.

Claire battled her own feelings as she watched the baby search for his reward. The mare turned toward the colt and gave him a push in the rump. He almost fell over but instead, his head slipped between her legs. Claire snapped a picture as the baby licked the teat and finally started nursing.

Paula let out a loud whoosh of air. "Oh, thank you, Lord." She looked upward as though praying, and Claire swore she saw Paula's eyes glisten.

Claire turned away quickly, so as not to invade Paula's private moment of compassion. She picked up her camera again and snapped glorious pictures of the colt happily feeding. Thank goodness the baby figured things out.

Their love for animals had united the three of them. Claire couldn't help but wish that Jeff had someone, a romantic partner, to share his horses with. He deserved that. She wondered if Lynette even understood his passion. Claire didn't know her well, but from the interactions they'd had so far, she doubted it. That didn't make Lynette a bad person, but it likely made her the wrong person for Jeff.

# CHAPTER NINE

Claire fixed her gaze on Jeff and they maintained eye contact. If he felt the same connection to her as she did him, he might understand the silent message.

He must have, because he immediately said, "Paula, before we leave, I need to find Gladiator's herd." Jeff knew Claire wanted to search for the gravestone.

Claire grinned. She imagined the expression that would soon be on his face when he realized he was wrong about the grave.

"I want to check on one of the mares in that herd anyway," Paula said. "She's about to deliver."

"Let's hope she doesn't," Claire said. "I don't think I can handle another nursing episode today."

Paula laughed. "Don't become a veterinarian then."

"Don't worry. I plan to concentrate on my photography studio."

An uncomfortable silence lingered in the air between them.

They packed their belongings without talking, and then followed a path that led through hills of desert-like sand and scrubby plants. Eventually the maritime forest appeared on their right side, and the beach on their left. The clear water of the Sound blended into the bright blue sky. Before long, they turned inland and reached the crossover point of the rivulet. Jeff led the way, with Paula close behind him, and Claire took up the rear.

How would Jeff handle the situation when he saw the grave next to the woods? He obviously didn't know the island as well as he proclaimed. Truth be told, when she had zoomed out to include the entire graveyard, she hadn't actually noticed the lone gravestone tucked between the trees. Then again, why would she notice? She hadn't expected him to question the photograph.

Before long, they hiked over the last dune and approached the graveyard. Paula headed toward the grazing herd, and Claire and Jeff stopped in front of the cemetery.

"Where is it?" Claire asked.

"I knew I've never seen that headstone before. It isn't here."

"Jeff, I swear I didn't alter that picture." She looked up at him. It was important that he believe her. "I just pointed the camera and clicked the button. The grave showed up in the photo, and I didn't think to question it." Goose bumps covered her arms.

"Maybe it was a reflection from the sun." He stared down at her prickly skin. "Claire, I know you didn't alter the photograph, but I don't believe in ghosts."

"I do. I definitely do."

"Why don't you take more pictures? That way, when it doesn't show up again, we can dismiss it as a funky accident."

"What if it does show up again?" she asked.

"It won't."

When her mind cleared enough to formulate a plan, she said, "Why don't you go with Paula, to keep her away from here? I don't want her to question why I'm taking pictures of the air."

"You don't want Paula to know we have a ghostly grave that only shows up in photographs?" He snickered nervously, as if to convince himself that the gravestone didn't exist.

"Very funny. Just keep me in view; I don't want to be left out here alone."

"Claire, you don't need to prove anything. And no way am I leaving you."

"So you think I might be in danger?" she asked to prove her point. "That sounds like you possibly believe the ghostly grave exists."

He rolled his eyes. "Take your pictures, but I'm not letting you out of my sight."

Claire walked closer to the graveyard and stared into the woods. She closed her eyes for a moment and tried to recall the details of the photograph. When she reopened them, she was staring at two trees that looked familiar. "This has to be where the grave is," she said to him. She inched closer and half expected the gravestone to appear suddenly.

When nothing happened, she sighed heavily and pulled the camera out of her pack. She would take pictures of where she thought the gravestone had been and hope for the best.

Claire aimed at the area between the two trees and snapped away, and then zoomed in to take a few close-ups. She found the camera hard to focus without a specific item to shoot at, and she hoped any engraving on the headstone would be clear enough to read. She wanted to know to whom the grave belonged. She tried not to think about the fact that she was taking pictures of something invisible.

Just then, a twig snapped from behind her and her heart raced from the unexpected noise. She whirled around to face Paula and Jeff.

"What are you taking pictures of?" Paula asked, sounding perplexed.

Claire swallowed hard and glared at Jeff. Why hadn't he warned her about Paula's approach? She had to think of a plausible excuse for snapping pictures of the woods. The other gravestones were too far away to use them as an excuse. "I like pictures of leaves, trees, branches, that sort of thing. Ordinary objects make interesting compositions if you zoom in on them."

Her answer seemed to mollify Paula enough to end her questions.

"Are you ready to leave?" Jeff asked, offering Claire an apologetic shrug.

Claire nodded and repacked her equipment. She couldn't wait to see the images she'd captured. Unfortunately, since Paula stood next to her, she couldn't look at the pictures on the camera's LCD screen. Claire was fairly certain she'd found the right location for the gravestone.

The second Paula walked away, Claire turned on Jeff. "Why didn't you warn me?" she whispered.

"I called out to you. You were concentrating so hard you missed my heads up."

He looked upset, adorable even, so much so that she had to forgive him.

"Come on," Paula encouraged. "Let's go home."

The return trip went fast. When they reached the dock, the women climbed from the boat and headed for the parking lot, while Jeff stayed behind to secure the lines. As soon as they were out of earshot, Paula smiled at Claire. In a low voice she said, "I know it's last minute, but Lynette's tenants are giving her a bridal shower next week. It's going to be in the back room of the Salty Mug. I hope you can come."

Was this a peace offering? It didn't feel like another chance to rub Lynette in her face. Claire supposed it didn't matter; Paula had extended an invitation, and she couldn't think of an excuse fast enough to get out of it. Besides, she'd look petty if she didn't attend. That wouldn't bode well for a new business in town. If she wanted to get to know the local women and fellow shop owners, so her studio stood a chance, then she'd have to go to the bridal shower.

"Sure. I'll be there." Claire hid her anxiety while currents of panic shot through her body. She had just accepted an invitation to the dragon's dungeon.

\*\*\*

Jeff held the truck door open for Claire while Paula peeled out of the parking lot, her truck stirring up dust.

"Do you care if I pick up Frank first?" he asked. Claire hadn't minded the first time, but then again, things had changed between them. He should have been up front about his engagement to Lynette.

"Not at all." Claire's face brightened, as if she actually wanted to see the dog. Maybe she liked Frank more than him. He didn't blame her if she did.

"You'll tell me what shows up on your camera, won't you?" He risked a glance her way while he drove along a flat back road.

"Maybe. You have to promise to trust that I haven't altered the photo, though." She smiled. "Otherwise, you need to take your own pictures."

He shrugged. "That implies you think the image will show up again. I bet it was a fluke."

She turned to stare out the side window. "Exactly. That's why you need to take your own pictures, because you aren't going to believe me." She whipped her head around to face him again. "Why don't you watch me upload them? That way you'll know I'm being honest."

He studied her for a quick second. "All right. It's not that I don't trust you, but I need proof."

"I understand."

Before long they drove up in front of his brother's house. His brother's wife, a slender brunette woman about Claire's age, pointed at the gravel driveway that led to Jeff's home.

"That's Tom's wife, Sally," Jeff explained as he waved. "He must have taken the kids and Frank to my house to visit the horses."

What would Tom think when he saw Claire in his truck again? Jeff never brought women to his house, other than Lynette, but to save time he wanted to pick up Frank before he drove Claire back to the studio. He knew Tom wouldn't ask why Claire was with him, but he'd wonder about it for sure. The only people that might openly question him would be his mom and maybe his sister, but if anything, they'd probably be happy that he hadn't dragged Lynette along.

Was it wrong of him to bring Claire here, to spend time with her, even if he kept their relationship on a professional level?

Jeff drove around the bend and pulled up outside his house. For some reason, the expression on Claire's face thrilled him when she saw his home, a four-bedroom Cape Cod. He'd had it built when he'd asked his ex-girlfriend Dana to marry him. She had wanted a newer, bigger house for the kids they'd planned to have one day. Now he'd likely never have kids. A dull ache spread through his body at the dismal thought.

Thanks to his family, they had played musical houses and had shifted around to accommodate him and Dana. Jeff had moved into his new house, Tom and his family had moved into Jeff's vacated house owned by their parents so it wouldn't sit empty, and his sister had moved from their father's house into Tom's old one. But when Dana left to return to the city, everyone felt disappointed. The fact that Lynette would move into the new house after the wedding irked everyone except him. Ultimately, his family would forget about how much they disliked Lynette after they had kids. But who knew when that would be?

He wanted to have children right away, but Lynette wanted to wait. Right now she wanted to concentrate on selling real estate and finding tenants for her rental properties. She was in her prime. She promised that they would have children, eventually.

He had to ask the question, though. If Lynette changed her mind about kids, would he resent his decision to marry her? He had to admit, the thought more than disturbed him. He wanted to hold his children, to play with them, to love them. He had so much love to give that the wait seemed almost intolerable, but he had to be patient. The first step, marriage, needed to start out on a solid foundation instead of on shaky ground. He wasn't so sure about the strength of their relationship, however, and couldn't help but question if he was making the right decision.

Claire screeched with delight. "Are all those horses yours?"

He looked around the farm and tried to view it through her eyes. The house had a nice-sized yard with a young magnolia tree in the front and a black fence around the back and sides. He'd wanted to fence in all of it and not even have a front yard to mow, but Dana had wanted a place to plant flowers. He hadn't complained. After all, he had a pasture full of horses.

"I have twenty. I have a few rescues from Pony Island that I adopted, and a few I'm keeping here until they find a good home. The rest of the horses are part of my breeding program. I have paint horses and quarter horses, and I have a black and white paint stallion that's so well trained you'd never know he was a stud. I can actually lead him around by the forelock, past a mare's stall, and he won't even look at her."

"I'd like to see that. I thought all males looked at women, and most of them do more than look." She chuckled but he didn't laugh. "Just a female joke. Sorry."

"We don't all look or cheat. I don't know who you've dated before, but not all men are jerks." Jeff believed most men were honest. He considered himself loyal; he'd never cheat on a woman. Did his confusion about Claire mean he was unfaithful? He noticed Claire's doubtful look and knew he had to say something. But what?

"Claire … if a man looks elsewhere, he isn't happy in the relationship he's gotten himself into."

"I'll buy that, but why can't the man be honest and end the relationship if he's miserable? I believe in sincerity, no matter how much pain it causes."

She had a point there, but things weren't always that easy. "What about honor?" he asked. "If you're committed to somebody and that person counts on you, it would be dishonorable and selfish to ruin everything you've worked toward together. Especially at the last minute." He'd said too much. Would she understand the implication he made about his own situation?

"If a person is truly unhappy, it doesn't matter how many people count on him, or the timing. That person owes it to himself to be happy."

"Men don't think like that."

"Then that's a shame. Personally, I wouldn't want to live a miserable life just because I didn't want to hurt someone's feelings. I also wouldn't want my fiancé to marry me if he was unhappy. That hurts everybody involved. There's a right way and a wrong way to handle the situation. Cheating is never the right way."

"Is that what happened to you? Did someone cheat on you?"

She stared at him for a moment. "Yes. More than one man." She opened the truck door and jumped out before he could question her further. He hopped out to follow her.

Frank bolted from around the house and just about knocked Claire down. Tom turned the corner next. "Frank sure likes you," he said. "I can't say he usually likes Jeff's female friends."

Jeff frowned at his brother. "Are you referring to Dana or Lynette?" He knew Tom didn't care for Lynette, and he'd suspected his brother hadn't cared for his past choices in women in general. But Tom's bluntness surprised him.

Claire looked shocked at the mention of Dana's name. "Thanks," she said. "I like Frank, too."

Tom left Jeff's question unanswered. "I think dogs sense things about people that we don't," Tom said as he looked at Jeff. "If an animal likes someone, they're usually a good person."

"I'll take that as a compliment then. Thanks, Frank." Claire patted the dog's wet head.

"He's been in the lake. That dog will retrieve a stick all day long if you're willing to throw one out there for him." Tom glanced down at the dog with obvious affection.

"Ms. Claire?" said a small voice from behind them.

Claire turned around and smiled at Kayla. "Hi there." She knelt down to the girl's level.

"Do you want to see the horses with me?" The girl dripped with enthusiasm. "Please?"

"I'd love to."

The little girl reached out, took Claire's hand, and led the group to the paddock fence. "That's Punky," Kayla said, pointing to a small horse eating grass. "And the one drinking water is Ginger. That blonde one is Blondie. Uncle Jeffie wants to find good homes for Punky and Blondie. Do you want a horse?"

"I'd love to have a horse, but right now I don't have a place to keep it." Claire truly looked sorry.

"You could keep it here if you want. Uncle Jeffie won't mind." The girl's face lit up with joy.

Tom grinned, seeming to enjoy Kayla putting Jeff on the spot.

"We'll find a home for them, Kayla," Jeff said. He slicked back the little girl's hair with his large hand. "That's a promise."

"Why are some of the horses wearing halters and short lead ropes?" Claire asked.

"They won't let us catch them until they've been with us a while," Jeff explained. "This way we can reach out and grab the rope. The leads are short so the horses don't step on them and get hurt. The two with halters on are rescues from two weeks ago."

"Oh! How old are they?" Claire truly looked interested.

"Blondie will be two next week," Kayla said, "and the other one is already two." The horses crowded the fence line and Ginger, an older horse, pushed the younger ones away and demanded Kayla's attention.

"I ride Ginger; she's mine," Kayla explained. "Someday I'm going to jump her over fences like Aunt Pam and Paula, and go on trail rides with Uncle Jeffie. Aunt Pam says I'm not ready to do that yet. First, I have to learn to ride better. Do you want to ride her, Ms. Claire?"

Claire glanced up at Jeff. "I'd love to sometime."

Jeff looked at his watch. "I have time to ride now if you want. I could saddle up one of my young mares and we could go on a short trail ride. At least you have on jeans and boots. What do you think?"

"Oh, I don't know."

"What else do you have planned?" Jeff asked.

"I wanted to ask around about my father this afternoon, and upload today's pictures. Besides, Shirley is probably wondering what happened to me."

Jeff detected a hint of excitement in her eyes about riding, despite her words, so he handed her his cell phone. "Since you never carry yours, here's mine. Call Shirley and check in, and then we'll ride for an hour or so. I promise Ginger is gentle."

"I'm not afraid; I've been riding all my life."

"Then you can ride Razor." He winked at Kayla and she giggled.

"What kind of name is Razor?"

"Let's just say he's my prized barrel racing horse. He has two speeds, walk and gallop. He's great on the trails."

"Come on, Kayla," Tom said, steering his daughter away from them. "It's time to go home." He whisked Kayla away and Jeff secretly thanked him.

Claire dialed the studio's number and talked with Shirley. When she hung up, she said to Jeff, "We were actually busy this afternoon. We sold several prints and a woman ordered a framed picture of Dante nursing in the pond."

"It's just a matter of time before people figure out you're a wonderful photographer. When the word spreads, you'll be swamped."

She looked at him sincerely. "Thanks, Jeff."

"Come inside for a minute. I need to change clothes before we ride." He placed his hand at the small of her back to encourage her toward his house. "You can admire your photo hanging on my living room wall."

She walked with him and when they entered the house, he was proud to show off his brightly lit home. He hoped she liked his house, and then he wondered why he cared. She confused him to say the least. It was easy to imagine her in this house with delicious smells coming from the kitchen, which he'd cook for her, of course. He envisioned meals served on the deck along with a pitcher of freshly squeezed lemonade. He could almost imagine a yard full of kids, their kids, as they played and screamed with delight. He sighed. Why did he allow the tormenting thoughts to enter his mind while he was engaged to another woman?

He couldn't help but ponder the question. Obviously, as he told Claire earlier, he was unhappy in his current relationship. What would happen if he indulged himself for once and allowed a future with Claire? Unfortunately, that was simple to answer. She would drag his heart through the mud, all the way back to Charlotte.

# CHAPTER TEN

Jeff changed into his favorite pair of faded jeans, then placed a well-worn cowboy hat on his head before he walked back into the living room. Claire stood like a delicate angel by the fireplace, studying the assortment of family photos lined up on the mantel. He reflected how some women looked masculine in a baseball hat, but not her. She exuded femininity, even while dressed in jeans and hiking boots.

Since she'd first arrived in Big Cat, she had turned his emotions upside down. He was normally a levelheaded guy, one who took pride in his loyalty to the people he loved.

He noticed she was looking at a picture of him. In the photograph, he was standing next to a younger version of his niece and nephew, who were riding bareback on a chestnut pony. Jeff walked up behind Claire, and when he reached forward to touch the frame and share a memory, he caught a whiff of her lavender-scented shampoo. He pulled his hand away from the frame. "Are you ready?" His deep voice cracked.

She turned quickly and almost bumped into him. For an awkward moment, neither of them moved. "Sure," she finally said, her voice equally gruff.

Jeff made for the mudroom and out the side door, followed closely by Claire and Frank. With the barn in sight, and some physical distance now between him and Claire, he regained his composure enough to think straight.

"Lynette mentioned you visited her dad at his bank a few days ago." For Claire's sake, he almost hated to mention his fiancée's name, but he wanted to find out how the search for her father was going.

She shrugged. "He didn't know my dad."

"Sorry. Like I said before, he's out there somewhere and we'll find him."

She grinned, her face revealing a vulnerability that made him want to pull her into his arms.

"Tomorrow after work," she said, "I'm going to visit some of the local quarter horse farms. If my father lives anywhere around here, breeders will know of him."

"There are lots of little farms nearby. That's a good a place as any to ask around."

"The horse world is small and everybody knows each other." She pinched her lips together, then tilted her head to the side. "I guess it's always possible my mother got the name of the town wrong, but I find it odd that she'd pick the name Big Cat if he didn't live here."

"Especially since it's such a small place."

"Exactly. And the name is uncommon."

She had a point. "I know a lot of the local ranchers, so if you want help, let me know," he offered. "I can go with you."

"I appreciate that, Jeff, but I want to find my father on my own. It's my personal quest."

He had to respect her wish, even though it deflated his sense of wanting to help. He really had no business trying to find her father anyway.

Jeff marveled at how different Claire and Lynette were. Lynette seemed to flaunt him as an accessory. She had a well-respected career, and he considered her an independent woman, but she was needy at the same time. She often required someone to prop her up emotionally when she was in the middle of one crisis or another, and she had a tendency to want him to do things for her. Lynette was also materialistic and shallow compared to Claire's down-to-earth way.

She broke his thoughts by saying, "Do you have a helmet I can wear?"

"A helmet," he repeated, unsure at first what she meant. "Oh, right, a riding helmet. You can use my sister's. Just remind me before we mount our horses."

Jeff grabbed two halters from a hook and they walked out to a paddock behind the barn while Frank stayed outside the fence. "You don't have to ride Razor if you don't want to. He can be a handful, but normally that's only when he's about to barrel race."

"He'll be okay. I used to ride my father's barrel racer. He used to rear up until I'd let him run. That horse was so fast. He'd lean into the barrels until I thought we'd fall over." The memories showed on her face and her eyes grew dreamy. "The few times I saw someone else race him, I realized he was scarier to watch than to actually ride."

"You must be a good rider then. That's him over there." Jeff pointed to a chestnut gelding with a perfectly brushed mane and tail.

"You take good care of your horses."

"I try. I have a lot of them, and I try to spend time with each one. I have a routine worked out where I bring my grooming box into the paddock and they come to me. They actually beg me to brush them. They want my interaction, which is far better than if I forced my agenda on them."

"Black Eagle was like that with our horses. He taught me the same philosophy and it makes sense. He insisted on developing a bond with the horses and making a connection with them. It makes a huge difference when they're eager to please."

"I'd say." Jeff locked his gaze on Razor and whistled. The horse whinnied and trotted to him.

Claire lowered her eyes and reached outward, palm up to greet the horse. "Hey there, buddy." The horse nudged her politely in answer. Jeff handed Claire a leather halter and she held it out for the horse to lower his nose into. "That's a good boy."

Jeff walked through a gate that led to the mare pasture, located a paint horse named Lacey, and whistled. She too trotted eagerly to him and lowered her head into the halter. Jeff glanced back at Claire and watched her stroke Razor's neck. Would Lynette mind if she knew he was about to ride with another woman, especially one that she viewed as competition? Would she be furious, or not care? The lack of an answer bothered him.

Jeff reasoned that he needed to work with the young mare anyway. He'd bring Claire along because she wanted to ride, and because he wanted the company. He got tired of riding alone all the time. Sometimes he wanted to share his sport with someone who cared about horses as much as he did.

After they tacked up, Jeff watched her mount Razor with ease. In one fluid movement she softly sat atop the saddle and Razor seemed happy. She hadn't poked him in the side with her toe when she'd mounted, and she hadn't plopped on his back when she sat. Claire and Razor made a good match.

Once they were well on their way, the trail opened into a large field. "Do you want to run?" Jeff asked. When Claire nodded, he said, "I have to warn you, though. Razor's fast, and he won't stop until we reach the end of the field. When we near the edge, you better lean back, because he will jam on the brakes."

"Got it." Claire didn't wait for him to initiate the gallop. She nudged Razor and the horse immediately took off at full speed.

He was amazed at her ease and confidence on horseback, and on an unfamiliar horse at that. She appeared fearless. Razor sped through the field and looked like a rocket.

She rode with impressive poise and balance, as though she had ridden Razor all her life.

"Come on Frank," he said to the dog. "We can't beat them but we can join them." Frank barked and Jeff nudged Lacey into a slower-paced gallop.

Sure enough, once Razor reached the end of the field, he skidded to a sudden halt. He tripped and collapsed onto his knees, however, instead of sliding gracefully as he always did. Jeff watched the ensuing disaster as if it played in slow motion. Claire lurched forward onto his neck. The horse's nose hit the ground and Claire sailed over his head as a circus acrobat might do. Her body did a complete flip, and she landed on her back. She lay there still.

Jeff urged Lacey to gain speed so he could reach Claire faster, but the horse couldn't run any quicker. By the time he approached Claire, his mare huffed for breath. Jeff jumped off before Lacey came to a complete stop and ran toward the unmoving lump.

"Claire!"

He knew better than to move her, in case she'd hurt her back or neck. "Claire! Answer me." She still made no movement or sound. "Answer me now." He fought off panic and forced himself to remain rational. He gently brushed her long bangs from her eyes. She winced. "Claire, talk to me."

Frank whined and licked Claire's face affectionately.

She moaned.

"I'm calling for help. Don't move." His heart hammered in his chest as he pulled his cell phone from his pocket and dialed 911. "I need an ambulance." He tried to remain calm and give the dispatcher the information she wanted and then added some specific details to increase the likelihood that someone would find them in the remote area. "If you come in from Highway 24, you'll see a street on your right, called River Landing. That road will dead-end into a dirt track. We're about a mile down on the right, in the field. Please hurry. She's barely responding."

Once the dispatcher was finished with him, Jeff turned his attention back to Claire, smoothing her hair to the side once more.

"I shouldn't have put you on Razor. Darn it, why'd I do that! He's normally so sure footed."

Claire moaned again but didn't open her eyes. She still made no movement at all. If it hadn't been for that small, painful-sounding moan, he'd be even more worried, if that were possible. He picked up his phone again.

"Tom, Claire fell off Razor and isn't moving," he said in a shaky voice. "I've called for an ambulance. Can you come out here to bring the horses back?" Jeff glanced at Razor, who appeared all right and now grazed in the open field.

"Oh, man!" Tom exclaimed. "Where are you?"

Jeff told him how to find them. "Please hurry. I don't want to leave the horses out here alone when the ambulance arrives. I want to ride with her to the hospital."

"No problem. I'll get Pam to help me."

"Thanks." He disconnected the phone and tossed it onto the grass next to him. His sister, always a source of comfort no matter what the crisis, would know what to do until the ambulance arrived. She was a nurse, after all.

"Hang in there, sweetie. People are coming to help." His heart ached to the point that it felt like someone had driven an ice pick into his chest. What, he asked again, was this woman doing to him? She was lying on the hard ground, hurt, all because he'd put her on his fastest horse. His warning about Razor's sudden stops, the horse's fall aside, hadn't been enough to protect her, to prevent this awful accident from happening.

Stop it. It did no good to blame himself; it was an unfortunate mishap, that was all. She'd be fine. She had to be. He wouldn't let anything bad happen to her, not if he could help it. But he already had. Claire was hurt.

Despite his thoughts, he reminded himself to remain positive. "Claire, you'll be okay." He said the words for her benefit as much as for his own. "Just like Mario, when I told you he'd figure out how to nurse, he did."

Just then, his phone rang. He glanced down, looked at the caller I.D., and groaned. He definitely deserved Lynette's untimely call. "Lynette, I can't talk right now."

"What's wrong? You sound winded or upset."

"I'm in the middle of something and can't talk." *Tell her the truth!*

"What's the problem?"

Here it comes, time to explain that he'd gone on a joy ride with another woman. He deserved this, he really did. The best he could do was to tell the truth and hope she'd understand. "We went on a trail ride. I wanted to work with Lacey. Claire rode along and fell off Razor. She isn't moving and seems to be hurt."

"Oh! Will she be okay?"

He had expected her to get mad, or yell, or something. "I don't know. Like I said, she isn't moving, and her eyes are closed." His throat ached. "Listen ... I need to go." He hoped she hadn't heard his concern and the affection layered in his voice. Concern seemed normal but affection was downright inappropriate.

"Keep me posted."

"Will do. And Lynette, thanks."

He had just shoved his phone into his pocket when the sound of a truck rumbled through the field off in the distance. He looked up to see Tom driving with Pam riding in the passenger seat.

When the truck stopped, Pam opened the door and ran to Claire. "Has she moved or said anything? Is she unconscious?"

"She's groaned a couple of times, that's it."

"Frank, move over." Pam pushed the dog aside. "Jeff, can you hold him? He doesn't want to leave Claire's side."

"Frank, come here." He grabbed the dog's collar and pulled him closer. "It's okay, buddy. She'll be fine."

The dog whined.

Pam tucked her short blond hair behind her ear, leaned close to Claire's face, and remained that way for what seemed an eternity. "She's breathing but it's slow and shallow." Pam gently touched Claire's wrist and took her pulse, counting the beats with her watch. "Her pulse is weak and erratic."

Jeff knew to check all those things, but he'd forgotten. In the heat of the crisis, because of his personal involvement in the situation, he'd forgotten almost everything he'd learned.

He had never felt such intense responsibility for someone else before, so this was unfamiliar ground. Other than the horses, he only had Frank to care for. He was a simple person, one who fed horses, refilled water, dumped a cup of dog food into a bowl twice a day, and let his dog out to use the bathroom whenever needed. All that would change for the better when he had kids, but for right now he settled for animals. They were much easier.

"Run your hands over her lightly to make sure there aren't any obvious breaks," Pam suggested. "But don't move her and make sure you look for any hint of blood on her clothes. It takes a while for it to seep through jeans."

He reached out to touch her bare arm and hesitated.

"Do it, Jeff!"

He touched her soft arm and ran his hands over her elbow, down to her fingers, and back up to her shoulder. He shuddered from the warmth of her unusually pale skin. So soft. Oh, gosh, he didn't want to touch her.

Claire groaned when his fingers grazed her face.

Pam pulled a stethoscope and blood pressure cuff from her tucked-in shirt and wrapped the cuff around Claire's upper arm. She stuck the stethoscope into her ears.

Jeff inhaled a long breath while he lightly touched her shoulder and arm. Then he ran his hand down her rib cage and around her shapely hip. His body temperature seemed to rise and he hoped Pam didn't notice the sweat beading on his upper lip.

"Anything out of the ordinary so far?" Pam's voice pierced his thoughts.

Jeff cleared his throat. "Um, no."

"Keep going then."

Pam took Claire's blood pressure twice and pulled away. "At least her BP is normal for now, but I don't like that she's unconscious. The ambulance needs to get here soon. It doesn't take that long to drive from Morrisboro. Where are they?"

A siren screamed off in the distance. "Claire, sweetheart, listen to me," Jeff said, and then swallowed hard. Now that help was nearby, he pulled his hand away from her upper leg. "The paramedics are almost here, so hang in there. I'll ride in the ambulance with you."

Claire groaned but still made no movement.

"That's right," Pam said. "You're going to be fine." She turned to Tom, who was standing nearby, holding the horses. "I want to get the horses out of here before the ambulance arrives. I can't leave the scene. Can you take them back to the barn?"

Tom nodded.

"Thanks for being here, sis." Jeff looked up at Pam and managed a pathetic smile. He saw the compassion in her eyes and knew she understood.

Without hesitation, Tom climbed on Lacey while holding Razor's reins in his free hand. He turned to look at the dog. "Frank, come on!"

Frank refused to move from Claire's side. "Go, Frank," Jeff said and pointed toward Tom. The dog licked Claire on the cheek and then ran halfway to Tom with his ears flat and his tail tucked. He stopped once to look back. "Frank, go on." The dog hung his head and obeyed.

Jeff barely noticed the limp as Tom led Razor off, still breathing heavily from the earlier gallop. Frank followed reluctantly behind them. They had just cleared the far edge of the field when the now silent ambulance pulled into view with its lights flashing.

The paramedics jumped from the emergency vehicle and ran toward Claire with their equipment. "I'm a nurse," Pam said to the closest paramedic. "Claire's pulse is weak and erratic, her blood pressure is normal, and her breathing is slow and shallow."

The man glanced at her and nodded. He conducted his own quick check of her vital signs. The other man jogged back to the ambulance. He removed a stretcher, which bounced and clanked along with him as he made his way back to Claire. They gently loosened her helmet and put a cervical collar around her neck. Then they cautiously slid a backboard under Claire, strapped her to it, and lifted her onto the stretcher and strapped her to that. Now that they had her secured, the men carefully rolled her away. Jeff walked alongside her, holding her hand as they bumped along the field to the ambulance.

Jeff didn't ask permission, he just climbed into the ambulance with Claire and sat down next to her. One of the paramedics stuck an IV into her vein and Claire winced.

Jeff reached for her hand again and held it tenderly. She surprised him when she opened her eyes and a small smile appeared on her mouth.

"I'm glad to see you're awake!" Jeff said, and released a long sigh. He squeezed her hand for encouragement. "You're doing a great job; we'll be at the ER soon."

Even though the ambulance traveled at a fast speed, it seemed to take forever before they reached Crystal County Hospital.

No sooner had the vehicle pulled into the circular drive, than the paramedics had unloaded the stretcher. They zipped through a set of double glass doors into the emergency room with Jeff walking alongside, still holding Claire's hand. The antiseptic smell of the hospital stung his nose in sharp contrast to the outdoor smells he loved. He recalled all the time he'd spent with Claire on the island. She had to pull through this.

They wheeled her into a room and transferred her, backboard and all, to a hospital gurney. A new crew took over. They took her stats all over again, all the while talking among each other.

A tall woman in scrubs seemed to be the key person in the room. She stood over Claire and asked, "What's your name, sweetie?"

Claire didn't answer.

"Do you know where you are?" Unfortunately, Claire remained silent. "You're at Crystal County Hospital in the emergency department. Can you talk?" When Claire only moaned, the woman said, "Can you wiggle a finger?"

Claire barely lifted her left index finger.

"You can't talk because of the pain?" the woman asked.

Claire lifted her finger again.

"Okay. Can you raise your right finger?" Jeff dropped her hand for a few seconds, and Claire responded by barely moving the finger. "Good. Can you wiggle one foot at a time? Good. Now I want you to lift your left finger when I touch something that hurts. Don't worry, I won't press hard." The woman touched different areas and Claire lifted her finger when the woman touched her head. "Do you have a headache?"

***

Yes, Claire did. She had the worst headache of her life. Why was she in the emergency department, and why was Jeff holding her hand? She strained to remember but her every attempt failed. She noticed a helmet in Jeff's hand. That jogged a fleeting memory of Jeff's horse, Razor. Weren't they supposed to go riding?

"Do you know why you are here?" the woman asked.

Claire barely shook her head. Something restrained her neck. She had no clue why she was the center of attention. Didn't she have somewhere she had to be? Oh, yeah. She wanted to ask around about her father. How had that landed her in the hospital? Claire winced from the pain of thinking. Then the memory of riding Razor popped into her mind.

"Try not to move your head; just wiggle your finger," the woman said with compassion laced in her voice. "You fell off a horse. Do you remember that?"

Claire frowned. *Please, someone stop my headache.*

The woman shifted her gaze to a man dressed in scrubs beside her. "I want a CAT scan of her head," she said, and turned back to Claire with a serious expression on her face. "You were

107

lucky you wore a helmet." Then the woman squeezed her hand, the one that Jeff wasn't holding, and smiled. "I'll see you after we get the results back."

Claire nodded slightly and managed a partial smile, thankful that the hospital staff was so friendly, and that Jeff had stayed with her. His warm hand lent her comfort.

His level of commitment astonished her, but that brought up an issue. Even though it was hard to remember things right now, she didn't forget that Jeff was committed all right, to Lynette. What would his fiancée think of him holding another woman's hand?

She didn't have to wonder long.

# CHAPTER ELEVEN

No sooner than the hospital staff had pushed Claire into a small sterile cubicle, a familiar voice rang through the air like a shot from a rifle.

"Jeff, there you are." Lynette darted into the room. Her heels clicked hurriedly on the linoleum and her black skirt rustled loudly. She acted as if Jeff were the one that had been hurt, yet Claire was the one lying on a bed with her neck in a brace.

Lynette stepped between them and casually forced him to drop Claire's hand. Then she stretched upward, pressed her lips into Jeff's, and demanded his attention. After an animated kiss, she said, "Is everything okay, sweetheart?" Lynette managed to glimpse down at Claire, who groaned not only from pain but also from disgust at how Lynette played Jeff.

He glared at Lynette as if she'd lost her mind. "Does everything look all right? Claire's hurt." Kudos to Jeff.

Lynette flashed a frosty smile at Claire, clearly stating, "He's mine, so back off." There wasn't a smidgen of concern on the stylish woman's face. Claire restrained a chuckle at the lipstick that stretched above Lynette's top lip from the forceful kiss she imposed on Jeff. Lynette was bound to be mortified when she noticed the imperfection in the mirror.

Claire had trouble believing he was engaged to this woman. If he liked that type of person, then he deserved the "it's-all-about-me attitude" that went along with her. She reluctantly reminded herself that Jeff wasn't hers to fight for. He was getting married in two weeks.

The man in scrubs from earlier approached Claire. "It's time for the CAT scan." He turned to Jeff. "Are you coming along?"

Jeff looked at Claire, then at Lynette. It would be interesting to see what choice he made. He was in a jam, and she found it intriguing.

Jeff shrugged, as if to lessen the impact his decision held. "Claire, if you don't mind, I'll wait here."

Claire managed a half smile. If he had accompanied her, she'd have to wonder about Jeff's loyalty as a partner. By his decision to stay, he proved he had integrity. She could argue that he'd taken the easy way out, the path of least resistance, but he'd made the right decision, even though she'd love to be the one he had chosen.

The man wheeled her down a maze of hallways, and Claire marveled at how he'd memorized all those turns. She'd get lost for sure.

"Have you ever had a CAT scan before?" he asked.

"No." After all this time, Claire had finally managed to say something. Her voice sounded quiet and husky, but the word was still audible, a definite improvement from earlier.

"It's painless and easy. We'll take a few pictures of your head and send you back to the ER. Nothing to be afraid of."

"Okay." She wasn't nervous in the least. In fact, she viewed the CAT scan as a welcomed reprieve before she returned to Jeff and Lynette. The tension in the room, since Lynette's arrival, had become almost unbearable.

Claire needed to convince Jeff to go home. He didn't need to stay, or to feel guilty. She didn't blame him or his horse for her fall. Claire remembered the accident now, mostly, and she specifically recalled Razor's fall at the end of the gallop. Simply put, she hadn't leaned back enough in the saddle and had lost her balance. If she blamed anyone, she blamed herself.

Jeff didn't need to be her hero. Claire had had enough heartbreak in the past, and to her annoyance, she apparently wanted to head down the rocky road of emotional pain again. Maybe her mother had been right all along, to avoid men altogether.

The CAT scan machine clicked several times, and when it finished, the man returned. "All done." He pushed her back down the never-ending hallways and returned her to the ER. He deposited her back into the room where Jeff and Lynette still waited. "The doctor will be in soon."

"Okay," she said with a scratchy voice.

"Claire, you talked!" Jeff said, clearly relieved.

Claire turned toward him and smiled. "I did. I'm not sure why I couldn't before, other than I had a headache." She rubbed the back of her head. "It was too much effort to talk."

Jeff returned to her side, reached out for her hand, but then retracted it. Claire noticed how Lynette's body stiffened from the far corner of the room.

"Jeff, why don't you guys go on home? I'm fine."

"Thanks," Lynette said as she took up residence next to Jeff. "Maybe we should do that. I still have work to do and it's getting late."

Jeff glared at Lynette, and then looked down at Claire again.

Not for Lynette's sake, but for her own, Claire said, "Really. I'm fine. Nothing seems to be broken."

He appeared undecided, as if he wanted to remain by Claire's side but knew he should leave. "When they release you, who'll drive you home? It might be best to have someone stay with you at your apartment tonight."

He was probably right. She thought for a moment before a plan slowly began to form in her mind. "I can call Shirley; she'll pick me up."

"I'm sure she's not at the studio this late," Jeff said. "Do you know her home number? I'll call for you."

Claire strained to remember, but Shirley's number refused to surface in her foggy brain. "It's in my cell phone."

"Where's your cell phone?" Jeff raised his eyebrows, clearly remembering that earlier she'd borrowed his cell phone to call the studio.

Her face grew warm. "On my dresser."

Jeff rolled his eyes.

Claire made a mental note to carry her cell phone with her from now on. After all, she paid the monthly bill in order to have the phone for emergencies, and every time she needed it, she'd left it behind.

"Don't worry, I'll find the number." He typed something into his phone. "I'll be back." He left with Lynette following close behind him.

Why couldn't he talk to Shirley in front of Claire?

Jeff needed to stop helping her. He had enough to deal with without the additional burden of feeling responsible for her.

He didn't need to be her hero.

Before long, he returned to Claire's side with Lynette still glued to him. "Shirley will be here soon," he said. "You can be thankful she agreed to help you; otherwise, you'd have to endure our company for the rest of the night."

That sounded more like a threat than something desirable. Claire viewed Lynette as borderline intolerable. Seeing her again drove home the fact that Claire needed to stop spending so much time with Jeff. The man was engaged. Time spent with him begged for trouble, no matter how she looked at it.

"Thanks for everything," Claire said to encourage them to leave. "Please make sure Razor's okay. He stumbled hard." Her eyes locked with Jeff's, and she didn't dare glance at Lynette.

Claire was fairly certain he wouldn't recognize her tender emotions toward him, but women definitely noticed such things.

When his face softened, she had to wonder if he'd noticed her undeniable feelings after all. He reached out and held her hand, despite Lynette's huff. "Keep me posted. Let me know the results of the CAT scan, and if you need anything, call me."

"I will."

At that, Lynette led the way out of Claire's room. Jeff glanced back and offered her a small wave. A caring man he was.

Shirley showed up almost immediately after they left. "Claire! What happened to you?" The older woman darted toward Claire and looked to be fighting off tears.

"I fell off Jeff's horse."

Shirley swallowed hard before she spoke. "He said you were in the ER and had an accident, but he didn't mention how severe it was."

"He probably didn't want to alarm you. But you don't need to worry. I'm tough and I bounce back fast."

Just then the female doctor walked in. "The results from your CAT scan show mild swelling of your brain. You've taken quite a blow to your head." The doctor looked at Shirley, then back at Claire. "You should be fine to return home; however, I want you to follow the discharge instructions I give you. Have someone stay with you and wake you up every two to three hours tonight. I'll give you a prescription for a painkiller if you need it."

"You're letting her go home with a swollen brain?" Shirley shrieked.

"Yes. There's no reason to admit her."

Shirley looked aghast.

"I'm fine, Shirley, other than a headache."

"Not according to what the doctor said. A swollen brain doesn't sound all right to me. But if you have to go home, I'll stay the night with you." Shirley rubbed Claire's hand continuously, as though to soothe away the pain.

"You don't need to stay the night. I'm fine," Claire said again.

The doctor raised her eyebrows at Claire. "It would be a good idea to have her there. Someone should wake you often. If they can't wake you, they need to call 911. Later, you'll probably hurt in places you don't even know you have, and you'll need help."

Claire looked up at the doctor. "Okay. I'll listen to doctor's orders for once. I'm not used to someone taking care of me, though." All her life she had practically raised herself, while her mother worked long hours to support them. Disturbing as it felt, however, Shirley's attention also felt comforting.

The hospital discharge went smoothly, and before long they pulled into the lot behind Claire's studio.

"Let me help you up the stairs," Shirley insisted.

"I appreciate your offer, but I can manage."

"Oh, please. You're just worried because I'm older and you're concerned I'll fall. Let me tell you something, Missy." Shirley shook her finger at Claire, who smiled. "I'm going to live until I'm a hundred and ten, so don't forget it."

"Yes, ma'am." Claire laughed. Secretly, she loved Shirley's spry spirit, but she wasn't about to admit that to Shirley, who might take offense. "I appreciate you driving me home and that you're willing to spend the night with me."

When they made it to the top of the steps and entered the apartment, Shirley took control. "Where do you want to rest?"

"In here's fine." Claire pointed to the couch. Right now she wanted to be near Shirley, and having a grandmotherly figure with her felt reassuring.

Shirley disappeared into Claire's bedroom and returned with a blanket and a pillow. "I'll make a pot of tea, and then we'll talk."

Talk? Claire wanted company, not someone to spill her thoughts to. Shirley pointed her finger at the couch, and Claire succumbed to the direct order by settling on the sofa and curling up against her pillow. Shirley went into the kitchen to put on a pot of water. How the older woman knew that Claire loved tea amazed her. They seemed to be kindred spirits, almost as if Shirley was the grandmother Claire never had and always needed.

Before the teapot whistled, Shirley pulled it from the burner and poured two mugs of decaffeinated green tea, a favorite of Claire's. She kept a wide variety of teas in a hand-carved, wooden box that Black Eagle had originally made for her mother. It was one of the few cherished belongings from her childhood. Shirley handed Claire a mug before she sat down in an antique rocking chair, also from her mother's small estate.

"So tell me about it," Shirley said.

"About what?" Claire's mind had drifted to Jeff and Lynette, and she wasn't sure what Shirley wanted to know.

"What do you mean, 'about what'?" Shirley asked. "I'd say you had quite an accident."

"Oh, that." For a moment, she thought Shirley wanted to know about the situation with Jeff. "I've had better rides. We galloped across a field, and at the end, my horse stopped and fell onto his knees. I lost my balance and ended up in the ER."

"I'm glad Jeff was there to help you."

"Me too. I should've leaned back more." Without a doubt, Shirley was setting her up for a discussion Claire didn't want to have.

"You know that he's getting married in two weeks, don't you?" Shirley drove the point home by narrowing her eyes.

Claire remained silent for a moment, and then said, "Yes."

"Lynette's been after him for years. His dad owns a lot of land, actually several hundred acres. I heard a department store is interested in buying the land, not that they would sell."

Claire didn't speak.

"Jeff's mother owned a steel distribution business. I heard she took a lot of the money out of the company before Tom took over. Supposedly, she gave Jeff and Pam a large chunk to compensate for giving Tom the business. My guess is Lynette wants to marry into the family to be part of the wealth."

"She doesn't love him?" Claire wrapped both hands around her warm mug to thaw the icy chill that suddenly ran through her body.

"She loves the idea of marrying him." Shirley took a sip of tea and swayed back and forth in the old rocker.

"Lynette seems to have her life together with all the rental properties and the real estate business," Claire said. "Why would she want more?"

"Come on, Claire. People always want more."

"Amazing. She has a sexy man who is devoted to her, and all she wants is his family's wealth. That makes me sick."

"You think he's sexy, huh?" Shirley flashed a knowing smile.

Claire ignored Shirley's perceptiveness. It felt good to have someone comfortable and safe to talk with, a grandmotherly type indeed. "So why does Jeff put up with her? He could have any number of women."

"That, my dear, is a complicated story." Shirley stopped the rocker and took another sip of tea. "Jeff had asked Dana Snider, his ex-girlfriend now, to marry him about three years ago. He was head over heels in love with her. Right before the wedding, she ran off, back to Charlotte. The poor man hid behind his island horses and his farm, and he avoided coming to town for at least a year. Around here that's hard to do. People tried to draw him out, but he wouldn't budge. Lynette cooked him casseroles and brought them to his house every day, and eventually she led him back to civilization."

"She cooks?" The image of Lynette in an apron shocked her. Claire saw only a selfish woman who wanted his wealth, not a loving homemaker.

"That's another interesting story. I heard she took cooking lessons from a country restaurant owner in Morrisboro. A rumor floated around that she wanted to learn to cook just so she could win Jeff's heart. You know the old saying—the way to a man's heart is through his stomach."

Now that resonated with the image Claire had of Lynette—manipulative. "But still, that doesn't make sense. Lynette doesn't seem like a content homemaker who'd like to cook."

"As you know, some women will do anything for a man," Shirley said. "And home-cooked meals usually work."

"Does she still cook for him? I mean, if she stopped playing the domestic wife, I'd think he would figure out what she was up to."

Shirley smiled. "No, I don't believe she does. Lynette is a busy woman, but as far as I know, Jeff hasn't complained. She's filled her schedule with listing new properties and managing tenants. Most important, though, she spends time overseeing the care of her grandmother, who has Alzheimer's disease and lives in a nursing home down the street."

"I had no idea. Will she inherit money from the grandma?"

Shirley smiled bigger. "You're a smart woman, and that sounds like Lynette, but I truly think she loves her grandmother."

"Hmm," was all Claire could say. "That's a side of her I can't really imagine. What about her father? He seems to be well off, too."

"I'd say he is," Shirley continued. "He's the president of the only bank in town and privately supports Lynette's business endeavors. All she has to do is give him a percentage of her earnings. It's a sweet deal if you ask me. And the more money she makes off her tenants, the more she invests in other rentals. She owns a large number of buildings in our town, most of them on Front Street. She's intelligent and definitely has good business sense."

"She even knows how to buy men." Claire's comment held a tart note she hoped Shirley wouldn't comment on. Truth be told, Claire wasn't ready to accept that Lynette had endearing qualities yet.

Shirley broke out in laughter. "My, you see right through people. I like that about you."

"Thanks." Claire stared at the ceiling. "Doesn't Jeff realize all of this? I don't understand why he asked her to marry him."

"And yet another interesting story; one you need to know. When you live in a small town, you know all the gossip." Shirley leaned forward and set her mug on a ceramic coaster on the coffee table. "Jeff sees more than you give him credit for. The man is not clueless. He knows what Lynette wants, but he's playing love safe. He wants a wife but doesn't want to be hurt again. By marrying Lynette, he has an automatic guarantee that she won't want to move away and force him to make a painful decision later. He will live and die here. He doesn't want to choose between his wife and family, and the horses, if his wife wants to move. Lynette will never leave this area."

A bright light bulb lit up a dark corner of Claire's mind, and she winced with pain. Without a doubt, she knew Jeff was attracted to her, but, because of a previous failed relationship, he denied himself a chance at real love. She posed a serious threat to his pretend and protected world.

But he cared about her.

She understood now why he was unable to reach out and give them a chance, because his fear numbed him. And he planned to forgo a chance for a happy marriage in order to protect the horses and his heart.

"Not only did Lynette flatter him with food, she proposed to him." Shirley looked at Claire with obvious interest.

"What!"

"That's right. She grew impatient and asked him to marry her. I think he saw it as the perfect solution for him, at least until you came to town. I see the way he looks at you, and so does Lynette. She told Paula this afternoon, probably about the time you had your riding accident, that she wanted you to leave town. She didn't like it that he'd rescued you from Pony Island that first night."

"What was he supposed to do, leave me over there?" Claire frowned. She seemed to be making enemies instead of friends. If it weren't for the possibility that her father might live in town, and the fact that she'd started a new business here, she wouldn't care. She'd leave. But that wasn't an option now. If Lynette turned people against her, she'd have to rely on business from the tourists. Would that be enough income to carry her through the year? She didn't think so. According to the rough figures she'd come up with, Claire also needed revenue from teaching photography classes and doing sittings. That meant she had to count on business from the locals if she wanted to succeed.

"Of course he wasn't supposed to leave you over there."

"So what about Paula? Why didn't he date her?" Claire asked. She sounded jealous, even to her own ears.

Shirley laughed. "Honey, Paula is his cousin."

Claire couldn't help but feel relieved. "Amazing." She thought about what Shirley had said. "Since you know everyone in Big Cat, do you know a man named Robert Kincaid?" Claire needed a father to love, so badly that desperation clawed at her. She had to find him.

"No, sugar, I don't."

# CHAPTER TWELVE

Jeff searched the Internet until almost midnight and his eyes blurred with fatigue. He'd traced Claire's father to a small town called Oldham, close to the Virginia border and on the Outer Banks. It hadn't been easy, but he'd stumbled on an old article in the town's newspaper archives. Surprised that the paper was online to begin with, Jeff silently thanked the educated employee who was up-to-date with modern technology.

He found the article interesting on multiple levels. Apparently, Robert Kincaid had married another woman after his estranged wife had disappeared some years before. The first wife's name, however, had been Loretta, instead of Virginia as Claire had said. The details didn't quite add up. In fact, the article failed to mention Claire entirely.

Jeff found that odd. Since the reporter went to the trouble to list Robert Kincaid's first wife, why hadn't he included the missing daughter's name? The possibility existed that the Robert Kincaid in the article wasn't her father, but there were too many coincidences to ignore. Interestingly enough, the piece went on to mention Mr. Kincaid's involvement with the wild horses on Corolla, and his longtime expertise as a quarter horse breeder.

Surprised Jeff hadn't heard of Claire's father before, he reasoned it was because Oldham was a few hours north of Big Cat.

Now that Jeff had a lead, he wanted to drive up there. As it happened, he had tomorrow off. He decided to go to Oldham first and then to Corolla, to see what information he could find. Perhaps someone knew Mr. Kincaid or could point Jeff in the right direction. Maybe he'd even get lucky and actually find the man.

Jeff rubbed his tired eyes. If he wanted to get an early start in the morning, he needed to get some sleep. He reflected that at least the weekend had ended better than it began. After the emotional drama of the wild foal's difficulty with nursing and then Claire's horrible riding accident yesterday, last night had ended with a huge fight with Lynette. To make matters more taxing, Lynette had returned today for two more rounds of arguments. She was bothered about the time he spent with Claire. He couldn't really blame her, but Claire aroused feelings he never thought he'd have again.

Jeff stood from his computer chair and headed toward the bedroom, ready to put this day behind him. He couldn't forget to include his sister's additional contribution to the tiring stream of events. Pam had popped in unannounced earlier this evening. She had wanted to make sure Claire had survived the accident all right and wanted to quiz Jeff about his friendship with her. Apparently, he had called Claire "sweetheart" during the crisis, when she was lying unconscious on the ground. His sister had noticed the endearment and the tender way he talked to Claire. As usual, Pam couldn't ignore the situation and had called him on his behavior. He denied everything and wrote off his reaction to Claire as being a severe case of cold feet about getting married, that's all. He seriously doubted it possible to care about another woman to any significant degree, ever again. Dana had broken his heart.

*** 

When Jeff went to shave his face at the bathroom sink the next morning, the reflection in the mirror startled him. He looked drawn and tired and had dark circles under his eyes. He'd continuously tossed around in his sleep and had relived the nightmare of Claire's fall. The sight of her limp body lying on the ground haunted him.

Jeff quickly finished getting ready, grabbed a quick bite to eat, and headed to his car. A few hours later, he pulled into the rundown town of Oldham. The downtown area consisted of one street with an aged grocery store, an auto repair shop, a greasy-spoon restaurant, and a few ramshackle shops. As he drove down the deserted Main Street, two local men sat outside the greasy spoon and watched him park in front of the newspaper office.

He climbed from his truck and waved to the two men. They ignored him and continued to watch Jeff's every move. He pushed open the glass door of the newspaper office and an old man with suspenders and dress clothes waved him in. The man sat at a cluttered desk and shoved a stack of papers aside.

What can I help ya with?" the man asked.

"I'm looking for information about an article I saw in your Web site's archives. It was dated ten years ago."

The man spit his tobacco juice into a cup and continued to chew. "You have to talk to my nephew, Jason. He does all that computer stuff."

"Where can I find him?"

The man spat again. "He ain't here right now, but he has one of them cell phones."

When the man didn't offer more, Jeff asked, "May I have the number? I'd like to talk with him today if possible."

The man opened an antique desk drawer and rummaged through a mess of papers before he pulled out an address book. He thumbed through a few faded pages and stopped. "Here it is." He rattled off the number, snapped the book shut, and slammed the drawer closed. He pivoted his chair away from Jeff and picked up a magazine.

Jeff ignored the dismissal and committed the number to memory. "Have you heard of a man named Robert Kincaid? The article mentioned he lived in Oldham."

The man turned back toward Jeff and reclined, but didn't answer at first. Eventually he said, "Who wants to know?"

The conversation felt like pulling teeth from a growling dog, but Jeff noticed the man didn't have many teeth to pull.

"Jeff Rhoades from Big Cat. Mr. Kincaid's daughter is looking for him, and I'm trying to help her find him."

"Never heard of Big Cat. Where's that?"

"A few hours south of here." Jeff inhaled slowly, despite the stale smell of body odor that enveloped the room, in a discreet attempt to remain patient. "Robert Kincaid used to have a farm nearby and raised quarter horses."

"Well, if you know all about 'im, why you askin' me?"

Jeff took another calming breath. "Because I want to find him."

"If you're wantin' to buy a horse, I'm sellin' one."

"No thanks. I just want to talk with him."

"I ain't seen Robert in a few years. Now, I got work to do."

At least Jeff had found someone who actually knew Mr. Kincaid. He counted that as progress. "Can you tell me where I can find him?"

"No." The man paged through his magazine again.

"I appreciate your help. I'll call your nephew."

As soon as Jeff left the building, he dialed Jason's number. He wanted to call before the man had a chance to reach Jason first. In his experience, surprise usually resulted in getting more information than might otherwise be expected. By the fourth ring, however, voice mail kicked on. Instead of leaving a message, Jeff closed his phone and backed up to peer in the window. Sure enough, the man had a phone pressed to his ear, undoubtedly talking to Jason.

Jeff opened the glass door again and smiled at the man. Seemingly shocked, the man stopped talking.

"Can you ask Jason if he wants to meet over lunch, my treat?"

Apparently caught off guard, the man actually asked his nephew the question. "He says he'll meet you in a half hour at the restaurant next door."

Jeff suspected Jason wouldn't be hard to identify, and would stand out from the other locals. If he knew how to archive old articles on a Web site, then he was educated, unlike the men Jeff had met so far.

"Appreciate it." Jeff turned and walked back out of the building. He had thirty minutes to kill. Who would be the next resistant local for him to try his detective skills on? Before long, the entire town would know he was here to ask questions, if they didn't know already. The two men he'd noticed earlier, the ones who'd sat outside the restaurant, were now missing in action. Jeff sauntered across the street to a dilapidated drug store.

When he walked in, the bell above the door tinkled. A man from behind the counter looked up. "How can I help you?"

Jeff flashed his friendliest smile. "I'm a friend of Robert Kincaid's daughter. I wonder if you know where I can find him."

"Robert doesn't have a daughter. He never did have kids, just horses."

Why did the paper, and now this man, deny that Robert had a child? Claire said she left home at age nine. Everyone in town should know about her. "Do you know where I can find him?"

"I haven't seen old Robert. He stopped coming downtown a few years back."

That's what the man at the newspaper office had said. At least their stories matched. "I see. Does he still live around here?"

The man didn't answer, only shrugged. The frustration of small-town dynamics caused Jeff to clench his jaw until it ached. Most people thought Big Cat was little, but it was innovative compared to this rusty town. No wonder Claire's mom had fled Oldham in the middle of the night. He could almost understand why she'd taken off the way she had.

"Thanks for your help." Jeff didn't wait for a response, not that he'd get one anyway. He stopped outside the door and noticed two men conversing over at the garage. He headed that way and the men suddenly became absorbed in working on a Volkswagen Beetle in desperate need of a paint job.

Jeff approached the garage entrance and poked his head inside. "Excuse me?" No one bothered to answer him. He stepped over the threshold and approached a man who had folded his upper body under the hood of a dented Chevrolet.

"Hi there," Jeff said.

The man stood and looked at him. "What can I do for ya?" He wiped his hands on an oily cloth and shoved the rag back into the pocket of his navy blue coveralls.

"I'm looking for Robert Kincaid, the quarter horse breeder."

"That might be kind of difficult, on account of he moved a few years back."

"Do you know where he moved?"

"He got remarried and his wife wanted to live by her sister. I can't remember the name of the town, but it was somewhere south of here, on the coast."

A lot of places fit that description. Jeff took a stab at the name. "Big Cat?"

"Yeah, I reckon that's it. It was named after a wild cat, a cougar maybe."

This was not a coincidence. Perhaps Robert Kincaid did actually live in Big Cat. But why hadn't anyone heard of him? "Do you remember anything else?"

The mechanic hesitated before he spoke. "Nope, other than he'd hurt his leg and gave up the horses. He couldn't take care of 'em no more."

That probably explained why Jeff didn't know him.

"Have you heard from him lately?" Jeff asked.

He noticed how the man stiffened and diverted his eyes. Jeff would bet he knew more than he was sharing—something important.

"Nope," he said again. He ran his hands up and down the side of his coveralls and avoided Jeff's direct eye contact.

"I appreciate your help." Jeff reached into his back pocket and pulled a business card from his wallet. "If you remember anything else, or if you ever need help, please call me."

The man looked surprised. "Yep."

As Jeff walked away, he glanced at the time on his cell phone. He had five minutes before he had to meet Jason. He headed over to the restaurant and pushed open the door. Two men and a woman, who sat in the far corner, stopped eating and stared. Though the tension in the room was thick enough to slice, Jeff seated himself at a booth by the window so he could see when Jason arrived.

A moment later, a young, pregnant server, obviously close to her due date, approached. "What can I get you?"

"An iced tea for now." He pulled out a greasy, plastic menu from behind the salt and pepper shakers. "I'm waiting for Jason, so I'll order when he gets here."

"Our specials are BBQ and hushpuppies, or chicken dumplin's. I'll be back with your tea." She turned and waddled off.

Jeff glanced over the menu and decided on the BBQ. He had just set the menu back behind the shakers when a thin, rather well-dressed man walked into the diner. He wore an air of professionalism that one achieved only from schooling, college actually, and not a local college, either. Undoubtedly, he was the one responsible for the newspaper's Web site and archives. The young man didn't hesitate and walked straight to Jeff. "I'm Jason."

They shook hands. "Jeff Rhoades. Thanks for meeting me." Jeff pointed at the bench across from him and Jason joined him.

"That's my job, to meet people. I'm a reporter." Jason flagged over the server. "Can I have an iced tea?"

"Sure thing." She repeated the specials for Jason's benefit, and then asked if they needed more time.

"I'll take the chicken and dumplings," Jason said.

Jeff ordered the BBQ and leaned back against the bench after she left. He decided to level with Jason. What did he have to lose? If anything, maybe Jason would empathize with Claire and give him something more concrete to go on.

But before he could say anything, Jason said, "So I hear you're looking for Old Man Kincaid?" He took his sweet tea from the server and drained almost half of it. Since she held a full pitcher in her other hand, his behavior must be routine.

"Yes, I'm looking for Mr. Kincaid." What did it matter if they discussed his reason for being here in front of the waitress? She'd probably heard the gossip by now anyway.

"What do you want him for?" The server refilled Jason's glass and walked off.

"A friend of mine, Claire Kincaid, is looking for him. I believe he's her father, and since her mother has died, she wants to find her only living relative."

"To my knowledge, he never had kids."

"That may be true, but there are a lot of coincidences that make me think he is her dad. Take his love of horses for instance. Claire's passion is horses, and she photographs the wild ones on Pony Island."

Jason's head popped up. "Really? Robert used to take pictures too, of the wild horses in Corolla."

"Yet another similarity."

The waitress approached their table with their food. That was the fastest service Jeff had ever received.

"He was also the president of the local horse foundation that oversees the wild horses," Jason continued. "Some time ago, though, he got bucked off one of his quarter horses. He had a hard time walking after that and had to stop riding."

"I read in your archives that he got remarried. By the way, your Web site is impressive."

"Thanks. My uncle insisted we didn't need one, but I'm going to take the paper over when he retires, and I feel archives are important. And, yes, Robert remarried."

"Do you know how I can find him?" Jeff shoved a huge bite of BBQ into his mouth. There was nothing like country cooking.

Jason raised his eyebrows and seemed surprised by Jeff's question. "He died a couple of years ago. I thought you knew that. I assumed your girlfriend wanted to find him to claim an inheritance."

It was Jeff's turn to be taken aback. That certainly explained the town's reaction to his arrival and their reluctance to give him information. They thought he was after the man's estate. And as far as Jason's reference to Claire as his girlfriend, he decided it wasn't worth correcting. He rather liked the way the word sounded.

"She doesn't want an inheritance. That's not what this is about," Jeff explained. "She wanted to get to know her father again. She hadn't seen him since she was nine."

"Sorry." Jason frowned. "His wife lives just outside of Big Cat. She kept her maiden name." Jason pulled out his phone and typed on the keypad to access a file of some sort. "Her name is Nancy Smith."

"I appreciate it. Do you know how he died?"

"His tractor overturned on him in a field when he hit a ditch. They tried to save him, but he only lived for a couple of hours. Please tell your girlfriend I send my condolences."

"I will." Jeff pushed his plate away, his appetite now ruined. He tossed money onto the table to cover both their meals and stood. "Again, I appreciate your help, Jason."

Jason nodded and continued eating.

All the way home Jeff contemplated how to break the news to Claire. He was about to singlehandedly destroy her dreams. He couldn't withhold the information, though, because she had a right to know. If he didn't tell her, he'd have to live with the secret, but if she ever found out, she'd never forgive him. No, he needed to tell her, as gently as possible. If she got angry, then he'd have to accept that as the price to pay for meddling.

# *CHAPTER THIRTEEN*

Jeff quickly showered and then headed straight to Claire's house. Even though the news would devastate her, she needed closure.

He knocked on the door. When she didn't answer, he knocked again, fully prepared to leave. The door eventually squeaked open and Claire peeked out at him.

"How are you feeling?"

"Other than sore all over and too sleepy from the painkillers to get out of bed most of the time, I'm fine. Now that the medicine has worn off, I've been up about an hour and a half. I think I'd do better without it." She shoved her hands into her pockets and looked down at her bare feet.

"Can I come in? I won't stay long."

She nodded and moved aside. He followed her up the steps to her apartment and mentally rehearsed for the hundredth time how to tell her about her father. The delicious aroma of a home-cooked meal filled the air and immediately distracted him. "What are you making?"

"Chicken potpie. It's a variation of a recipe passed down for generations on my mom's side."

A pang of remorse stabbed him. She talked about generations of her family with a dreamy expression on her face, while he wrestled with how to explain the truth about her father. The reality would tear apart her idealistic fantasy of meeting him again.

"Have you eaten?" Claire shoved her hand into a mitt and opened the oven, which released more delicious potpie smells. She pulled out a casserole dish and set it on the stovetop, and then with her hip, she closed the oven door.

"It's been hours since I've had lunch." What little he'd actually eaten.

"Why don't you stay for dinner? I made enough to freeze a bunch of meals, so I have plenty."

"You don't have to convince me." Perhaps it was best to wait until after dinner to tell her the bad news. After all, she'd gone to the trouble to cook, so he should have the decency to let her enjoy the meal.

"The potpie needs to set a little bit." Claire placed another plate along with silverware on the table. "How's Razor doing?"

"He's fine. I had to call Paula to come out and look at him."

"Oh?"

"He could barely walk and was dragging his right toe in the dirt. At first I thought he'd broken or chipped a bone, but his leg wasn't swollen. Paula thinks another horse kicked him in the shoulder and we didn't notice it. That's why he fell."

"And the fall made it worse?"

"It did. She gave him a steroid shot and said he should be much better in a couple of days. In a week, he should be back to normal."

"He was lucky."

"I'd say you were both lucky. What were the results of your CAT scan?"

"Just mild swelling of the brain. Nothing much."

His eyes widened. "Like I said before, you're one tough woman."

She shrugged off the compliment. "What do you want to drink with dinner? Iced tea, bottled water?"

"Water's fine." When she started toward the pantry he held up his hand. "I'll get it." He opened the door and narrowed his eyes. "What's up with the half-scattered cans and the perfectly aligned ones?"

Her face turned red and she cleared her throat. "That's kind of a long story. My ex-boyfriend said I lacked spontaneity. I moved some of the cans out of place to prove him wrong."

Interesting. He decided not to pass judgment or to ask for further explanation. He didn't need to know any more personal details of her life, because the more he learned about her, the more endearing she became.

When they sat down and Jeff shoved a forkful of creamy potpie into his mouth, he groaned with delight. How was it possible that Claire could cook too? Did she do everything perfectly? "This is wonderful. Where did you learn to cook like this?"

"Remember, my mom used to work in the restaurant business. She learned to cook before she was promoted to manager. On her time off, we embellished the diner's recipes until they became our own creations. Those were some of my favorite memories. She eventually bought her own small restaurant."

"If she cooked half as well as you, I bet her restaurant served the best food in town. I can almost picture you cooking together." Jeff savored another bite.

"Thanks. My mom was a kindhearted person. That's why her behavior never made sense. I don't understand why she took me from my bed that night. Her behavior doesn't match her personality." Claire pushed her picked-over dinner aside.

*Tell her, Jeff; tell her*, he urged himself. She'd brought up the subject, which presented the perfect opportunity to disclose what he'd found out.

"You didn't eat much. Shouldn't you be eating Jell-O or soup or something?" *Tell her!*

"That's all I've had since my accident. Tonight I wanted real food."

"Are you feeling all right?" He didn't want to tell her the news if she needed to lie down.

She stood and set her dishes in the sink. "This is the best I've felt since Saturday. I'm fine." She glanced at him and her expression grew serious. "What's the matter? You have something to tell me, don't you? And it's not about my concussion." She walked back over to him and stared directly into his eyes.

"Claire?" He stood and put some physical distance between them. It would about kill him to tell her. He looked away as she watched him intently. He probably should offer support and hold her hand, or maybe comfort her to lessen the impact. That felt wrong, though. He didn't have a right to that level of intimacy. Then again, could he get more intimate than telling her the truth about her father?

"First off, I want you to know my intentions were innocent," he said while his gaze met her intense eyes. "Since your riding accident kept you from looking for your father, I decided to search for him on the Internet."

She frowned. "I appreciate your help, but I told you I want to find him alone. It's my personal mission. Besides, I've searched the Internet and haven't found a trace of him."

"Well, I got lucky. I had to dig deep but I found an old article about him. I tracked him down to a small town a few hours north of here."

The frown faded and her face lit up with excitement. "Really?"

He gazed down at his sneakers. Oh, gosh, he hated what he had to tell her. "It's not good, Claire. I wanted to go up there and—"

"Yeah, let's go up there," she interrupted. "I can close the shop tomorrow, or ask Shirley to cover for me."

She wasn't listening. "Unfortunately, we can't," he said.

"Oh, that's right. You work most days and plus, you're wedding is coming up. How could I forget?"

Was that a dig? He heard the edge in her voice but chose to ignore it for now. "No, that's not what I meant." Despite his earlier decision not to touch her, he took her petite hands in his. "Claire, I drove up there today. I wanted to surprise you. But—"

"You went up there without me?" Her voice held a note of anger but he also detected a hint of curiosity.

If the fact he drove up to Oldham alone upset her, he could only imagine her reaction when he told her the devastating news. "Claire, hear me out. As I said, I went up there with good intentions. I talked to whoever I could, although most people wouldn't actually answer my questions. I did find out a few things. The article mentioned that Robert Kincaid remarried and someone confirmed that as true."

"How could he do that when he was married to my mom?"

"I don't know. Maybe she divorced him and never told you about it."

Her face turned stone cold. "Then my father would've known where she was and he would have found me."

True. Jeff believed Robert Kincaid had known all along where his daughter lived and had never tried to see her, although he had no proof. "I'm not sure what happened with that. But there's some bad news."

"What?" she asked in an icy tone that matched her expression.

"Your father had a tractor accident, and they tried to save him. Unfortunately, he didn't make it."

She yanked her hands from his. "No. You must have found someone else, not my father. He knew all about tractors, so that would never happen to him."

"I know it's a shock, but accidents can happen to anyone. Look at you on Razor. You ride well and you still fell off." He wrapped her in a hug, but after a moment she wrenched away.

***

Claire wanted Jeff to leave so he wouldn't see her rarely exposed vulnerable side. She hated that helpless feeling. The more he saw her in a weakened state, as he had when she was lying in the hospital, the harder it was to push him away. "You need to go. Now!" she said in a harsher voice than she had intended. But if her anger made him leave, all the better. She glared at him for emphasis but knew her reaction revealed years of pain, and fear of abandonment.

"Let me stay. I can help you through this."

"There's nothing to get through. You've helped enough." She didn't want his understanding, his hugs, or his affection. "I want you to leave," she managed to say. If the circumstances were different and he was available, then she might be tempted, but with his wedding looming around the corner like a monster, she'd have to be desperate to let him near her. Forget it.

Jeff hung his head low and then left quietly.

Claire sank to the floor and stared at the wall. What an insensitive man! He let her feed him dinner and then bam, he hit her with a hurtful lie about her father, a father he couldn't possibly have located. Jeff didn't have enough information to find someone she had searched for extensively. What made him think the poor man he'd dredged up was her dad anyway? Did he have proof, or had he based his conclusion on some ancient article?

She shook her head, refusing to be alone in the world. That wasn't the plan. She wanted to find her father and reunite with him. She had lost too many years without him, and now that her mother had confessed that he lived in Big Cat, he was supposed to welcome her into his life. The man Jeff had located didn't live in Big Cat, so he'd found the wrong man. It was as simple as that. Her father couldn't be dead! Did Jeff have any clue about what his outlandish claim did to her emotionally?

Men just didn't get it, at least not Jeff. He had pushed his way into her life only to wreak havoc and chaos. She felt so angry she could ... could what?

She let out a painful, long sigh.

To Jeff's credit, he had been honest. She could imagine his apprehension with telling her what he'd learned, so why was he forthcoming? Because he cared. The poor guy had spent his day off driving up the coast in search of her father, and she'd thanked him with a swift kick right out the door.

Claire curled into a ball on the tile floor and started crying, years of unshed tears running down her cheeks. She bawled like a child because Jeff had insisted her beloved daddy had died.

The answers to her past were gone now, dead with her mother and father.

She must have sobbed for at least an hour, although it felt like an eternity. She barely heard the soft knock on the door. To her surprise, Jeff crossed the room, scooped her up off the floor and into his strong arms.

"Shhhhh. It's okay." He carried her to the couch and rubbed the back of her head until her sobs turned into occasional gulps for air. "I'm here for as long as you need me. I won't leave you."

"But... but... you're marrying Lynette next weekend. You are leaving."

"Claire, there are things you don't understand. Let's talk about that another time. Right now, you're in pain and I'm here to comfort you. Accept my support."

Without thinking, she snuggled closer to him and buried her face into his outdoorsy-scented neck. She loved the way he smelled, loved the way he felt, loved ... She reluctantly reminded herself not to love anything about him. He would hurt her as all the men in her past had. She pulled back and he wiped the tears from her cheeks. She wiggled free of his arms and sat opposite him on the couch.

Eventually Jeff said, "Claire, I should go home. It's late and I have to work early in the morning. I'll check in with you tomorrow."

She nodded. "I have to work, too." She hadn't gone downstairs to the studio since her accident because of the pain, but she planned to work tomorrow. Shirley had been sweet to spend Saturday night with her and then to run the studio by herself the last couple of days, but Claire didn't want to take advantage of the older woman. No matter what, she planned to work a full day tomorrow.

"Don't overdo it. You've been through a lot lately."

Claire pushed too hard sometimes, but to spend another useless day in her apartment sounded dreadful.

Jeff helped her from the couch and slid a strong arm around her back. With the other, he helped her stand. "I'll help you to the bedroom."

*** 

When Claire rolled over to shut off the buzzing alarm, she felt like a Mack truck had run back and forth over her. If she thought her body ached before, today there were no words to describe her pain. But painkillers were not an option. They made her sleepy and knocked her out for most of the day, and she didn't want to miss any more work. Ibuprofen would have to suffice.

She crawled from the bed and took a slow shower, but the hot water didn't come close to easing her muscles. She groaned when it came time to bend down and dry her feet. She hadn't fallen off a horse since she was a kid. Right now, the resilience of her childhood years seemed eons ago.

Eventually Claire made it downstairs to the studio. When she opened the door to the shop, Shirley greeted her with a smile and a steaming mug of peppermint tea. How had the woman known to have a mug of tea ready precisely at the moment Claire came downstairs?

"From the way you're moving, I'd say you shouldn't be here right now."

"Good morning to you, too." Claire reached for the mug and drank a long, soothing sip.

"By the way, I fed your cats the past couple of days, but I haven't been out there this morning."

"Thanks, I'll get them." Claire took careful, measured steps through the studio to the small kitchen. When she bent over to pull a container of cat food from the lower cabinet, she grunted. She was too old to be falling off horses. Why hadn't she leaned back in the saddle? Claire opened the back door to the awaiting cats, and they ran toward her, meowing. "Hey there, kiddos. Did you miss me?"

The friendly cat whined.

"Me, too." Claire groaned again as she bent over to pour some food into the pan. The cats hung back a safe distance. "One day you're going to let me pet you," Claire said to the friendly one. She wanted to touch them, rub her hand across their thick rough coats, but she hadn't known them long enough to build their trust. Maybe she had set her hopes too high, like yearning to be with Jeff. Maybe someday her desire would come to fruition.

The cats dove into the food as if they hadn't eaten in days. Claire chuckled. She adored them already and suspected she had a lot of love to give someone. In her case, she played relationships safe by bonding with animals. They were loyal and didn't sleep with your neighbor, nor did they marry someone out of convenience. Cats and horses were much safer, indeed.

Claire went back inside and attempted to frame more photographs while Shirley tended the few customers that drifted into the shop. Yesterday they had received two more orders for the framed photograph of Dante nursing in the marsh pond.

When Shirley finished with the customers, she walked up to Claire and stood next to her. "Maggie and Betty, the two women who ordered the framed pictures of Dante, almost got into an argument with Mildred, who'd bought the last print in the bin.

They calmed down when I told them they could order as many prints as they wanted."

"I guess that bodes well for business. I'll make more copies then." Evidently, other people were touched by the precious moment that Claire had hoped she'd captured in that photograph. Appreciation for her art made her feel talented and acknowledged.

"And tourist season is just beginning," Shirley said. "So far it's mostly the locals who want to buy your pictures. Wait until the tourists see them."

Despite the tension between Clare and Lynette, the locals still wanted to patronize her shop. It actually surprised her, based on the amount of recent sales from locals, that no other photographer had opened a studio in Big Cat before now. It seemed the horses were even more important to the people of this area than Claire had first realized.

She'd also sold a couple of prints of the cemetery. Claire thought back to Jeff's reaction to the photograph of the mysterious gravestone and couldn't wait to upload the newest pictures that she'd taken over the weekend. Too bad for Jeff, but she didn't plan to invite him over to watch her upload them as she'd promised. If he didn't believe the gravestone existed, then he'd have to take his own pictures. Seeing him last night had been awkward enough. She wasn't used to crying, much less in front of someone she was attracted to.

But before she could upload the images, she had prints to frame and paperwork to catch up on. Maybe with some luck, she'd have time to work on the gravestone pictures tonight before she had to leave for the Salty Mug.

Claire had almost forgotten about Lynette's bridal shower. That ought to be a tension-filled event. She didn't look forward to Lynette tossing the wedding in her face once again, nor did she welcome the idea of watching Lynette open skimpy lingerie, one piece after another. And she refused to imagine Jeff's face when he saw Lynette's perky little body in next to nothing. The thought of them in bed together made her almost physically sick.

She hoped Jeff realized, before he stood at the altar, the mistake he was making, but the journey was his.

# CHAPTER FOURTEEN

Jeff dialed Nancy Smith's phone number. Her number ended up unlisted, but he'd gotten lucky because one of the people he'd called after his search had given him the correct number.

The phone rang at least four times before an older-sounding woman answered. "Hi, I'm Jeff Rhoades from Big Cat. I'm calling on behalf of a friend who knew your husband, Robert Kincaid."

"Oh, then honey, you're a friend of mine."

"Thanks. I have a bunch of questions I'd like to ask. Would you mind if I came by to meet you?"

Without hesitation, she answered. "No, not at all. I'd love the company. When and what time, sweetie?"

His heart went out to her. If she was older, maybe she didn't get many visitors. "Around six o'clock tonight? Unless that's too short notice."

If Ms. Smith met him tonight, that would take his mind off the bridal shower. If he wasn't around, then Lynette wouldn't try to talk him into attending. He imagined a bunch of women ogling over party trays and scanty underwear. With his luck, they'd hire a sexy man to romp around the room and flaunt his muscles. No thanks. It all sounded downright embarrassing.

He could easily fill his evening with an abundance of different activities, from cleaning stalls to helping Claire find out more information on her father. He wanted to ease her pain. Whether his meddling would prove to be a distraction or part of his confusion, he didn't know. He respected that Claire wanted to learn about her father on her own, but Jeff had made a mess of things and needed to fix them. Otherwise, he wouldn't forgive himself for destroying her dream.

"I'll be here," Nancy said. "I don't go many places these days. When you get older, it's easier to stay home."

Again, her comment concerned him, because he had expected a woman in her late fifties. He had a moment of doubt as to whether he'd found the right person, but he had mentioned Claire's father by name, and she hadn't corrected him. Maybe Mr. Kincaid had married someone older.

"Thanks, ma'am. I'll see you tonight." Jeff clicked off his phone and tried to concentrate on what he wanted to accomplish the rest of the afternoon. He really needed to return to the island to administer more birth control. He thought about asking Claire to join him but then remembered she was in no shape to walk around the island.

He wondered how she felt today. He dialed the studio's phone number but hung up before he pressed the last digit. No, he shouldn't call her and lead her on, even though his intentions were purely innocent. Or were they? What exactly did he want from her? His mind fogged over and absolutely refused to think about that difficult question.

***

By early afternoon, Claire had been too busy in the studio to finish framing the prints the two women had ordered much less eat lunch. Finally, she sat down at a small table in the back to eat a sandwich while Shirley covered the studio for her. It had been a good decision not to take the strong prescription painkiller this morning. If it had wiped her out today, with business being what it was, Shirley would have had trouble keeping up alone.

Claire's overall pain had improved somewhat, thanks to the ibuprofen and all the moving around she had done. Maybe there was truth in what her mother used to say. "Claire, your muscles will stiffen if you lie down for a long time. You need to get up and move."

Shirley walked into the back and leaned against the table, interrupting her thoughts. "What a busy day."

"No kidding," Claire replied. "By the way, are you going to Lynette's bridal shower?" She tried to look nonchalant when she asked, but it wasn't as easy as she'd hoped.

"Only her tenants are invited, so no. That's fine because I need to paint my toenails tonight." Shirley made a show of flashing her sandaled foot to Claire.

Claire's jaw dropped at the comment. When she noticed Shirley's smile, she laughed. "So there's no love lost between you two, is that what you're saying?"

"Pretty much." Shirley pulled out a chair and sat down. "We used to own one of the houses downtown, and when we were ready to sell, we listed it with Lynette. But when one of her business clients wanted to buy it, the whole transaction turned into a nightmare. My husband insisted to his grave that we paid for too many repairs and didn't get nearly enough for the house. The buyer sold it as commercial property for almost double what he'd paid us for it. My husband and I didn't have friendly feelings about how the deal went. But I try not to hold grudges. Honestly, I just don't care for the woman, bless her heart."

Claire soaked up the information without commenting at first. Then she said, "Well, I'm sorry that happened. It doesn't seem right, and I can certainly understand why you don't want to go to the bridal shower."

"Are you invited tonight?" Shirley asked. At Claire's nod, Shirley continued. "So how do you feel about that?"

"About what?" Claire feigned innocence.

"Oh, come on Claire. Level with me, honey."

It actually calmed her to know Shirley cared enough to ask. Since her mother died, she'd kept her feelings to herself. Those feelings included the pain of her mother's death, the sting of her ex-boyfriend's betrayal, and her confusion about Jeff. Shirley had proven to be trustworthy and obviously had Claire's best interest in mind.

Claire decided to confide in her friend. "Shirley, I think I love him. What do I do?"

"Oh, my." Shirley sat down next to Claire and reached for her hand. "I suspected that's how you felt. Have you told him?"

"No. How can I do that? He's about to marry someone else."

"What do you have to lose?" Shirley squeezed her wrinkled hand, the joints knotted from arthritis, around Claire's hand.

Claire absorbed the warmth. "He has to reach his own conclusions, so he doesn't resent me later. I shouldn't have to change his mind." She wasn't about to chase him. Either he wanted to be with her, or he didn't. "Besides, it's not fair to dump my emotions on him right before his wedding."

"True, but what if he loves you and doesn't know how to get out of the mess he's in? Jeff is an honorable man. He might decide to go through with the wedding because he believes in living up to his commitments."

True, but why be married to a "commitment."

"I understand all that," Claire said, "even if I don't like it one bit. Lynette's a convenience."

"As I said before, Jeff's afraid of being hurt again." Shirley placed her free hand on Claire's shoulder for a moment and looked straight into Claire's eyes. "He loves Big Cat, loves his family, and his horses. He doesn't want to give that up."

Shirley's touch radiated comfort. "I'm not asking him to give up anything. In case you haven't noticed, I love this area and the horses, too." Claire diverted her eyes. Oh, she missed her mother. Claire managed to meet Shirley's direct eye contact again and found comfort from the empathy she saw there. "I also realize we barely know each other. But I believe when you meet your soul mate, you know it."

"I think you're right. He recognizes the bond the two of you share. It scares him, and it should. He's about to get married," Shirley said. "I also think he knows he's about to make a big mistake. Tell him, Claire."

"In his mind, I'm a risk," Claire whispered. "He probably wonders why he should take a chance on me."

Shirley sighed. "He's not much of a risk taker, that's for sure. Having said that, shouldn't you be honest and let him make the decision? Don't make it for him."

"I'm uncomfortable telling him how I feel. I'd rather sit back and hope he comes to his senses."

"Then I'll hope for the best, too." Shirley looked truly sad. "I'm here for you, sweetie."

"Thanks," Claire said. "I'll keep myself busy until next Saturday. After that, there's no use pining after a married man." When Claire stood and tossed her half-eaten sandwich into the trash, Shirley frowned.

The rest of the afternoon went by surprisingly fast, considering her pain had started to increase once again. After the steady stream of shoppers had slowed and she'd finished framing the two immediate orders, she retreated to her apartment to get ready for the bridal shower.

First, however, Claire wanted to upload the graveyard photos to her computer. That way, once she returned from the party, the pictures would be ready to view. Eager to see if the grave showed up again and if the close-ups revealed a name, she started the upload and headed into the bathroom.

Claire lingered in the warm shower, and then managed to dry off without too much discomfort. But when it came time to lean over and pull on nylons, she groaned. Eventually she decided to go without. She dressed in a simple but classy black dress with her long hair pulled back in a twist. It was important to look conservative, especially since Lynette's renters were throwing the bridal shower. It would require some effort to maintain that polished demeanor while Lynette opened slinky lingerie, but Claire had to rise to the challenge. Her heart and career depended on professionalism.

When she walked outdoors for the first time in days, she had to reach back inside the doorway to grab an umbrella. A fine mist fell and the sky held gray clouds with the promise of more rain. The weather fit her mood.

Claire glanced at her watch. Perfect. With a few minutes left to stroll down the block to the Salty Mug, she'd be exactly on time. Her plan to avoid the pre-party chatter served as a feeble attempt at self-preservation. Even so, jitters danced in her belly, and she pretended to ignore them along with the pain that jabbed at her heart. If the bridal shower bothered her this much, maybe she'd skip the wedding altogether. Perhaps no one would notice her missing, no one except Jeff. By then it wouldn't matter what he thought. He'd be married.

As she approached the front door of the restaurant, Jenni walked up behind her. "Hi there, Claire. I haven't seen you around the ferry lately."

Claire smiled, even though she wondered why Jenni was here. Since she wasn't a tenant but still had an invitation to Lynette's party, did that make her an ally, or an enemy?

"I haven't been to the island recently," Claire replied. Actually, it hadn't been that long, but she didn't want to divulge that Jeff had taken her over there. Just in case Jenni couldn't be trusted, she wanted to keep any possibility of future gossip to a minimum.

"Bob did it again."

"What do you mean?" They walked inside the restaurant and toward the back room where a large group congregated.

"He left a man on the island."

Claire jerked up her head. "You've got to be kidding? How did that happen?"

"The same way it happened to you. I told him you were out there, and he insisted he picked you up. He blamed me, said I forgot to check you off the list."

"Unbelievable. So was the man okay?"

Jenni smiled. "Other than being beyond mad, he's fine. He reported Bob to the paper as you had threatened. Didn't you see today's headlines?"

Claire shook her head. Her focus had been to make it through the entire day at the studio, so she hadn't thought to read the morning paper.

"Bob's already feeling the squeeze. People are walking right past our ticket booth, all the way to the other side of town, and taking the *Sea Horse Ferry*. One man even shook his paper at Bob and yelled something ugly. Guess they didn't want to be left behind to spend the night out there."

"Good. I'm glad his rudeness and neglect have come back around to haunt him. But since he's your boss, why are you telling me this?"

"I quit after he blamed me for leaving the other man behind. That's why I'm here tonight. My brother Keith is planning to sign a lease with Lynette. He's going to rent dock space two slips down from my ex-boss."

"Doing what?" They set their presents on a table decorated in white, already crowded with fancily wrapped packages.

"We're about to become Bob's competition. Keith wants to own his own ferry business, and I'm going to help him for the summer."

Claire barked a loud laugh. "Good for you!"

"Thanks," Jenni said and smiled. She picked out a nearby table just far enough from the center of action, but close enough not to be rude. "Do you want to sit with me? I might go crazy if I have to endure the party alone." Her tone implied she'd prefer a tooth extraction.

Jenni proved to be a friend.

"I have an idea," Claire offered. "I heard the owner of the *Sea Horse Ferry* wants to sell his business. If you bought an existing company, you wouldn't have to start from scratch." That first day they had met at the dock, Jenni had reached out to her by taking an interest in helping Claire to find her father. Claire wanted to return the favor.

Jenni flashed Claire a smile. "Fabulous idea. I didn't realize George's business was for sale. Do you think it's too far on the other side of town?"

"The town isn't that big. And you just said that people were walking to the other end to avoid using Bob's ferry."

Jenni tilted her head. "You're right. It's only a few blocks really. That seems like a long way when you're from here, but visitors don't usually mind. Most tourists stroll up and down the street all day long to shop."

The scenario was perfect. "And neither ferry is centrally located," Claire said. "They're both on opposite ends of town. I think you'd be fine."

Several women giggled from the center of the room.

"By the way, did my leads about your father pan out?" Jenni asked, without taking her eyes off the group of laughing women. Did the clique bother her too?

Claire frowned. "Well, your tips helped rule out some things. Actually, I found out he's dead."

"Oh, Claire! I'm so sorry." Jenni reached over and hugged Claire.

They separated when Lynette walked up, smiling as if she owned the world. "Hi there, Jenni. I see you met Claire, our local photographer." She said the last word as if it were a despicable job, perhaps equivalent to scrubbing toilets.

"I sure have, and she's wonderful." Jenni sent Claire a conspiring look.

Claire secretly thanked Jenni for her willingness to stand up to Lynette on her behalf. Actually, if Claire could leave the bridal shower without creating gossip, she'd do it. Then she reminded herself that if she viewed the party as an opportunity to network a bit, and displayed a confident attitude, then it wouldn't matter what Lynette said about her in town. If she remained positive and friendly, she'd bet that people would eventually gravitate toward her.

"Lynette," Paula said as she approached with a somber expression on her face. "Your grandmother is lost in the bathroom and won't come out. When I tried to help her, she swung her fist at me."

"Not again." Lynette turned back to Claire and Jenni. "See you later, Jenni." Lynette ignored Claire and walked off toward the bathroom.

Claire had to laugh off Lynette's rudeness. The woman was obviously insecure about Claire's presence at the shower—and understandably so. She perceived Claire as a threat, and maybe there was validity to her concern.

"Claire, it's nice to see you again," Paula said.

Relieved by Paula's guarded but somewhat friendly remark, Claire said, "You, too. How's the foal doing?"

Paula lips turned down into a frown but the concern didn't quite reach her eyes. Maybe that was good news. "I went to the island today and he's nursing well. He looks much stronger than he did on Saturday."

"That was a bad situation," Claire added, "and I'm glad he figured it out." Claire noticed another group of women watching as Paula and she talked. Maybe if Paula deemed her safe, they would follow suit and be friendly too.

An older woman screamed as Lynette led her from the bathroom. "Grams, here's your seat. I'll even tie a balloon to your chair." The hunched over woman complied and sat in a chair next to the gift table.

Paula said under her breath to Claire, "We should probably get this party started. You never know how long she will behave."

Lynette kissed her grandmother affectionately on the cheek and sat down next to her. The older woman patted Lynette's leg. "Honey, I love you. Please, don't ever leave me."

Lynette's face turned gentle but worried, like that of a young child afraid to be alone herself. Perhaps the painful reality that her grandmother was the one mentally leaving the world, frightened her. "Grams, I'm not going anywhere."

Claire had to admit, albeit reluctantly, that the scene unfolding before her eyes was touching, and that Lynette actually had endearing qualities. For a person Claire wanted to resent, it became difficult to do so when Lynette treated her feeble grandmother with such tenderness. It was easier to dislike Lynette, to picture her as a manipulative schemer, who misled Jeff into an unwanted engagement.

Paula moved the party along by handing Lynette one gift after another to unwrap. Thankfully, most of the presents were specialty items from the local shops instead of suggestive lingerie. The conservative presents made sense since it was the shop owners, instead of close personal friends, who were the gift givers. Claire's present was the picture she'd taken of the container ship in the fog. She knew Jeff would like it, even if Lynette didn't.

When Lynette had opened her last present, her grandmother belted out a scream.

"Grams, let's go home." Lovingly, Lynette rubbed the elderly woman's arm and stood. "Sorry, but I have to leave. Thanks for coming everyone." She turned to Paula and said, "I'll be back to clean up, but I need to bring Grams back to the nursing home while I can still control her. She probably needs her medication."

"Where's Jeff?" Paula asked. "He's usually good at helping with her."

Lynette gave a one-shouldered shrug. "I can handle Grams alone. Besides, I don't know where Jeff is. He hides out a lot lately." Lynette flashed Claire an accusatory glance, one that rippled through Claire's body.

Silence filled the room, and even Grams grew quiet. Claire had a momentary hot flash from the heat of the stares. She found it unsettling to be the *other* woman, the interloper, the woman who threatened Lynette's happy life. Before now, the thought had never crossed her mind. She couldn't help but wonder if the bridal shower would force her to view Lynette and the situation differently.

# CHAPTER FIFTEEN

"Ms. Kincaid, I'm Jeff Rhoades." He reached out to shake the hand of the woman who possibly had known Claire's father. "I spoke to you on the phone earlier."

"Please, call me Nancy, and do come in." Nancy opened the screen door and stepped aside. Despite her wrinkled skin from hours in the sun, she was younger than she had sounded on the phone. She appeared warm and friendly with her thick gray hair wrapped into a tight bun at the nape of her neck.

When Jeff stepped into the small house, he noticed the old and comfortable-looking furniture in the living room, and the sparse and neatly placed knickknacks on the fireplace mantle. The near wall held an array of wooden-framed photographs. He stepped closer and marveled at several pictures of a handsome man with tanned skin and light brown hair, standing next to a different horse in each photograph. Undeniably, Jeff knew he was staring at Robert Kincaid, although the man held no physical resemblance to Claire.

"Have a seat," Nancy said. "I'll bring in a tray of cookies and iced tea."

"Please, let me help you," Jeff offered. She nodded and he followed her into a compact kitchen. A young woman, about his age, sat at a scarred wooden table and filled a baking sheet with mounds of cookie dough. Jeff had to do a double take, because at first he thought the woman was Claire. Could she be a sister Claire knew nothing about? Then he remembered the newspaper reporter in Oldham had said that Robert Kincaid never had children.

"Jeff, meet my daughter, Robin."

His expression must have given away his confusion, because Nancy immediately qualified her statement. "Actually, she isn't my real daughter; I just think of her as one. Robin is our foreman's daughter, but since Robert died, he isn't our foreman anymore. He's a friend."

When Jeff remained quiet, trying to add up mentally what Nancy had told him, she took that as a cue to keep talking. "Robert died in a tractor accident, so we moved from our farm. It's just outside of Big Cat. I couldn't do all the work to keep it up and running. Honestly, I didn't even want to try. Robert was the farmer, not me."

"I'm sorry to hear about Mr. Kincaid." Jeff looked first at Nancy and then at the young woman, who was watching him closely now. "It's nice to meet you, Robin. For a minute there, I thought you were my friend, Claire. You look just like her."

Both women looked alarmed and stared at Jeff. When no one spoke, he asked, "Did I say something wrong?"

"You said your friend's name is Claire?" Nancy asked.

"Yes, Claire Kincaid. I didn't mean to bring her up this way, but seeing Robin caught me off guard."

Nancy pulled out a chair and sat at the table. "Well, I'll be …. I haven't heard Claire's name in years."

Jeff studied Robin's wide eyes, but when she didn't offer an explanation, he had to ask. "Are you and Claire related?"

"You might want to sit down," Nancy suggested, pointing at a chair cattycorner to Robin.

Jeff gladly complied. He noticed Nancy had forgotten the cookies and tea, and Robin had pushed the baking sheet aside.

"Robert had been previously married, to a woman named Loretta. She had a little girl named Claire."

"Wait a minute. Sorry to interrupt, but Claire told me her mother's name was Virginia."

Nancy shook her head with disapproval. "Is that what she calls herself? Her name is definitely Loretta, and we lived in a small town on the North Carolina-Virginia border, called Oldham." There was a definite edge to Nancy's voice now. "Maybe she called herself Virginia to disguise her name, so Robert couldn't find her. He never did have luck locating her, even though he tried. It was sad, really." Nancy grew quiet for a moment, somber and lost in memories, then she turned away to collect herself. When she looked back, she said, "Anyway, we all grew up together, and some years after Loretta left, I married Robert."

Jeff's heart ached for the older woman, and for Claire.

Claire wasn't going to like this.

"Where is she? Claire, I mean." Nancy asked with a hint of hope glittering in her damp eyes. "Why didn't she come with you tonight?"

Jeff grimaced. Claire was a proud woman with moral integrity, and she was spending the evening attending his fiancée's bridal shower, most likely because she felt obligated. He admired her principles. After the obvious dislike between Claire and Lynette, he was surprised Claire attended the shower. He couldn't help but wonder if she went because she wanted to meet people to increase her business, or out of loyalty to him? Did it really matter?

Here he was, sitting in a kitchen, talking with people who knew her father. Why?

He cleared his voice to answer Nancy's question, as though admitting the truth aloud would decrease the guilt he carried for being there. "She's actually at a bridal shower—my fiancée's shower." His face grew warm and he knew it burned crimson. Unfortunately, saying the words made him feel worse.

Nancy studied him. "Really? I'm sorry to be so blunt, but I assumed Claire was your girlfriend."

Jeff's stomach churned. "No, we're just good friends."

Nancy raised her eyebrows. "You haven't mentioned where Claire has been all this time, or how you found me."

Thank goodness for the change of subject. "Her mother took her to Charlotte, but when she died, Claire moved to Big Cat. Recently."

"Died?" Nancy's eyes grew red from unshed tears. "How?"

"Ovarian cancer. On her deathbed, she told Claire that her father still loves her and that he lives in Big Cat. Claire moved here to find him." He leaned toward Nancy and whispered, "You can imagine how devastated Claire felt when she found out he'd passed away too."

"He isn't dead."

What was she talking about? "I thought you said—"

"Robert wasn't her father. Black Eagle is."

Jeff's mouth fell open. "Black Eagle?"

Unbelievable. He turned to look at Robin, who sat quietly at the head of the table. "That means you are Claire's sister?"

Robin nodded. She remained silent, but her unspoken words said enough. She had a sister, one she never got a chance to know.

Jeff once again found himself in a bad position. He'd have to inform Claire of the information he learned tonight, even if she resented his interference. He had set out to find her father, and to find answers. Well, he'd certainly done that.

How would Claire handle this new development?

"Half sister actually," Robin explained, tucking a long strand of black hair behind her left ear, just as Claire always did. "We had different mothers."

"Her mother was Loretta," Jeff said as he looked at the ceiling for a moment and then back at Nancy. "Please enlighten me. Claire thinks Robert was her father. I assume his name is on her birth certificate instead of Black Eagle's."

"That's right. Robert and Loretta had married, and eight months later, she had a baby. Robert knew the baby wasn't his because he and Loretta had waited until their honeymoon before they … you know." Nancy blushed and looked down at the scarred table for a moment, tracing her finger along a scratch. She looked back up with pain in her eyes. "Robert confronted Loretta, and she admitted that she'd had an affair with Black Eagle before the wedding. Loretta had gotten cold feet and they had broken up for a short time. Loretta didn't know she was pregnant when she married Robert, and when the baby came the three of them decided it would be best for everyone if Robert became the legal father. They agreed to keep the truth between them.

"Back then there was a lot of prejudice against out-of-wedlock babies in our small town," Nancy continued. "In this particular situation, because the baby's father was Native American, it would have been even worse. The whole family would have been scandalized. They believed it best that Claire never know, so she could have a normal childhood. Black Eagle wanted to remain foreman, so he could stay close to his child, and Robert kept him on as long as he promised never to tell Claire he was her father."

"Amazing." Jeff tried to hide the bitter edge in his voice. "Claire would have wanted to know. She spent most of her childhood without a father."

"It's unfortunate, I know. Things didn't work out as planned. Loretta loved Black Eagle, and when he got married to someone else, she couldn't handle living next to his wife and later their child, Robin. Loretta stayed around for a while, a couple of years, but then fled."

"Are you telling me Claire has met her sister?" Jeff pulled his gaze from Nancy and glanced at Robin, who refused to look at him.

"Yes. Robin had just turned two when Loretta left."

When he turned back to Nancy, he noticed her hands were shaking. "I can't believe someone thought this deranged plan made sense." He clenched his jaw and forced his temper down.

"I agree. Robert tried to find Claire but gave up quickly. After all, he wasn't her real father."

"What about Black Eagle? He just ignored all of this and didn't bother to search for her?"

Nancy smiled empathetically. "Of course he looked for her, but without the Internet back then, it was hard to find people. He couldn't leave the ranch often, because of his responsibilities. Whenever he did, he went looking for Claire but never found her."

"What about now, why isn't he still looking? Did he write her off like everyone else has?"

"You must really love Claire. There's no need to raise your voice at me; I'm innocent in all this. I didn't understand the situation until I married Robert and he confided in me."

"I'm sorry." Jeff didn't dare comment on Nancy's assessment about his feelings for Claire. He hadn't worked through the possible truth in his own mind, and he certainly wasn't ready to admit anything to Nancy. "Of course none of this is your fault, and you are being an enormous help."

Nancy's body visibly relaxed and her lips curled into a small smile.

Jeff softened his voice. "If you don't mind me asking, where is Black Eagle now?"

"To answer your first question, on occasion he still searches for Claire. He drives up and down the coast whenever he can. He thinks she'll remember her roots and come back here, looking for Robert. He doesn't have the resources to travel far, but he has looked for her. Robin has also searched on the Internet, but she hasn't found anything, either. To answer your next question, I sold our old farm to Black Eagle, and his family raises horses on it."

"How odd. I'm in the horse business and I've never heard of him."

"I know the horse world is small, but evidently not that small if you don't know him." Nancy stood and walked to the refrigerator. She poured three glasses of sweet tea and brought them back to the table. She pushed one toward Jeff and handed another to Robin.

Robin stood, walked to the counter, and returned with a checkered, cloth-lined basket stuffed full of fresh-baked cookies. She offered the basket to Jeff.

"Thanks," he said. Jeff took a long drink of iced tea and bit into a still-warm cookie. "These are great." He held up the cookie to Robin, who smiled. "So is Black Eagle still married?" he asked Nancy.

Nancy set down her glass. "Yes, he is."

"That means Claire has a father, a stepmother, and a half sister. She thinks she's alone in the world. She'll be surprised, to say the least, to know she has an entire family."

"I know he'd love to see her. Let me give you his phone number." She walked over to the counter, wrote the number on a piece of flowered notepad paper, and handed it to Jeff. "I'll tell him that we talked today. Please let Claire know that he loves her; he always has."

"That's exactly what Claire's mom said, only Claire thought she meant Robert."

"Maybe it's not too late to fix this awful mess," Nancy said. "Robin's mom is aware of what happened, so there are no surprises on our end. My suggestion is to give Claire time to absorb all this without pushing her."

He seriously doubted that time could heal Claire. "Thanks for telling me the truth." Jeff turned toward Robin. "Are you okay with Claire calling your father? This must be somewhat of a shock to have her back in the picture after all this time."

"Yes," Robin said. "I have no memory of Claire, of course, but I grew up knowing about her."

Nancy managed a genuine smile. "Once Loretta left and Claire's reputation wasn't at stake in town anymore, Robert felt there was no reason to keep the secrets."

"I'm glad he didn't." Jeff despised secrets, although lately life seemed full of unspoken truths.

"Mr. Rhoades?" Robin asked. "If you'll follow me home, I have a box for you to give Claire. My dad's been holding onto it for years, and he'd jump at the chance for Claire to have it."

"I'm sure she'd appreciate it." He looked at Nancy again. "I do have one more question for you, if you don't mind."

"Honey, I don't mind." Suddenly Nancy looked ten years younger. Perhaps she felt relieved to unburden herself after all these years of secret keeping.

"Where is Mr. Kincaid buried?" For Claire's sake, he had to know.

A moment of silence filled the room before Nancy answered. "That's another secret, but I'll tell you because I'm sure Claire needs closure."

"I appreciate that." Jeff leaned in closer, as if to keep others from overhearing another hurtful truth, to the woman who'd trusted him enough to share her painful past.

"He's buried on Pony Island," Nancy almost whispered. "He'd always said he wanted his final resting place to be undisturbed by people, and near the horses."

Jeff drew back as if she'd slapped him. "People are allowed to be buried on the island?" He thought he knew everything there was to know about the little island he held sacred.

"No, that's the secret. Black Eagle buried him there in an unmarked grave. It's located near the old graveyard."

Jeff swallowed hard and realized the impact of what Nancy had told him. He needed to get to Claire, and fast, before she looked at the close-up photos of the mysterious gravestone. The unmarked tombstone was Robert Kincaid's.

# CHAPTER SIXTEEN

Claire walked through the shadowed streets alone. The mist had turned into a light rain but she didn't bother to open her wet umbrella. She tried to focus on something positive instead, but found the task difficult. The realization that Lynette was almost likeable bothered her more than she wanted. Lynette's vulnerable side, the one that showed such affection toward her grandmother, had taken Claire aback. Her surprisingly loving behavior made Claire understand how she was intruding on the woman's wedding, and threatening the stability of her future.

Whether she liked it or not, she had to accept Jeff's decision to marry Lynette. Bluntly put, his happiness wasn't her business.

She also needed to accept the sad reality that neither she nor Jeff wanted to take a chance on love again. Jeff preferred to take the safe road, and that she understood all too well.

Opening the door, she left the damp umbrella to dry on the entryway floor, and then climbed the steps in slow motion. She needed more ibuprofen to ease the pain in her muscles. Too bad the anti-inflammatory wouldn't ease the wretched pain in her heart. She'd get through this wedding somehow, one hour at a time, even one minute at a time. Then, once the couple said, "I do," she'd let go of the pipedream, scary as it was anyway, and bury her grief. She excelled at that.

Once upstairs, Claire headed straight to the stovetop and turned on a burner. When the teapot whistled, she poured a cup of water and dropped a decaffeinated tea bag into her favorite pottery mug. Then she walked down the hallway to the small office. When in distress, she always immersed herself in a pile of work. That strategy had been her lifesaver in the past, and she'd rely on it again for the upcoming week.

Claire sat at the perfectly organized desk and scowled at its neatness. Her ex-boyfriend had been right. She was too organized, too boring. She reached into a cubby and grabbed the few business books she liked to read in her downtime, and spread them across the desk. She stared at the slight mess she'd created and felt a little better, a little more carefree.

When her tea had cooled a bit, she took a sip. The hot liquid slid down her throat and slowly melted away her anguish. She always drank a lot of green tea, a reassuring security blanket, when she needed solace. Her mother had used the same tactic and had passed it on to Claire.

She looked up at the ceiling. *Thanks, Mom. You're always here when I need you.* Her mother's perfume wafted imperceptibly through the air.

Enough of feeling sorry for herself. Claire shook the computer mouse to wake up the system and clicked on the file to view the new images of the graveyard that she'd uploaded earlier. Sure enough, the photos had loaded. In the first picture, to her disappointment, she had cut off at least half the gravestone. Thankful she had taken more shots, she pulled up the next picture.

\*\*\*

Barely Claire heard the doorbell ring. When she didn't move, she thought she heard the front door of her apartment open. She tried to push aside the blurry fog that shrouded her brain, and strained to recall if she'd locked the door. Apparently she'd forgotten. When Jeff appeared in the office doorway, she looked up. She saw him run to her side, alarm written on his face, and her mind swirled in different directions.

"Claire? Are you all right?"

She remained silent.

"You looked at the photos, didn't you?"

She nodded numbly. She attempted to force the words out, any words, but only a breath of air escaped.

"Was your father's name engraved on it?"

"Yes," she managed to say. "How?"

"I can't explain how his grave showed up in the photograph, but I can tell you that Black Eagle secretly buried him on the island."

More secrets. What else could possibly go wrong in her life?

She stared at Jeff. Soon he'd be married to someone else. She needed to be smart and push him out of her heart.

"Why are you here, Jeff?"

Between the concerned expression on his face and the way he set his jaw, he evidently had more bad news to share.

Claire frowned at him as he reached out toward her. No, she didn't want his affection; he belonged to another woman. She pulled away so fast she felt like a snake ready to strike in self-defense. Not only did Claire find her voice, she found her anger. "You have a fiancée, go be with her."

Jeff jerked back, his eyes filled with hurt. "I came to tell you I found your father."

Anger boiled up inside her and spilled over. "I've found him, too. I just saw his name engraved on a headstone, and he's buried on Pony Island." Heat burned her cheeks and face.

"No, I mean I really found him. He's alive."

"How dare you lead me on, in more ways than one. Leave me alone."

He moved backward and bumped into the wall. "I'm not lying about your dad, and I've never led you on."

"Really? Then why are you in my apartment, trying to hold me? What would Lynette say if she knew?" The words spewed from her mouth before she could stop them. "I've had my share of unfaithful men, and I'm sick of the hurt. You shouldn't be here, Jeff; that's wrong. I'm a big girl and I don't need your help."

If she pushed him away fast and hard, the pain might hurt less. It felt almost good to be the one who did the rejecting for once.

He backed away into the hall, his face red with anger. "Fine, I get the message. I'll stay away from you, but before I go, I need to tell you about your father."

"I don't want to know. Just leave." The words hissed from her mouth in a tone she didn't recognize.

He turned around sharply and left. Seconds later, Claire heard the apartment door slam shut. The blood pounded in her ears and when she stood, she felt lightheaded. She held onto the wall to make her way to the couch. *Get yourself together, Claire. Now!*

She was a survivor, but she wasn't sure she could handle yet another heartbreak.

***

The next morning Claire awoke in a state of confusion. She must have fallen asleep on the sofa, fully dressed. At first she couldn't remember how she got there. Turning over onto her side, a stab of pain shot across her back and throughout her body. Involuntarily, she groaned. A night of sleeping on the soft cushions hadn't been conducive to healing her sore muscles.

Then the memory of last night flooded back. This time she groaned with grief.

She closed her eyes and reopened them, hoping the fight with Jeff was just a bad dream. Unfortunately, she was still lying on the couch with the light streaming in through the living room blinds. A sudden thought made her jolt upright, despite her soreness. She must be late for work. As if on cue, the phone rang.

The caller I.D. displayed the studio's number. "Good morning, Shirley." Claire's voice sounded deep and scratchy.

"Sweetheart, I'm sorry to call, but I wanted to check on you. You're never late for work."

Not wanting Shirley to know she just woke up, she swallowed hard to clear her voice. "I'll be down in a bit."

"Lynette keeps calling. She sounds desperate."

Claire's thoughts immediately turned to Jeff. He'd left angry last night and she hoped he was safe, otherwise she'd never forgive herself. "Did Lynette say what she wanted?"

"No, just that it's urgent."

Unpleasant thoughts taunted Claire's mind. "I'll call her when I get downstairs. I want to take a shower first."

An unrelated idea, assuming Jeff was okay, pressed on her mind. She had an immediate desire burning inside her to visit her father's grave. "Shirley, I know this is last minute, but could you run the studio today? I need to go to Pony Island. I have something important to do."

"Of course I don't mind," she said. "Honey … it's none of my business, but I hope you've come to your senses. Are you going out to the island to tell Jeff how you feel about him?"

"Actually, I plan to stay as far away from Jeff as possible."

Shirley sighed loudly into the phone.

"I'll be downstairs in a minute."

As Claire walked through the door of the studio, the phone rang. Shirley answered and hesitantly handed it to Claire. "It's Lynette again," she whispered.

Claire nodded. "What can I do for you, Lynette? Is everything okay?"

"I need your help," Lynette said with a rush of words. "Our wedding photographer's sister is ill and the doctors don't think she'll make it. He has to leave town." The fast-paced sentences were a sharp contrast to her usual slow drawl, but her tone was still sweet as molasses. That meant one thing. She wanted something from Claire.

"Sorry to hear that. How can I help?" Claire immediately regretted asking the question.

"I want to hire you to take his place."

Claire's head reeled. How was she supposed to take wedding pictures of a man she wanted for herself? Why endure that kind of pain willingly? Sure, she happened to be the only photographer in town, and she wanted to maintain her professionalism, but that wasn't reason enough to take on Lynette and Jeff's crisis. Besides, Claire had hoped to avoid the wedding altogether.

"Jeff wants to hire you," Lynette said, practically pleading.

After a moment of self-reflection, Claire realized she felt compelled to accept the job, but only because she cared about Jeff.

"Okay," she said firmly. "I'll photograph your wedding, but if your photographer returns to town in time, he needs to do the assignment instead of me. Agreed?"

"Absolutely!"

Claire resented Lynette's enthusiasm. Suddenly it became difficult to breathe; Lynette had locked her into attending the awful wedding, and into being the only photographer. What was wrong with Claire for accepting Lynette's dreadful scheme?

Claire ended the call quickly. She needed to escape the closed-in walls of the studio before she burst. She hurried into the kitchen and packed her daypack with snacks and water.

"Bye, Shirley. And thanks," Claire yelled toward the main room. She blushed when Shirley appeared in the entryway and caught her before she scooted out the back door.

"Be safe, child. And think about what I said about Jeff. Don't run from your feelings."

"I've got to go." Claire hurried onto the patio with her daypack and power walked toward Bob's unreliable ferry service. Before she reached the ticket booth, she ran into Jenni.

"Are you going to Pony Island?" Jenni asked, and pointed to Claire's daypack.

Embarrassed that she'd actually use the ferry again, she said, "I am. I'm looking forward to the day you and Keith open your ferry service."

"Then consider today your lucky day. We talked to George, and he arranged for us to operate his ferry temporarily, with his guidance. It's kind of a trial run to make sure Keith wants to buy the business. You can be one of our first customers."

With the new ferry service in operation, she'd no longer have reason to accept rides to the island from Jeff. Her heart betrayed her and sank heavy in her chest. Using the ferry was probably a smart choice anyway, but the finality hurt.

*** 

Before long, Claire sank onto the sand in front of her father's invisible grave. She threw one broken shell after another in the general direction of where his headstone should have been.

"Dad, why did you have to go and die? I need you. I have questions I want answers to. For starters, why did Mom leave with me in the middle of the night? Why didn't you look for me? I want to know!" She threw another shell and it hit a tree. "Why didn't you love me enough to find me?"

No one answered except a distant call of a bird and a whinny of a horse. "Stay quiet, then. Take the easy way out, just like you always do."

The light rustling sound of sea grass moving made Claire turn around in time to see Jeff approaching.

He looked up in surprise when he noticed her.

"Jeff. I don't mean to be rude, but can't you leave me alone?"

"I had no idea you were here. Besides, I'm working and you're in my office."

She huffed at him.

"And by the way, anger doesn't become you."

"Whatever." She turned away from him and hoped he'd go away.

"You should know that Robert wasn't your father."

Claire whirled around and glared at him. Of course Robert Kincaid was her father. How would Jeff know anyway?

Jeff stood there awkwardly with his hands crammed into the pockets of his pants. Too bad he looked so sexy.

"I didn't get the chance to tell you last night, but *Black Eagle* is your father."

Claire's heart thudded to what seemed to be a complete stop, and when it began beating again, it was thumping so loudly she could hear the pounding in her ears. "What? He was my father's foreman, not my dad. You have no idea what you're talking about."

Jeff sat down on a clump of grass next to her. "I realize you're upset, but if you hear me out, you might find the new information interesting."

Claire gave up and collapsed onto her back in the sand. Exhaustion and defeat overcame her. "Go on then, tell me."

Jeff scooted a little closer, but not close enough to touch her. "Before your mom married Robert, she had a strong case of premarital jitters. They broke up briefly before the wedding, and she had a fling with Black Eagle."

Her brain tried to squeeze out what he was saying, but he'd hit a nerve. She didn't want to hear about how her mother cheated on her father with Black Eagle. Then a thought popped into her head. "Is that what you're having with me, premarital jitters?"

Jeff narrowed his eyes at her. "Claire, I know you're angry about my wedding, but there's a lot you don't understand."

"I have all day. Start explaining." She pulled her arms up behind her head to appear casual, although her belly knotted like a tangle of neglected yarn.

"I thought you wanted to hear about Black Eagle?" he asked.

"Let's talk about this first." Uncomfortable, she pulled her arms down, crossed them, and waited.

His face grew gentle. "Fine. I owe you an explanation. My goal is to marry Lynette because she'll never move from Big Cat."

"Your goal? How romantic."

He ignored her sarcasm and said, "I won't marry someone who will eventually demand to move back to the city."

"Is that what you think I'll do, insist on moving back to Charlotte?" If that was how he felt, he didn't know her at all.

"Yes. I give you six months and you'll want to move."

Claire shot off the sand so fast it knocked him backward. "Fine, then. Our discussion is over."

"Claire, wait. We need to talk about this rationally." He tugged her arm and gently pulled her back down to the ground. "Please hear me out."

Claire's legs and arms quivered from the inside out. Jeff had a way of igniting her temper. "I can't," she managed to say.

"Try."

When she didn't move away, he seemed to take that as a sign of resignation. "A couple of years ago my ex-girlfriend dumped me a month before our wedding. She ran back to Charlotte. In retrospect, I'm glad she ended our relationship before we were married." He looked around the island and frowned. "I love it here, Claire. I feel close to my heritage, and I take my job of protecting the horses seriously. They mean as much to me as my own horses. And then there's my family. I love living next to them, all of us on the same land. Pony Island feeds my soul."

His words touched a tender, painful spot in her heart. She looked away. "I understand that."

"I'd rather sacrifice having a loving marriage than be forced to leave my home. That might sound odd, but I can't help it. With Lynette, it's almost a business arrangement. She'll marry into my family's wealth, and I'll have a wife who won't force me to move away. Before I met you, my plan sounded reasonable."

*Before he met her*. That sounded almost promising. In a roundabout way, he just admitted he had feelings for her. A delirious exuberance made her laugh and before she thought twice, she reached across the sand and kissed him full on the mouth. The kiss was sweet at first, then hot. Their wet lips parted and his warm tongue touched hers briefly. When Claire gasped, they pulled away.

"I'm sorry. I didn't mean to do that," she said, breathless.

He moved farther away as if she'd shocked him with an electrical charge. "Whew. I'm not sure where that came from, but I liked it."

Claire's head felt as if it were spinning and she barely heard his words.

Changing the subject was much safer than discussing what just happened. She cleared her throat, hoping the effort would allow her to speak. "Um, you were telling me about my mom's premarital fling."

"Right." His face flushed. "Your mom didn't find out about her pregnancy until after the wedding, and the three of them decided you'd be better off with a family, without anyone knowing what had happened. They also didn't want to be scandalized in their small town."

"I see. So everyone thought I shouldn't know who my real father is. How thoughtful."

"Claire, what are you afraid of?"

She stared at him. "Snakes, wild animals—"

"No. What are you really afraid of?"

She sat there for several minutes and stared at the invisible grave. "I don't want to be alone, without family."

"So you're afraid you won't have love, acceptance, and trust? And you feel rejected by men, especially your father?"

His assessment stole her breath. He'd hit so close to home, had honed in on fears she hadn't known existed. "Yeah, something like that," she said with a soft voice.

"Claire, you can't bring back Robert Kincaid, but Black Eagle loves you. Why do you think he stayed on as foreman after all that happened? He wanted to be near you. He didn't abandon you; your mom took you away from him. She loved Black Eagle, and when he married and had his own child, your mom couldn't deal with it. She ran."

"Wait a minute. He has a child ... a girl?"

"That's right. Do you remember her?"

She looked up at the bright blue sky with fluffy white clouds and sighed. "Yeah. I can't remember her name, but I remember pretending she was my baby doll. I used to love to feed and hold her."

"Her name is Robin and she's your half-sister."

"Oh! My sister," she said in awe. That thought hadn't occurred to her until now. "I have a sister, and a father. Unbelievable."

"That's right. Nancy gave me Black Eagle's phone number. By the way, his wife knows all about you, so feel free to contact him. I've met Robin and she's delightful. But there's something you should know."

"More? I'm already on overload."

"Sorry, but this is important. It bothered me that I didn't know Black Eagle, even though he breeds horses, so I asked Lynette about him. I still don't know him, but she does. In fact, she invited him to the wedding. He can't make it to the actual ceremony, but he'll be there for the reception."

She groaned. "That means I'll have to see Black Eagle then."

"Have to see him?" He furrowed his eyebrows, apparently confused. "What do you mean? I thought you wanted to find your father."

"All these years I've thought of Robert Kincaid as my father. I have to think about this before I jump into meeting Black Eagle. I process things slowly."

"Are you afraid of rejection again?"

Claire felt like a vulnerable child who wanted her daddy, but was too afraid to reach out and embrace him. "I guess. I'm afraid he'll say 'No' and turn me away."

"Trust and believe in yourself, Claire. You have to understand how to make yourself whole, without your father. Then if he rejects you, you'll be okay."

"How did you get to be so wise?" She wished he could see his own situation as clearly as he did hers. She guessed it was easier to be objective about someone else than to analyze one's self. "You're right, but I have no idea how to make myself whole. I thought finding my father was the answer."

"You'll figure it out. The answer is hidden somewhere inside you." He reached forward and kissed her slowly–a warm, loving, unhurried kiss. He was most likely trying to make her feel better from the emotional trauma she'd been through lately. That's all his kiss was. Maybe.

When a voice interrupted them, Claire jerked away.

"Excuse me?" Paula stood not ten feet away with her arms crossed and a stern look on her face. "What are you two doing?"

# CHAPTER SEVENTEEN

"Paula. Why are you here?" Jeff asked.

"Working," she said with a tone of disapproval. "Obviously something you aren't engaged in. Speaking of engagement, I heard you were supposed to get married next weekend. Or have you forgotten?"

"Of course I haven't forgotten, not even close." Jeff clenched his jaw and worked it back and forth. In fact, the thought of marrying Lynette was never far from his mind. If he could back out, he would.

"Listen, Paula," Claire said. "It was an accident. It won't—"

"That didn't look like an accident to me," she interrupted. "You both seemed very content, like you've kissed before." Paula backed away. "If you're unfaithful now, Jeff, what kind of husband will you be?"

He shook his head, trying to reject her words. "If you must know, that was the first time I've kissed her." That was actually the truth, because Claire had kissed him the first time. Deliberately, Jeff sat upright and leaned away from Claire. He felt like a teenager getting caught making out with someone's daughter.

"And I resent being called unfaithful." He drilled his gaze into Paula's. He wasn't about to allow her to belittle him, to judge him.

"Then what would you call it?" Paula challenged.

He squeezed his eyes shut for a moment. When he reopened them he said, "Actually, you're right. My behavior is inexcusable, and I owe Lynette an explanation of what happened." He leaned back on his elbows, not meeting her glare.

First he had to understand what happened himself, before he could explain his actions to someone else, especially his fiancée. He didn't know what had gotten into him; he firmly believed in fidelity.

He risked a glance at Claire, but she sat staring at Robert Kincaid's invisible grave. She had her knees drawn up underneath her, her arms wrapped around them. A pang of empathy coursed through him. Claire had a lot to deal with right now. Not only had he overwhelmed her with the news about Black Eagle, they had also crossed the line with that unbelievably tender kiss.

He still felt the heat where her lips had touched his. Now, however, he sensed a distance between them. He was yet another man who had let her down.

"If you don't tell Lynette, I will," Paula threatened.

"I need to get back to my studio," Claire said, obviously uncomfortable. "See you at the rehearsal dinner. I'll be there to take pictures." With that, she walked away.

***

If Claire forced herself to take a bird's-eye view of her life, then she'd have to admit it had taken a downward spin at a dizzying speed. She needed to take control, and fast, before the situation worsened, if that were possible.

Jeff hadn't helped. Their spontaneous kiss had surprised her and left her even more confused. Unfortunately, it had also awakened a sense of excitement and longing. Jeff made her feel vibrant, made her almost believe she could love again. She had acted on a foolish impulse.

She needed to stay away from him until the rehearsal dinner, until she had to take pictures of the happy couple toasting their upcoming wedding.

And the thought of seeing Black Eagle again. Jeff's comments troubled her. He'd said she had to be self-assured, and needed to trust and believe in herself. How was she supposed to do that? Maybe the time had come to analyze her childhood and to be thankful for what she had instead of what she lacked. Many kids grew up without a father.

As far as Robert Kincaid, she'd always relied on him as someone who would eventually rescue her from loneliness and make her feel secure. She had to admit, though, that she'd never actually visualized her father's face when she fantasized about finding him. Maybe on a subconscious level, her mind had known Black Eagle was her real father.

So why did it hurt so much that Robert Kincaid was dead, and that she had been lied to her entire life?

Without a doubt, she wasn't ready to see Black Eagle yet. She had always admired and respected him, but she'd never contemplated the possibility that he might be her father. For the first time ever, she saw her resemblance to him—the dark straight hair, olive skin, and distinct profile. Her mother had had dark brown hair, albeit lighter than Claire's, but her complexion had been paler than Claire's. Robert Kincaid's skin had always been tan, so she assumed she had inherited her olive skin color from him. Now she knew better.

Even though Jeff had explained her mother's reasoning for withholding the truth about her real father's identity, she couldn't help but resent the well-intentioned secret. Claire despised secrets. She gave Jeff credit because at least he didn't plan to hide their kiss from Lynette until after the wedding like her mother had done. His willingness to face the inevitable confrontation took confidence, which she respected.

She wondered what Lynette would do when she found out about the kiss. Claire had a signed lease and didn't think her landlady could legally revoke it. At the very least, renting from her had become less than ideal. Claire was making enemies fast in a small town where her livelihood depended on local support in addition to sales from tourists. She couldn't afford to turn the town against her. Lynette seemed well respected and she guessed the locals would take Lynette's side if they had to choose.

Maybe she should pack up and move farther north, maybe to the Outer Banks. She could photograph the wild horses there. Since Robert was dead anyway, what difference did it make if she stayed in Big Cat? Big deal if Black Eagle lived nearby. She hadn't known he was her father until now, and he hadn't made any effort to find her. So what was the point?

To her surprise, her stomach tightened at the thought of moving elsewhere. She really wanted to settle down, and Big Cat, with its barrier islands and horses, already felt like home. She belonged here. She'd even started to make a few friends, such as Shirley and Jenni, and until today, Paula.

The kiss popped back into her mind. His strong arms around her set off a powerful explosion of feelings. She'd never felt anything like that before, and from his intense reaction, she'd bet he had experienced the same thrill she had.

She pulled her cell phone from her pocket. With a powerful urge to leave the island as soon as possible, she dialed Jenni for an early departure.

"Give us about fifteen minutes or so," Jenni said. "We're dropping off another group farther north on the island."

"Thanks. Please hurry." As soon as Claire hung up, an accusatory female voice sounded from behind her. Claire turned around to see Paula, standing on the top of the nearest dune, with her hands on her hips.

"I knew you were trouble from the beginning." Paula spat out the words. "The first day I met you, I knew you wanted Jeff."

"Nothing is going on between us," Claire explained firmly. Despite her emotional upheaval, she climbed the dune to stand at the same height as Paula, so as not to be at a disadvantage. "Jeff felt sorry for me because he had some bad news to share. That's all."

"It looked like more than sympathy. Lynette won't be happy about this." Paula stood taller and looked down her nose at Claire.

"I'm sure she won't be." Claire suspected Lynette's reaction would be irrational at best. That concerned her since Lynette happened to be her landlady. By kissing Jeff, she had made a big mistake.

"You messed up this time."

"Why does everyone tiptoe around Lynette? Are they afraid of her temper, or is it because she owns half of downtown, and people want to stay on her good side?" Surprised by her own blunt words, Claire had to fight back a small smile.

"Excuse me?" Paula asked with her shoulders squared. "I recommend you stay away from Jeff. If you don't, your happiness here will be short lived, guaranteed."

Claire considered her warning. Her growing concern for the future of the studio gnawed at her insides, but her independence remained important, too.

She turned away from Paula without another word and slid down the dune. What else could she say? Sometimes silence said enough.

It was a short walk to the cove, where the ferry had dropped her off earlier. She sat on the warm sand and waited, lost in thought about everything that happened. Before long, the ferry pulled into the cove.

"What happened to you?" Jenni asked when Claire reached the boat. Before she could answer, Jenni turned and looked off in the distance. "Oh, I see you ran into Paula."

"Yeah. I'm not her favorite person right now." Claire stepped into the cold water and climbed aboard.

Jenni's brother reversed the boat's engine and with a roar, they pulled away from the island. "I wouldn't think she'd befriend you," Jenni said. "After all, her best friend's fiancé happens to be

Jeff. I can understand her concern, especially since he's been off finding your father."

Taken aback, Claire studied the woman who sat beside her. Was Jenni the friend Claire had thought? "How did you know Jeff found my father?" Claire questioned.

"He asked Lynette about Black Eagle, and once that happened, word travelled fast. If he is your father, you're lucky; I've heard he's a good man."

"A good man," Claire repeated.

"And don't worry, if Lynette gives you trouble about Jeff, I'm on your side. She might be friends with the Big Cat socialites, if you can call them that, but most people find her annoying. I have to warn you, though. If you get on her bad side, and I'm pretty sure you're headed that way, she'll make your life miserable."

"Great." She shrugged off the concern, for now. "So you know Black Eagle?"

"No." Jenni wiped water from the boat's spray off her sunglasses. "I've never met him. I think he keeps to himself."

"Jeff said he didn't know him either, and he's even in the horse business." A spray of water shot over the entryway, closed off by only a line, and soaked Claire's shorts and part of her shirt. She moved to the far side of Jenni to avoid getting wetter. Between the cool water and the wind caused by the speed of the boat, she had to cross her arms to keep warm.

"That's interesting," Jenni said. "You'd think he'd know him."

Keith expertly guided the boat into a weathered slip. Jenni tossed a line to George, who pulled them in closer.

They climbed from the ferry and passed a man painting the ticket booth blue and yellow. A white flag, with a brown Islander Pony hand painted on it, flapped in the sea breeze and clanged against the flagpole. The sound reminded Claire of her childhood visits to the beach.

"Nice touch, Jenni. You move fast."

"Thanks. Someday I hope to have my own business to doll up, as my mother said."

Jenni would be a good business owner. "If you give me a handful of your ferry brochures," Claire said, "I'll put them in my studio to hand out to customers."

"They have the Sea Horse Ferry's name on them, but that's okay for now, until Keith buys it," Jenni said. "I'd be happy to set out your brochures, too. A little cross-promotion could help us both."

Claire smiled. Yes, she could count on Jenni. If things got ugly with Lynette, which they most likely would, Claire would need all the allies she could find. "I'll run some over tomorrow before my class starts." She had a lot of work to do before then.

"What class is that?"

"It's on basic photography."

"I've always wanted to improve my photography skills, if you can call it that," Jenni commented. "With the boat runs I'm doing, I'd love to photograph the cool things I see. This morning two dolphins jumped close to the boat, and a herd of horses ran along the beach."

"You should give the class a try. If you don't like it, I'll give your money back."

"So you have openings?" She walked behind the ticket booth, grabbed a small stack of brochures, and handed them to Claire.

"Of course, I'll always have room for you." Claire filled her in on the details and left. Maybe her business had a chance, if Lynette didn't try to wreck it.

***

The next day, Claire had just finished framing several different prints of Mario. When she turned off the music she listened to while working, she overheard Shirley's conversation with a customer.

"No, I want one of those wonderful shots of the Islander Ponies that I've heard Claire is so good at snapping. It's for Jeff's wedding present."

Claire walked up and politely interrupted. "I have just the one for you. I'll be right back." She turned around and walked back to the framing area to retrieve the perfect gift for Jeff. She carried a large framed picture of Mario back to where the woman waited. The photograph captured the fragility of the colt as he first learned to nurse, captured the protectiveness of his mother. Claire wanted a print for her own apartment, whenever she got the chance to frame one for pleasure.

"We thought the colt might die," Claire explained to the woman. "He was too weak to nurse. But as the photo proves, he figured it out finally."

"This is perfect," the woman said, looking at the picture with a grin. "Jeff will love it."

Lynette, on the other hand, might not appreciate the photo as a wedding gift.

"The horses are his life," the woman continued to say. "He'd do anything for the Islander Ponies."

"I can relate to his loyalty," Claire said. "I feel strongly about them myself."

Shirley stood close by, quietly observing Claire's interaction with the woman. Claire wondered who she was.

The woman studied her. "You might not remember me. I'm Jeff's sister, Pam. I helped you right after your riding accident. Jeff called me and I brought the horses back to his house, so he could go with you to the hospital."

Claire had no memory of Pam, but she was grateful nonetheless. "Thanks." Claire flashed a warm smile at the other woman. "I appreciated having him with me at the hospital until Shirley arrived."

"How are you feeling?"

"Much better. I'm still sore, but nothing like I was at the beginning of the week. How's Razor?" Claire hadn't thought to ask Jeff earlier today, mainly because their encounter had taken her by surprise, in more ways than one.

"He's fine now. Paula declared him sound and ready to be ridden again."

The mention of Paula's name made Claire wince. Unfortunately, Pam seemed to notice her reaction. Even though she gave Claire what seemed to be a knowing smile, she didn't comment.

"Anyway, I'm glad you're okay," Pam continued to say. "You were lucky you wore a helmet. Anytime you want to ride, please let me know. You should get back on a horse right away, you know, so you don't develop any fear. That happened to a friend of mine, and she quit riding altogether."

Pam was right. "Thanks. Maybe I'll do that."

"Actually, everybody is taking off work next Friday to take it easy before the rehearsal dinner that night. Why don't you come by and we'll go for a short ride?"

Claire wasn't mentally prepared to step foot on Jeff's land anytime soon. "I can't do that. I've missed a lot of work lately, and Shirley has been a saint. I need to give her some time off."

"Thanks, but I'm fine," Shirley piped in. "I bet that day will be slow around here. Go ride, honey. It'll be good for you."

"Then there's no excuse," Pam said. She grinned as though she was up to something.

"Well, I guess it's a smart idea," Claire said with some reluctance.

"Great. How about ten o'clock, in front of Jeff's barn?"

"Okay. Thanks for the offer." Claire walked behind the counter and rang up Pam's purchase after Shirley had suspiciously busied herself dusting the rack of prints behind her. "Would you like that gift wrapped?" Claire asked Pam.

"Yes," Pam said. "Please pick out whatever you paper you like the best."

Claire pulled out a generous amount of shiny silver paper decorated with white wedding bells and began wrapping. She forced herself to focus on the positive—the gift was mostly for Jeff. He would undoubtedly treasure the picture and it would hang somewhere in his house, where he would see it often. That thought brought her a small amount of solace.

"Here you go." Claire handed the present to Pam. "My helmet and I will see you next week." Pam chuckled and left.

The rest of the afternoon Claire prepared for her class. She wanted to gather a few photos that demonstrated unique lighting. She thumbed through a bin full of prints and pulled out a picture of the stallion that she had taken the night the ferry had left her stranded. The gorgeous sunglow outlined the stallion in burnt orange. It provided a perfect example of how she used light to transform an otherwise ordinary picture into a piece of art.

"So fill me in on why you look so glum," Shirley said from across the room.

Claire looked up startled. "I'm not moping. I'm in deep concentration. I want to pick out the right combination of prints for my class tonight."

"Sure you do. Does your mood have anything to do with the wedding?"

"No." Claire looked back down and continued to search through the bin. She pulled out a lighthouse picture with swirling fog that she'd taken years ago, and set it aside. The light played an interesting role in that print. It added an air of mystique to the photo. "Can't a person be lost in thought?"

"No, not when you take in consideration that the man you love is about to walk down the aisle with someone else. I'm concerned about you, child."

"Shirley, we've been over this before."

"Whatever happened to the concept of marrying for love?" Shirley asked.

"Love disappeared years ago with repetitive lies from men and women alike. It's only a figment of people's imaginations."

"If you're talking about Black Eagle, I assure you that withholding the secret wasn't just his fault. No one knows him well, but he seems to be an honorable man, who deserves a chance to explain."

Claire stood perfectly still. "Does everyone in this town know my business?"

"Of course. And I'll tell you something else. Lynette despises Black Eagle on principle, even though she barely knows him, but she desperately wants his land. Developers want to buy it to build an upper-end subdivision for people who can afford second homes near the beach.

"Lynette had wanted to buy it from Nancy Smith before she sold it to Black Eagle for next to nothing. The fact that Nancy refused to sell it to her for more money just about caused a war. Since you are Black Eagle's daughter, you are automatically an enemy. And you're after her man. That doubles the likelihood of a full-blown battle with her."

"I am not after her man. He's about to marry the woman, so she wins." Claire clamped her arms across her chest. "If Lynette despises Black Eagle, why did she invite him to her wedding?"

Shirley raised her eyebrows. "Do you really need to ask me that?"

Unbelievable. Would Lynette lower herself to such deceit? "She's befriending him to get what she wants?"

"Of course she would," Shirley answered with certainty in her voice.

"Like I said before, she wins," Claire said. She wasn't about to fight for a man. Either he loved her or he didn't. "She can have Jeff."

A strange smirk passed across Shirley's face. "And you're planning to trail ride on his property, with his sister, the day before his wedding." Shirley winked and a smile brightened her wrinkled face. "I'd say you owe Pam a "thank you."

"Do you think she has ulterior motives?"

Shirley grinned bigger. "I'm simply saying that you have an opportunity to convince Jeff that he's about to make a huge mistake."

"Shirley," Claire scolded.

"It wasn't my idea."

Suddenly Claire felt guilty. "Why would Pam do that? Doesn't she like Lynette?"

"Think about that for a minute. Why would she want her brother to marry someone whose only interest is her family's wealth? She's protecting her brother." Shirley sat in a nearby chair and pressed her palms into her dress to smooth it.

"You have a good point." Claire leaned against the photo bin. "But it's not my job to save Jeff from making a mistake. I came here to find my father, a man who turned out to be somebody else. That's hard enough to deal with. I don't want to get involved in everybody's lives." Claire wasn't sure she liked small town living after all. "I especially want to avoid romantic relationships. That makes me the wrong person to get involved in this mess."

"Is that so? From my vantage point, you are exactly the right person."

\*\*\*

Claire's photography class started out well. Seven students showed up and eagerly listened to her every word. Jenni was the most enthusiastic of the group and asked intelligent questions about composition and lighting. She showed great promise. The class was intense and well focused, until the studio door shot open.

Angry heels clicked across the floor and headed directly for Claire. Lynette stopped just short of her and glared. "You have crossed the line this time," Lynette exclaimed. "How dare you kiss my fiancé."

Several people gasped and one person giggled, probably Jenni.

"How dare you strut into my class and make a scene," Claire chastised. "I suggest you leave, right now."

"I suggest you stay away from Jeff. Your lease has been terminated." Lynette tore up the contract in her hands and dropped the pieces onto the floor.

"We will talk about this later, in private." Claire took hold of Lynette's arm and tried to lead her toward the door.

"There is nothing private about you trying to steal Jeff." Lynette jerked her arm away. "Everyone in this room sees what a tramp you are."

Claire tried to remain in control of her rising emotions. "Call names if you wish. I recommend that you leave while you still have some dignity left." Laughter sounded from the students.

"I still expect to see you at the rehearsal dinner, as we agreed. I'd hate to tell everyone how unprofessional you are if you back out at the last minute." Lynette abruptly clicked her heels back to the door and left.

Claire wondered why Lynette still wanted her to photograph the wedding events, unless she wanted to rub Jeff in her face.

When the class ended, Jenni approached Claire. "What are you going to do about your lease?" She pulled up a stool and sat down, her freckled face creased with concern.

Claire rolled her eyes at the drama. "She can't tear it up. I have a copy."

"That might be true, but she can destroy you." A wicked grin replaced Jenni's serious look. "There are no other buildings available to rent downtown, except for one. It's across town, next to the maritime museum. I've heard it's about to be listed for lease with a real estate agent because the tenant is moving out. But the owner wants to renovate the building first."

"Let me guess, Lynette's company will manage it."

"Sure, but I bet if you approach the owner beforehand, he would consider renting to you without Lynette's involvement. The building is perfect for a studio. It has large windows with a gorgeous view of the inlet and lots of natural light. Like I said, it needs some work and the apartment above is outdated, but with your creative touch you could make it cute."

"Who's the owner?"

She flashed a devious smile. "Jeff Rhoades."

# CHAPTER EIGHTEEN

Friday arrived too soon. Claire had mixed emotions about horseback riding at Jeff's farm with his sister. Butterflies circled in her tense belly, and breathing became more difficult with each mile she drove toward his house.

To add to the emotional mix, she planned to ask him about the possibility of renting his building. Even though she had a signed lease, did she really want to stay in her building when her landlady planned to make her life miserable? She wanted to find somewhere else to rent. If she wanted to stay in Big Cat, which she did, she'd have to ask Jeff for help. She had a hunch that if the decision were his alone, he would lease it to her.

The problem was Lynette. Would he defy his future bride and lease to someone she'd just supposedly evicted? It seemed likely that if he did, it would cause a serious rift between Jeff and Lynette. But if he refused, what would Claire do? Too bad she had no other options on Front Street. She wondered if Lynette had another renter in mind for Jeff's building and was counting on the lack of vacancies to force her out of town. And away from Jeff.

As Claire drove down Jeff's gravel driveway, her stomach tensed even more. The impulsive kiss, a mishap for which she accepted full responsibility, went against her natural grain. Usually she had to work hard just to be mildly spontaneous.

When Claire pulled in front of Jeff's house, Frank bounded up to her car, barking joyfully, his tail wagging fast. Claire opened the door and he all but climbed in to give her a tongue bath.

"He likes you."

Claire looked past the dog and saw Pam, who stood there dressed in khaki-colored riding pants and tall black boots. "I like him, too," Claire said. She grabbed her helmet off the passenger seat and climbed from her car.

"You can ride my horse today, if you want. He's older and gentle." Pam headed across the yard toward the barn and Claire followed.

"If you don't mind, I'd like to ride Razor." Claire wanted to settle a niggling fear before it grew bigger.

Pam stopped short and turned toward her. "Are you sure?"

"I need to do this."

"Okay." Pam continued to walk toward the barn. Claire trailed behind and secretly scanned the area for any sign of Jeff. He was nowhere around. The depth of her disappointment surprised her, considering the entire drive over here she'd fretted about seeing him.

"If you're looking for Jeff, he's grooming the horses out in the field."

My, she was perceptive. "Is he riding with us this morning?" Claire asked, feigning nonchalance. She had no idea why that question had slipped from her lips, other than her mouth had clearly defied her.

Without turning, Pam said, "Absolutely. He needs to take his mind off the wedding tomorrow."

"What do you mean? Isn't the groom supposed to look forward to his wedding?"

"You'd think."

When they reached the field, Jeff's gaze met Claire's. "Hi there," he said with a hint of warmth in his eyes.

"About our—"

He shook his head and stopped her mid-sentence. Either he didn't want to talk about the kiss, or he didn't want his sister to know. Claire found it hard to believe, with the gossip most likely running rampant through town, that Pam hadn't already heard about what happened. Perhaps that's why she invited Claire here to begin with.

"Claire wants to ride Razor," Pam interjected. She saved them from an uncomfortable moment of silence.

Jeff smiled. "He's already brushed and ready to be saddled."

Claire stared at him. How had he known she'd want to ride Razor?

Before long, they were riding through the woods in single file, along a narrow stream. Jeff led the way, and Pam brought up the rear a fair distance back. Since Claire followed right behind Jeff, she couldn't help but admire him. Had he looked so good in a western saddle before? His faded jeans fit him perfectly, and with his sexy cowboy hat tilted slightly on his head, he looked as if he had been born to wear it.

"My horse is limping," Pam called to them after about an hour. "I need to go back, but you two continue on."

"You shouldn't ride alone," Claire said, twisting in the saddle so Pam could hear her. "We can go back with you."

"No, I insist. I've ridden these trails hundreds of times alone. I'll be fine." At that, Pam turned her horse around and walked away.

"Her horse isn't limping," Claire said.

"Hmm. That's interesting." Jeff's voice sounded odd, somewhat mysterious. He immediately dropped the subject and started to whistle to an unfamiliar tune.

A while later, Jeff asked, "Do you want to stop and eat lunch? I know the perfect spot."

Muted warning bells went off in her head, begging her to listen. A picnic lunch sounded too cozy, with the two of them sitting together and no one else to buffer the conversation. What would they talk about?

She could easily turn back and eat later, but her stomach growled in protest. Thanks to her nervousness this morning, she hadn't eaten much breakfast.

"I guess so."

Jeff didn't seem to notice her hesitation. He guided his horse across the shallow stream, emerged on the opposite bank, and waited for Claire to cross.

She cued Razor to follow, and thankfully, he stepped into the water without an issue. She once rode a horse that would take at least an hour to step into a creek, and then once he did, he'd try to race to the other side. Razor showed no signs of resistance, in fact he seemed to enjoy it. He even stopped for a moment to paw the water and splash them both. Claire laughed and urged him forward and out of the creek. Once she was behind Jeff again, she followed him on a wooded trail that led to a tiny clearing.

He glanced back at Claire and pointed to a fallen, moss-covered log that lay at the edge of the grassy area surrounded by woods. "Do you want to stop here?"

"Looks like a great spot." Too perfect, maybe.

Jeff headed over to the inviting little hideaway, a sanctuary for two. When he dismounted, Claire slid off Razor and led him next to Jeff's horse to keep the animals near each other. She made a point not to get too close to Jeff and to avoid his gaze.

He pulled halters over the horses' bridles and tied them to separate trees. Then he unloaded his saddlebag and handed Claire an insulated lunch bag before he pulled out a small quilt. He glanced at her as he spread it on the ground.

"So, have you called Black Eagle yet?" he asked innocently enough.

Claire emptied the lunch sack onto the blanket. Wrapped sandwiches, grapes, crackers, and cheese greeted her. She smiled at the bottle of wine with two paper cups, instead of three.

She ignored his question and instead asked one of her own. "So Pam's ride back to the barn was part of the plan?"

Jeff looked up. "Actually, yes. I wanted a chance to talk with you. I doubted you would ride with me if I had asked."

"You're right. So what's so important that you had to lure me out into the woods alone?"

He sat beside her on the blanket. "Are you going to ignore my question about Black Eagle?"

Claire exhaled loudly. When Jeff focused on something, he refused to let it go.

She didn't want to admit that she'd thought about Black Eagle a lot over the past week. In fact, she had simply tried to survive since she'd found out the truth, had tried to absorb the disturbing reality that her life was one big lie. At first she denied the truth, and then anger had taken over. She'd even gone so far as to suspect that Jeff had lied to benefit himself somehow. What an absurd notion.

She leaned on one hand, away from Jeff. "No. I'm not ready to call him yet."

Jeff popped a grape into his mouth. "How are you going to handle tomorrow when you see him at the reception?"

"You mean now that I've been roped into being there because I have to photograph your wedding?"

"Nobody roped you into anything. You agreed."

He just didn't get it. Lynette had no doubt finagled the situation, at least to some degree, so that Claire would end up the photographer. The situation had presented the perfect opportunity to rub their marriage into Claire's face. Of course Jeff wouldn't see the manipulative plan; he was a man, after all. Shirley had told her that men never see women's nasty and scheming ways, but Claire saw right through it. Lynette had devised a brilliant plan to make sure Claire attended the wedding.

"That's right. I agreed to be the photographer. Whatever." Claire picked at her sandwich. She no longer had an appetite.

"So what are you going to do?" Jeff asked eventually, interrupting her thought process.

"About what?"

"Are you okay? You seem distracted," Jeff commented.

How observant. "Let's talk about you for a minute," she said. "Tonight is your rehearsal dinner, tomorrow is your wedding, and you're out here horseback riding with me to distract yourself. How do you explain that?"

"I never said I needed a distraction."

"No, you didn't, but your sister did. What are you running away from, Jeff?" Claire tossed her sandwich onto the blanket.

He shrugged. "My sister is nosey and likes to butt into my business. She's been doing that since we were kids."

Claire watched him closely and caught a glimpse of a small, scared boy. Maybe his sister knew him better than he wanted to admit. "What are you afraid of?" she asked.

"Let me see ..." He stared up at the sky before answering. "I think you said you were scared of snakes and wild animals ..."

"I also said I didn't want to be alone, without family, but we aren't talking about me. So what is your true fear? What are you hiding from?"

He stared at her as if he didn't comprehend the question. "Heck, I don't know."

"Then try this out. You've been hurt before, by someone you deeply loved and trusted, right before your wedding. You felt abandoned by your fiancée when she left for the city."

He frowned.

"You've hinted that your mother is domineering, and your sister butts into your life. I imagine your father is the laid-back, quiet type. Maybe subconsciously you feel abandoned by him too because he doesn't stand up to your mother, and never has. He leaves you to deal with the overbearing women in your family, who happen to love you very much. That's where Lynette comes in. Instead of loving someone and risking abandonment again, you want to marry a woman who poses no threat to you."

Jeff winced.

"Did I hit a nerve?" When he didn't answer, she continued. "You will miss out on having a loving marriage, a warm, caring relationship, and your children—"

"Stop. You've proven your point. Why do you care what I do?"

How was she supposed to answer that?

She decided on the partial truth. "You're my friend. Of course I care what you do and the decisions you make." She cared too much. Now was the perfect chance to follow Shirley's advice and tell him exactly how she felt. But that still seemed wrong.

"You should care about your quality of life," she said in a guarded voice. "If you marry for convenience, then you're taking the easy way out."

"Just like avoiding Black Eagle?"

Ouch. "That's different. I'm not marrying Black Eagle and settling for less, just because I'm afraid to want more from a spouse."

"Boy, you woke up this morning in quite a mood. Fine, if you can handle the truth, I'll tell you."

She leaned back on her elbows and waited. When he didn't say anything, she said, "I can handle it."

He leaned forward, inches from her face, and said, "I realize the mistake I'm about to make. In part, it's for you."

She gasped. "That's absurd." How dare he blame her for his inability to tell Lynette he'd changed his mind? What nerve.

"If I back out of my wedding now, everyone will accuse you. Your business would die off so fast you wouldn't know what hit. Then, you'd have to move again, farther from your dad."

And farther from Jeff. Of course he'd feel abandoned again, and if he wanted a relationship with Claire, he'd have to leave his beloved hometown to follow her.

"I don't want you to move away," he whispered.

Any words that formed in her mind had vanished. And his face was still so close to hers.

"So I'm doing this for you," he said.

She leaned away. "You mean you're marrying Lynette to save my business?"

"It didn't start out that way. But that's a big reason now." He moved away and shoved the rest of his sandwich into his mouth.

"Thanks, but don't do me any favors. I'd rather see you happy than have you marry someone you don't love ... for me." How ironic.

"You don't know the half of it," he said with his mouth still full. "Besides, all I want to do is help you."

She forced her gaze to meet his. "Actually, if you want to help me, I can think of a better way."

He chewed quicker and then swallowed. "What's that?"

"I've been theoretically kicked out of my building, and I need to rent studio space and an apartment."

His eyes grew bigger. "You want to rent my shop?"

"Yes. Lynette stomped into my class last night and verbally evicted me." She looked directly into his eyes and challenged him.

"She can't legally do that."

"She can if we both agree to rip up all the documents, including my copy. Just like our lease never existed. Then I wouldn't have to deal with her directly anymore."

"Do you know what you're asking?" He frowned. "Don't take this the wrong way, but she won't like it if I override her decision, if I rent to you."

"And do you plan to let her run your business, too?"

He clenched his jaw. "What's that supposed to mean?"

She purposely hit him where it hurt. She'd had about enough of his hands-off approach. "Do you want another bossy woman in your life?"

"No one will take over my buildings. And I wouldn't say she's bossy."

"Then what is she?"

He didn't answer.

This was her last effort to help him see the truth. Then, if he still didn't understand, she'd have no regrets.

"What if she tries to take over all your real estate and absorb it into her business?" Claire asked. "Don't you get her manipulative ways?" She had stepped way out of bounds, but once she'd crossed over the line, she found herself caught up in the momentum. "What about the Islander Ponies? Do you think she understands your passion?"

"What I see is you trying to change my mind about marrying Lynette. And then you more or less asked me to rub you in Lynette's face by renting my shop to you."

"I'm sorry." She crammed what remained of their lunch back into the bag and stood. "I just want you to be happy."

"And I want *you*," he said.

Claire gasped and froze. The bag dropped to the ground with a thud. Jeff jumped to his feet and stood by her, reaching out to hold her hands.

"But ... I can't have you." His eyes held what appeared to be tremendous pain. "Before I met you I committed to someone else. I can't disrupt my wedding at the last minute for someone I barely know. I'm sorry, Claire."

Her heart plummeted from a soaring height and crash-landed in a crumpled heap next to the bag at her feet. She turned her back to him, untied Razor, and left Jeff behind. All her pain, from her mother's death, Robert Kincaid's death, the lie her life had been, and now Jeff's impotent confession, erupted and overflowed like a volcano.

She trotted, not wanting to run Razor again thanks to the accident, wherever the trail allowed, so she could put some distance between her and Jeff. They had ridden to the clearing at a leisurely walk, but she planned to return to the barn as fast as possible. That way she'd have Razor untacked and be gone long before Jeff showed up. It seemed the horse understood her sorrow and he behaved exceptionally well. By the time she rode into the barnyard, her face was wet with tears of the past.

Claire wouldn't allow anyone to hurt her again. She would concentrate on what she had come to Big Cat for, but with one major change. She no longer needed to find her father; Jeff had done that for her. That didn't mean she had to accept Black Eagle in that role, or actively pursue a relationship with him. She would focus on saving her studio, and she didn't need to rely on others to help her; they only hurt her instead. It was back to her old beliefs, back to mistrusting everyone.

She had to face the strong possibility that she'd have to relocate after all, unless there was an affordable shop available outside the downtown area. Lynette dominated the real estate business in Big Cat, though, so even if Claire found another store to rent, it was likely Lynette managed it. Worst case, maybe she'd just stay in Lynette's building. She did still have a binding contract.

Claire hopped off Razor and hugged his sleek neck. "Buddy, thanks for the ride. I hope we've forgiven each other for our riding accident." She patted his neck.

"So how was your ride?" Pam asked. "I see you came back without my brother."

"He'll be along shortly."

"Why is your face wet? Don't tell me he still insists on marrying Lynette?"

Claire glanced up into Pam's friendly face. "I just don't get it. He seems smarter than he's acting. Why doesn't he see the reality of the situation?"

"I'm not sure if you mean the reality of Lynette using him," Pam said, "or the two of you being soul mates, but Jeff is afraid. The more he feels the more he runs. Trust me, he isn't stupid or timid. That man would rather let you walk away than address his worst fear."

"You mean his fear of trusting in love again?"

"Yes. You scare him. You remind him of the one person he loved. It about crushed him when Dana left and moved back to the city. He could have handled her cheating on him better than what she did. Pride can be overcome but she hurt him much deeper."

"Why did you ask me to ride today? Were you setting me up from the get-go?"

"I didn't exactly think of it that way. I asked you to ride because I wanted you to get back on a horse again. I also wanted to give Jeff one last chance to see reason. He was the one who asked me to ride away after an hour or so."

"Why did he do that?"

"He didn't say, but I think he loves you."

# CHAPTER NINETEEN

Claire showered vigorously to wash off the pain of the day, so it wouldn't add to her lifelong collection of hurt. The soap felt like a heavy weight and the water stung as it hit her overly sensitive skin. Right now life was a burden.

She planned to dress, go downstairs to help Shirley for the rest of the afternoon, and continue to cope with the overpowering sense of dread. Then, since she had no choice, she'd dress as professionally as possible for tonight's rehearsal dinner. If Mr. Jeff Rhoades wanted to ruin his future by refusing to see logic, then there wasn't a thing she could do. He was in charge of his own life. Right now, she had to lick her wounds and pull herself out of a black mood.

Claire could probably learn from Jeff's stubborn behavior. She had to admit there was a distinct correlation between his dilemma with Lynette, and her own situation with Black Eagle. She'd argued with him earlier that the circumstances were different, but the underlying issues did have strong similarities. Claire was just as afraid to reach out and accept the love Black

Eagle and his family offered, as Jeff was afraid to open his heart and accept the love Claire could give him.

She finished dressing and eventually made her way downstairs. Self-reflection was good to a point, but she'd spent enough time thinking; she had a business to run. Shirley usually managed to cheer her up, so maybe her unwavering warmth would help Claire feel human again.

"You look horrible," Shirley commented as soon as Claire entered the studio.

"Thanks, that's what I wanted to hear."

"I guess the horseback ride didn't go well?" Shirley walked over and touched Claire on the shoulder.

That one small act of affection was nearly Claire's undoing. She swallowed hard to regain her composure. "You could say it was informative."

"Why don't you sit down and I'll bring you some tea. Be right back." Shirley disappeared and when she returned, she had two mugs of already steeped green tea. How did she always have the tea ready and waiting for Claire as soon as she came downstairs? The temperature was just right.

"Thanks, Shirley. A friend is exactly what I need right now." Claire caught a whiff of her mother's cologne and knew she was once again watching over her.

"Do you smell that perfume?" Shirley asked, sniffing the air.

Claire smiled. "It's my mother. She visits when I'm sad and when I drink her favorite tea. I know that sounds kind of strange, but it's true."

"I have an aunt who used to visit me. She hasn't done that in a while, though." Shirley glanced up, as if greeting Claire's mother. "I wonder why my aunt stopped visiting me. Anyway, what happened today with the trail ride?"

"Oh, nothing really. Jeff and I talked and he told me the same old story."

"So the wedding is still on?"

Claire nodded. "He said he wanted to marry Lynette because of me." Claire stared into her mug.

"What?"

"He said if he called off the wedding, everyone would blame me, and my business would sink faster than a leaking ship. He said he wants me to stay in Big Cat, so I can be close to my father."

"Do you believe he's right?"

"I believe to some degree it's true, but he's mostly fooling himself. His ego can't handle rejection again." Neither could Claire's. That's why she wanted to avoid Black Eagle.

"What are you going to do?" Shirley asked.

"Nothing."

"What do you mean, 'nothing'?"

"Shirley, it's his life." She tried to keep the frustration from her voice but it proved to be impossible. "He has to make his own choices. It's not my place to interfere." Claire took a long sip of tea and closed her eyes for a moment. She savored the mild flavor and took comfort in the familiarity of her mother's scent hovering nearby.

"What bothers me," Claire continued, "is that Lynette is never going to understand his passion for horses, or understand how much they mean to him. The first time he has an emergency that involves them, she will throw a fit."

"That concerns me too," Shirley said. "That will be one tough problem to work through."

"But that's their issue, not mine. I hope for their sake Lynette learns to accept his enthusiasm and love for horses."

"Honey, I need to ask you something." Shirley's expression grew more serious, which hadn't seemed possible until now.

Claire studied her. "Of course. You can ask me anything."

"I heard Lynette evicted you." Shirley frowned and picked at her fingernail before she looked up. "Is it true?"

Small town dynamics shouldn't faze Claire. "She tried to evict me, but she can't unless I agree to move. We have a lease. But I can't leave right now because I have nowhere to move."

"Will your business survive?"

"Yes, it will. One way or another, we'll be fine," Claire said. "I promise." She hoped she hadn't made a promise she couldn't keep.

Shirley sighed. "Thank goodness. By the way, Jenni came in today looking for you. She'll be at the rehearsal dinner tonight as her brother's date. Evidently he's one of the groomsmen."

*What a relief,* Claire thought, *I'll have a much-needed ally.*

\*\*\*

Jeff glanced in the mirror and straightened his tie. He was never one to like getting dressed up to go to dinner. Unfortunately, Lynette loved it and wanted to dine at fancy restaurants all the time. He preferred to eat at home and wear jeans. Dressing casual was one of the many reasons he loved his job. He was a cowboy at heart and wearing a ranger's uniform every day was his idea of professional attire.

He shot a glimpse at the bedside clock and groaned. In less than an hour he'd have to pretend to be happy, pretend to be thrilled about the wedding. Lynette deserved better than what he offered. She deserved someone who loved her wholeheartedly.

Tonight was the first of many long nights ahead. He'd always imagined cozy nights in front of the fireplace, or hours spent playing board games with his significant other. He'd pictured family dinners at the kitchen table, instead of formal meals for two in the dining room. And kids. Marriage included a yard full of kids, chasing a dog. It would be a long while before Frank had that chance, if ever.

Poor Frank. He'd be lucky to sleep in the house when Lynette moved in. Jeff stood taller and set his jaw. His dog was his family, the child he would probably never have. Lynette would have to come to terms with Frank.

His mind drifted back to Claire. He'd thought about her all day long. It was obvious that he'd hurt her earlier, and that hadn't been his intention. She'd never know what it cost him to watch her ride away. Part of his heart had torn off and followed her.

Pam yelled up the steps and broke his thoughts. "Are you ready?"

"I'll be down in a minute." He grabbed his suit jacket and glanced in the mirror once more. How much would a woman he didn't love passionately change him? Marriage was all about change, but when you loved someone, it made the bite easier to chew. He waved goodbye to the man he knew, and walked down the steps.

"There you are. Why, don't you look handsome?"

"Thanks, sis." He leaned down and planted a stiff kiss atop her head.

"What was that for? You act as if we're going to a funeral instead of a rehearsal dinner."

That was exactly how it felt.

"Jeff, if you're this miserable, think what the rest of your life will be like. Don't let your integrity steer you the wrong way. People will eventually accept whatever choice you make. If you want out, stop the rehearsal tonight."

"I can't do that, sis. I've given my word, and that's what I live by."

"That's stupid, Jeff. If you don't love the woman, then don't go through with the wedding. You both deserve more."

"I know. Are you ready to go?" He gently took Pam's arm and led her out the door. "I can't stand to be late."

Lynette was always late.

"And I want to stop by Claire's first. I need to give her something," he said. "Let's go."

*** 

Jeff suffered his way through the rehearsal at the church, possibly the longest hour in history. The blur of instructions barely registered in his mind as the minister droned on.

Finally, they were on their way to the restaurant. He'd actually been relieved when Lynette had insisted on riding with her parents. Pam rode in his truck to keep him company, and all the way to *The Dockside*, they didn't speak. Instead, his thoughts zeroed in on Claire.

From this night forth, he had to think of Claire as an acquaintance. He really couldn't even think of her as a friend, because his attraction to her would be disastrous and ruin his marriage. There was no room in his marriage for three people, a mistake he had seen other men make. People might think him old fashioned, but his core principles were something he couldn't change. Heck, he didn't want to change them.

He pulled his truck into the gravel parking lot and dropped his sister off at the door. He found a parking spot at the far end, climbed down, and slammed the door shut. He would give almost anything right now to leave the rehearsal dinner behind and take a long walk on the beach.

He appreciated the array of stars in the sky on this cloudless night, appreciated the sound of the water as it lapped against the dock. It was too nice a night to sit inside, with tiny candles and artificial lighting. He much preferred to be true to his soul and dine outside with the night air and the tiki torches. But Lynette had planned the dinner without his input.

As he approached the restaurant door, Claire, who carried an armful of camera equipment, rounded the corner of the building. They almost collided. "Um … hi." He sounded like a nervous kindergartner, seeing his dream girl alone on the playground.

She nodded politely and continued walking.

"Here, let me help you carry that," he offered.

"No thanks," she said in a bittersweet voice. She adjusted the awkward load in her arms as best she could while dressed elegantly in a silky shirt, skirt, and heels.

If she wouldn't allow him to help, he could at least open the door. He lengthened his stride and reached the entrance first, opening one of the heavy, double doors. She glanced at him, curtly said thanks, and walked through. He kept in step with her quick pace. "Claire, I'm sorry about today."

"No problem. I understand that you have to do what feels right."

"That's a skewed viewpoint. I have morals I have to abide—"

Just then Lynette slithered up to Jeff. She slid her pale arm around him as she kissed his cheek. "Hi, darling. I wondered when you'd get here. I see you've been hanging out with Claire again."

*\*\*\**

Claire turned to Lynette, and in her most nonchalant voice, she said, "Just because two people walk in together doesn't mean they've been hanging out. If you'll excuse me …."

She could hear Lynette behind her. "How rude. I don't know why I hired her."

Jeff said in a deep, protective voice, "Give it a break, Lynette."

Claire walked to the long table and a few people acknowledged her with a smile or a casual greeting. Jenni wasn't there yet, so Claire set up her tripod and camera. She didn't understand why someone would want to have pictures taken of a rehearsal dinner anyway. However, if Lynette wanted visual memories of a bunch of people shoving food into their mouths, so be it. Who was Claire to complain? The job helped pay the bills.

It didn't take long to set up what little equipment she had brought, and unfortunately, Jenni still wasn't there by the time Claire finished. She looked around and grew more uncomfortable by the minute. Everyone socialized, enjoying the celebration, and she stood alone as the hired help. She felt like an observer, watching a bad movie with an even worse ending.

If her somber mood tonight indicated anything, tomorrow would be unbearable. To add to her emotions, she would have to see Black Eagle again, ready or not. What if he rejected her publicly? Undoubtedly, her heart would break into tiny pieces.

She contemplated the scenario for a moment. Hadn't she proved to be resilient, a tough survivor? After experiencing the loss of her mother, then Robert Kincaid, and in some ways Jeff, she had already proven she could endure abandonment. She'd simply glue the pieces back together and her heart would be even stronger than before.

What a liberating thought. She had to admit she was mildly curious about Black Eagle. Was he still the same warmhearted, patient man who had sat beside her for hours under a shade tree, observing horse behavior? Had he put his real daughter up on a horse's back early on, as he had Claire? A jolt of jealousy shot through her, and then a surprising sadness because of the years wasted. She was pretty sure sadness derived from love.

Maybe she was finally ready to see him.

She couldn't help but wonder if her sister would be at the wedding reception, too. She marveled at the thought, which brought her full circle. She had a sister. Yes, a sister.

Claire had to fight the natural tendency to resent her mother for withholding the truth. But if she compared her mother's situation to her own feelings, the confusing ones she was experiencing about Jeff, she could almost understand and empathize with her. Her mother had chosen to hide in Charlotte instead of dealing with Black Eagle's marriage to another woman. Claire was all too familiar with watching the man she loved marry someone else.

Just then Jenni approached. "Hey there, Claire Bear."

The nickname startled her. A long-lost memory zoomed to the surface: Black Eagle used to call her that when she was little. She would run to him, climb on his lap, and giggle as he bounced his legs like a horse. *Claire Bear.*

"Claire?" Jenni asked.

Claire swallowed the thick lump in her throat so she could speak clearly. "Yeah. Am I glad to see you?" She tried to keep her voice even.

"It's been rough, huh?" Jenni gave her a quick hug, apparently unconcerned about the handful of stares they were receiving from Lynette and her clan.

"Not too bad." Liar. Claire wasn't capable of discussing her innermost feelings right now, not while she worked, and definitely not in front of all these people.

"You're handling all this better than I would," Jenni said.

Paula walked up and forced a smile. "Claire, I had the pleasant opportunity to meet your father yesterday. It turns out the other veterinarian in town takes care of his horses."

Claire raised her eyebrows at the mention of Black Eagle.

"Lynette was with me yesterday when I had to make a farm call out to his place," Paula explained. Her words were innocent enough, but her voice held a note of sarcasm. "His usual veterinarian is on vacation, so I covered for him."

"Oh." Claire wondered where Paula was heading with the conversation. Whenever Lynette was involved, things seemed to deteriorate fast.

"Yeah," Paula said, still smiling. "He mentioned that he wanted to sell some of his land to her. She's wanted to buy it for years. He offered enough property so he could in turn buy the building you're renting, so you can stay there. But of course, Lynette isn't interested in selling her downtown properties, especially one on Front Street."

Black Eagle was willing to sacrifice his land for Claire in order to save her business? Amazing. Such generosity was all the proof she needed to know he loved her. Paula's ill intentions had a positive effect on Claire. A warm glow began to radiate from the center of her chest and her fingers started to tingle.

Instead of replying to Paula with the snappy retort she no doubt expected, Claire said, "Thanks, Paula. I'm thrilled to hear that. How generous of him."

Paula's face hardened. "He wanted to help you, since you've been evicted." She added emphasis to the last word. "Where do you plan to move?"

"Nowhere. I have a contract, and I choose to stay where I am." Claire stood confidently. She reminded herself that everything would be okay. Paula didn't need to know how anxious Claire felt on the inside.

"I offered to rent my place to her," Jeff said as he walked up behind them. He scowled at Paula. He must have overheard enough of the conversation to want to protect Claire from Paula's wrath.

Claire glanced up, surprised at first by his offer, but then quickly recovered. "And I declined. Thanks, but I'm perfectly happy where I am."

He blinked, obviously surprised she turned down his offer.

Jeff had his chance to agree to the idea earlier, and he'd let her ride off on Razor. She'd had enough of the engaged-but-suffering-hero act. Let him try to save someone else for a change.

As far as moving, she had a legal document that allowed her to stay put. Lynette seemed almost desperate to run Claire out of town and force her to end her friendship with Jeff. For once, Claire realized how much control over the situation she had. If Lynette wanted to play hardball, Claire was in the game.

"Well, Lynette says you have to be out by the end of the week," Paula declared, clearly an authority on the subject.

"That's great for Lynette. She can call my lawyer if she wishes." Claire refused to budge. She had a business to run, and now belonged to a family who lived in town.

Paula turned on her heels and strode away. Mission accomplished.

"Claire," Jeff said, visibly amused by Claire's performance. "Don't challenge Lynette. You can just rent my place."

"Thanks, but I'm fine," Claire said casually, as if the pending eviction were no big deal. Maybe he wanted to avert a battle between the two women, or maybe he actually saw a glimpse of Lynette's true colors. Whichever the case, and before this was over, Lynette would show her true side. Claire suspected that whenever Lynette didn't get her way, she threw a king-sized fit.

Well, Jeff was a big boy, and handling Lynette was about to become his challenge.

After Jeff walked away, Jenni said, "Claire, Lynette will make your life miserable if you stay there."

"Thanks for the warning, but I can handle it."

Lynette's father tapped his spoon on a glass and everyone hushed. He gave the required toast, and to Claire, it sounded more like a business presentation than a congratulatory speech. She snapped a few pictures and tried to focus on the job at hand, as opposed to the fact that this time tomorrow, Jeff would be married.

Dinner consisted of roasted chicken, sautéed green beans with pecans, and garlic mashed potatoes laced with fresh rosemary. When the server overlooked Claire, Jeff motioned to include her in the meal. That was a kind gesture, but the exclusion hadn't really bothered Claire. Her job was to take pictures. Besides, she didn't have much of an appetite anyway.

Lynette leaned into Jeff and whispered loudly enough that Claire overheard her. "How is she supposed to work if she's eating? We're paying her a lot of money to take pictures."

"It's not that much money," he said. At the waiter's questioning glance, Jeff nodded.

Lynette frowned. "I don't think we should provide dinner for an employee."

"Sorry, but I disagree. As far as I'm concerned, she's a guest too, and she agreed to do us a favor at the last minute."

Claire smiled politely at the server when he set a plate at an empty place at the table. Suddenly, she found her appetite. "Thank you. It looks delicious." She didn't look at Lynette. True, she was working and shouldn't eat, but if she gave in to Lynette now, she might as well resign herself to moving to another town.

Jenni leaned over and muttered, "She's a piece of work."

Claire forced a smile and didn't say a word. If she kept silent, no one could overhear. She glanced over at Jeff, who smiled while he talked with his future father-in-law as if he were enjoying himself.

After a few bites, Claire pushed her plate aside and stood to take more pictures. She clicked one of a laughing Jeff, one of a flirting Lynette, who hugged on Jeff's best friend from out of town, and one of a scowling Paula, who seemed bothered by a conversation with Lynette's mother.

When the dinner finally ended, Jenni helped Claire pack her equipment and load it into the trunk of her car. "What are your plans for the rest of the night?" Jenni asked.

Claire wrapped her arms around herself to keep the chill of the night away. "I guess I'll go home, read a good book in the bath, and go to bed early. How about you?"

"I'll probably go over the ferry's books. Do you want to come over, so you aren't alone? We could watch a movie," Jenni suggested.

"Thanks, but I'm fine. I guess I have to accept the inevitable, and after tomorrow, I'll move on." No matter how painful it was. "I'll allow myself one more night to feel sad and then that's it. There are plenty of men out there who like horses, and I'm young enough to find one." Surprised by her own answer, Claire realized the progress she'd made. When she'd first come to Big Cat, she was dead set against romantic relationships, but somewhere along the way she'd changed her mind.

"That's a healthy way to think about it. Mourn for a night and let it go."

"Yeah," Claire said with newfound empowerment.

"You don't realize how lucky you are."

"How so?" Claire asked, taken aback.

"You're attractive, smart, self-confident, and you make a living doing what you love. I envy you."

Funny, but she had never viewed herself that way. "You have your own business, too. So why envy me?"

"Because you're living your dream. I'm just helping with the ferry business, but my dream is to own a coffee shop. When I figure out the money part and a business plan, then I'll open my own business."

"Jenni, that's a great idea. That fits you perfectly." A group of people left the restaurant and stopped in the parking lot to chat, Jeff and Lynette among them.

He looked over but Claire didn't pay him any attention. She concentrated on her conversation with Jenni.

"Where do you want to set up your coffee shop?"

"As you know," Jenni said, "there are no available buildings to rent right now, except Jeff's. That's too big a place for what I need, and too expensive. If you decide to move out of Lynette's building, please let me know. Your studio would be ideal for a coffee shop. It's next door to the bookstore."

"Okay, but I doubt I'll move anytime soon." She risked a glance at Jeff, who stood next to Paula. Lynette laughed and touched Jeff's best friend on the shoulder. The man backed away a step.

"I don't want to accept any favors from Jeff," Claire said. "Besides, he'll be married to Lynette tomorrow, and she'll probably run his business affairs in one way or the other."

"Hmm. That's a shame for him. You're right, though; why move if she'll be your landlady either way? Maybe it is best if you stay in the studio until something else becomes available."

"Yeah." Claire ignored Jeff's stare as he walked by.

"Try to have a good night. If you need me, just call," Jenni said.

"Thanks, I'll do that." Claire gave Jenni a quick hug and then climbed into her car. It promised to be a long night. Somehow, some way, she had to come to terms with the wedding tomorrow.

# CHAPTER TWENTY

Claire let herself in the back door of the studio and made her way to the cabinet that held the cat food. When she reached inside for the container, her hand hit a box instead. Confused, she pulled it out, folded the flaps back, and stared down at a bundle of yellowed envelopes. Someone had written Claire's name in angled script across the front, but with no address, and Black Eagle's name in the upper left corner.

Letters? Why were they in her cabinet, and who had put them there? Black Eagle's wife immediately popped into her mind, but that seemed unlikely since Claire hadn't met her yet. Black Eagle might have put them there, but that didn't match his straightforward way. Shirley was also a possibility, but that seemed doubtful as well. The only person who made sense was Jeff. Maybe he'd gotten the letters from Claire's stepsister the other night when he'd met her. But how had Jeff put them in the cabinet without Claire noticing? She thought back to the key hidden under the flowerpot by the back door. She had used it the night he had driven her home after he'd rescued her from the island.

But when had he put the box there? They had gone riding together in the morning, and then she'd helped Shirley out the rest of the afternoon. If Jeff had stopped by, Claire or Shirley would have seen him. He must have dropped by the studio on his way to the rehearsal. She'd been upstairs getting ready for the rehearsal dinner and wouldn't have noticed if he'd entered the studio's back door. Somehow, he'd known to put the box in the one place she'd look—by the cat food.

Before Claire allowed herself to read the letters, she wanted to feed the cats. She grabbed the food container and carried it outside. The friendly cat stopped rubbing against the chair and pushed against Claire's leg.

"Good kitty," Claire said to the meowing cat. "That's the first time you've ever touched me. You're starting to trust me." Ironically, Claire found herself building friendships with people, too, such as Shirley and Jenni. When Claire bent down to touch the cat, it scooted away. "That's all right. I'd say you've made improvement." Anxious now to return to the awaiting box of letters, she filled the cat food dish and walked back inside.

Claire inhaled a deep breath to prepare for what she might read. Then she let her breath whoosh out like air escaping from a balloon.

"Okay, here it goes," she said to herself. She slid open a drawer next to the sink and grabbed a butter knife to use as a letter opener. Then Claire settled onto the floor and pulled out the bundle of letters. She hesitantly slipped the rubber band from around the sealed and aging envelopes.

With her hands shaking, she opened the first envelope, pulled out a handwritten note, and carefully unfolded it.

*Claire Bear,*

*I searched but I can't find you. Your mother hurt me a lot when she left town. I thought she might do that but I hoped she would stay. I guess I do not blame her for running away, because the agreement between us was wrong. I want you in my life. Please find me someday.*

*Your father,*
*Black Eagle*

The back of Claire's throat ached, her eyes stung, and swallowing suddenly became difficult. She held proof that Black Eagle was in fact her father, instead of hearing the startling news secondhand through Jeff. Not only did she have a box of letters from her past, she'd just read that her father had looked for her. The letter said so.

It amazed her how, after she'd made the decision to pursue Black Eagle, she'd found the letters. As she concluded earlier at the rehearsal dinner, she was a survivor. She had nothing to fear, though, because according to the letters, Black Eagle wanted to see her again.

Claire thumbed through the small stack and opened a more recent letter.

*Claire Bear,*

*I am still looking for you. If I don't find you, I hope one day you will find me. I do not have the money to travel far but that does not mean I haven't searched. My other daughter tried to find you but had no luck. I wish for you to come home. I will keep writing notes because it makes me feel close to you. I love you my bear.*

*Your father,*
*Black Eagle*

She read one letter after the next, and they were almost identical in content. He still seemed to be the caring, tender man she remembered, which actually didn't surprise her. People rarely changed. Her heart swelled with love and a stray tear ran down her cheek. Tomorrow, Black Eagle would wipe the painful tears of the past away.

***

The next morning, Claire awoke revitalized. She had slept the best she had in years. Again, she'd dreamt about Robert Kincaid, but this time, instead of hearing his muted voice, he spoke loudly, as if he stood next to her. "Claire, I want you to be happy, to love Black Eagle, and never to resent your mother for taking you away. I believe you now understand her reasons. Always remember, I love you." When he said goodbye with finality in his tone, Claire had reached out and tried to touch him, but he'd disappeared.

She sat in bed now, feeling oddly refreshed and confident. Everything seemed so clear, even Jeff's wedding. With new understanding, she appreciated the reasons why he wanted to marry Lynette. She even realized that his fear had frozen his ability to think rationally.

What a wonderful time they'd spent together, she reflected, and for that, she was grateful. Jeff had taught her that she could love again.

By finding her father, he had given her a precious gift.

The phone shrilled and broke her thoughts.

"It's Jenni," her new friend said. "I wanted to make sure you're okay after the rehearsal dinner last night."

"I think I am," Claire said with conviction. "Of course, for my own selfish reasons, I'd prefer Jeff not marry Lynette. But the choice is his to make. When Jeff found out the truth about my father, he in a way freed me to love again. I'll never forget that." She could finally let go of the burden of feeling fatherless all those years.

"You are a remarkably strong woman," Jenni said with admiration.

Claire was a lot stronger than when she'd first moved to Big Cat, for sure. She didn't need to lean on some loser boyfriend as she had in Charlotte, or to hide from relationships altogether. She was more independent than she'd ever given herself credit for.

"Thanks, Jenni. It's time for an attitude change—my attitude. I'm going to march into Jeff's wedding as a professional photographer, do my job, take this wonderful opportunity to meet Black Eagle, and then leave." Yes, that was exactly what she needed to do.

Her refreshing mindset empowered her. She was no longer a lost little girl who looked for her daddy in a sea of people. He lived right here, just outside Big Cat, and he wanted her in his life. That filled her with confidence.

"Good for you! I hope Lynette is just as professional. Once she marries Jeff, maybe she'll forget about evicting you."

"I doubt that, but I'll do my part. Instead of challenging her, which is probably a losing battle anyway, I'm going to call a truce. Maybe if I back off from Jeff entirely, she'll feel less threatened."

"I like that plan," Jenni said. "That way, you won't have to rely on Jeff and his building, either. Your life will be a lot more stress free if you can somehow make peace with Lynette."

Yes, indeed, but it was the word "if" that concerned Claire.

\*\*\*

Unfortunately, it was the last morning of a single man's freedom—his freedom—and it had arrived before he knew what hit him. Funny how he'd always thought his wedding day would be exciting, exhilarating even, but that reality had turned out to be quite different. He needed to listen to what his common sense was telling him.

Jeff stood in the shower and ran his hands over his face. He scrubbed harder and tried to wipe away the image that refused to fade in his mind. Last night at the rehearsal dinner, Claire had looked almost impassive. He didn't know what he'd expected, maybe that she'd be hurt or even angry—not that he preferred either of those reactions—but unemotional was downright infuriating. He didn't understand why he cared about her reaction, but he did. Maybe he wanted to know that she truly loved him.

His normally amiable father would box his ears if he got wind of his thoughts. His dad was as Christian as they got and would find Jeff's attitude appalling. It wasn't that he necessarily wanted Jeff to marry Lynette; he just wanted Jeff to get married and to be happily committed.

He finished his shower and stepped onto the bare floor. Frank lay next to the sink and began to lick water from Jeff's toes. He couldn't admit his straying thoughts to even his dog. "Frank, enjoy bachelorhood for one more day, because I have a feeling this is your last morning in this bathroom. I promise that you won't sleep outside, but licking water from my toes ..."

Frank whined as if he understood.

"I know, big boy. I thought I was doing the right thing by agreeing to marry Lynette. Heck, I had no idea you'd like Claire better."

Franked jumped up and barked.

"Come on, give me a break, buddy."

Frank jogged from the room, snubbing him.

"Fine, act like that," he yelled after the dog. "You'll come around when it's time to eat." Frank didn't return, so Jeff dried off, walked into his bedroom, and dressed in his favorite pair of faded jeans, the ones with frayed holes in the knees. "Lynnette will probably throw these away."

He straightened his back and squared his shoulders. "But not if I don't let her. If I marry Lynette, that doesn't mean I have to give up everything. Did you hear that, Frank?" He raised his voice again. "You can still lick the water from my feet if you want."

Frank warily walked back into the bedroom.

"That's right. If Lynette doesn't like it, she needs to marry somebody else. She has to accept who I am, dogs, horses and all."

Frank barked his approval.

Jeff stuck his bare feet into his ragged loafers and walked outside to feed the horses. Pam was already there, one step ahead of him as usual.

"My, don't you look perky this morning," she said.

"Give it up, Pam. I know what you mean and the message gets old."

"And grumpy, too." Pam filled a large bucket full of pellets and carried it to the fence line. She measured the mares' feed with a scoop and dumped each one into individual buckets hanging along the fence. Each horse knew which pail belonged to her. "Shouldn't you be happy, excited, booming with male pride today?"

"Stuff it, sis. Can't a man wake up tired?"

"Not on his wedding day. Maybe that's a sign you're about to do the wrong thing. You don't see the evidence even when your body tries to warn you." She walked over to the Gator, loaded the back end of the utility vehicle with hay, and took off toward the gate. He met her there and opened it so she could drive through.

He joined her in the field and spread several piles of hay around. "Sometimes life is more about giving things up than taking," he said. "Have you ever thought of that?"

"No. I think that's a cheap excuse to avoid going after what you want. You're afraid, scared of love."

Jeff gritted his teeth. "You hit a man where it hurts. Thanks. I can always count on you for empathy."

Pam sent him a wicked grin. "I don't think you really want my empathy. You know in your heart what you want and you're running out of time."

***

Claire sat downstairs and worked diligently on the studio's accounting. They had made decent sales this past week, partly due to Jeff's wedding, and with spring break beginning, tourist traffic had picked up as well. Once she added more photography classes and sittings, her business would be in the black in no time. Of course, she had to play it smart and save for the slow season. Unfortunately, the largest expense, besides Shirley's wages, was the building she rented from Lynette. If only she could find a cheaper place to rent.

The bell tinkled above the door and in walked Shirley. "Hi there," Claire said. "Thanks for coming in today. What would I do without you?"

"You'd be just fine on your own," Shirley said. "But just in case, I came a little early so I could give you emotional support and some words of encouragement." She pulled out a chair and sat next to Claire.

"Thanks. What wise words do you have for me?" Claire pushed a stack of papers aside to give Shirley her full attention.

"As I said before, the attraction between you and Jeff is obvious. There are approximately two and a half hours before the wedding. What are you going to do about it?"

"Nothing. Maybe I've matured; I don't know." Claire paused. "I understand and accept why he's making the right choice for him. His decisions aren't my business. If Jeff wants to hide from his feelings, that's his choice. Sure, I want us to have a relationship, but not enough to wreck a wedding."

"That's very logical. Why not give in to passion?"

"Because passion doesn't last; love does. Passion is the beginning stage, and then the relationship grows to a new level. If things didn't work out with Jeff and I messed up his wedding, he would always resent me. That would crush me."

"And that's why he likes you. Lynette enjoys controlling people, whereas you truly care."

"I do, but as far as Lynette's concerned, I have to let that go. I need to lie low, out of Lynette's grasp, and concentrate on running my studio."

"Well, I understand and wish you the best, as always. Your studio is becoming successful, if this week is any indication. And today you will meet your father. Mission accomplished."

"That's right," Claire said with conviction and smiled. "By the way, did you hide a box of letters in the cabinet with the cat food?" She was almost certain Jeff had put them there but wanted to ask Shirley just in case.

"Why would I do a thing like that?" Shirley immediately stood and walked toward the kitchen. Thankfully Claire had removed the box last night and had brought it upstairs to her apartment.

"Never mind." Claire raised her voice so Shirley could hear her from the other room. "You answered my question." Claire walked to the doorway of the kitchen and asked, "Shirley, since Jeff invited you to the wedding, why did you agree to work instead?"

"Like I said before, sweetie, I don't care for the woman he's marrying." Shirley had her head stuck in the cabinet as she looked for the box.

"Your decision isn't based on me, is it?"

"No, honey." Shirley stood and looked over her shoulder at Claire. "I never planned to attend their wedding. And I don't see a box in the cabinet."

Claire stacked her equipment on a table close to the back door. "Forget about the box. Anyway, I know this is last minute, but I could use an assistant at the church today." She regretted her decision to photograph the wedding and wanted a friendly companion to accompany her. Besides, extra help would be beneficial.

When Shirley fell silent, Claire tried to convince her. "It would be a great chance for you to learn about photography, and we could close the studio for the day." Even though she didn't want to close the shop on a Saturday with tourist season beginning, she really didn't want to be at the wedding without a comrade, either.

Shirley helped carry the light stuff out the back door. "Not in this lifetime. You agreed to endure that awful wedding, not me. I'd much rather work here today. Think about it, though; there might not be a wedding if you'd tell him how much he means to you."

"It's how *he* feels that matters," Claire said with confidence. "Jeff has to come to his own conclusion. He doesn't want to marry Lynette, but he hasn't figured out how to let the guilt go."

"You are a smart woman." Shirley shrugged and looked resigned.

"Thanks. I'm going upstairs to get dressed. I need to get there early to set up."

"I wish you luck today."

Claire leaned forward and gave the older woman a hug. "Thanks for everything. I don't know what I'd do without you."

"It's nothing. Just be careful today."

"I will." With that, Claire quickly finished loading her car, and then went upstairs to shower.

Afterward, she dressed in an expensive, tailored suit and a sexy, low-cut blouse. Sure, she'd let Jeff make the mistake of his life, but she wouldn't make it easy for him.

# CHAPTER TWENTY-ONE

Pam fussed over Jeff's tie in the back room of the church. She yanked it to the left, then to the right. He began to believe she was trying to choke him. "Sis, that's enough." He took her small hands and held them gently. "The tie was perfect five minutes ago."

"Sorry. I can't believe you're getting married. I apologize for trying to talk you out it. If you're happy, then so am I," Pam rambled. "Besides, I want to be an aunt again."

Jeff stiffened. Now wasn't a good time to explain that Lynette wanted to postpone having children for the time being. He'd just found out about her decision, which she'd casually mentioned to someone else at the rehearsal dinner.

Pam noticed his tension and apparently understood what it meant. They were usually sensitive to each other's body language, and he couldn't hide much from her. "She doesn't want kids?" Pam asked.

"Eventually." He had to be honest with her. "Maybe never."

"Are you kidding? I can't believe it." Pam grabbed hold of his tie again and pulled him closer. "Listen to me, brother. I know how you want kids. Don't settle for someone who can't give you what your heart desires. It's not worth it. It's better to be alone than to settle for someone you love only as a friend, and who doesn't even want children."

His body went numb. She was right.

"I know you. If you wanted out, you'd feel bad abandoning Lynette now, but this is your life we're talking about. Think seriously about this, Jeff."

He could feel a single tear wetting his left eye, but he didn't dare wipe it away and call attention to it. He also didn't utter a word because he knew his voice would betray him.

Pam released his tie and retrieved her purse from nearby. She dug in it for a moment and then handed him a handkerchief. So much for hiding his emotions. He grabbed the cloth and dabbed his eye. "Can I keep this?" At her nod, he folded it into a tight square and shoved it into his pocket—in case he needed it later.

Their father approached with a bright smile that revealed his pride. "Glad to see your wedding has you choked up, son." He patted Jeff on the back.

Jeff and Pam cast each other a look, and a silent message passed between them. They agreed not to mention their previous discussion to their father. It wasn't likely he'd understand, and at a very minimum, he'd offer a bunch of unsolicited advice. He'd just had his fortieth anniversary with Jeff's mother, and although she was domineering, his parents seemed happily married.

His father removed his glasses, wiped them on his handkerchief, and put them back on his wide nose. Then he cleared his throat. "Jeff, your mom says not to faint in front of everyone. That would embarrass her."

"Thanks for bringing that to my attention," Jeff replied in a tense voice.

"That's why Mom's not in here," Pam said, "because she makes comments like that. I asked her to help Lynette with her dress."

A knock sounded and Jeff's cousin, Jimmy, cracked the door open. "Lynette wants pictures of y'all in the dressing room, so she wants to send in the photographer."

"That's fine," Jeff's father replied cheerfully.

Even if Jeff did want to back out of the wedding, how could he stand to disappoint his father? Today seemed to be one of the happiest days of his dad's life. Maybe he wanted to relive his own wedding day to Mom. Guilt singed the corners of Jeff's mind, and left behind a faint, sickening smell he hoped was obvious only to him.

Claire breezed into the room as if she were carefree and unbothered by today's events. She exuded professionalism, all right, dressed in her black suit with her shiny black hair clipped back. And that sexy top she wore! He grew even more annoyed when she set up her tripod and began dictating what poses she wanted.

"Jeff, stand over there and shake hands with your father." When he didn't move immediately, she smiled at him. "Why, don't you look handsome? You make the perfect groom. Now, stand by your father."

He listened, but scowled.

"Do you think a smile is possible? It's such a joyful day, much too exciting for such a dour look," Claire scolded.

"Excuse me for a minute," he said to his father and Pam. He walked over to Claire, grabbed her elbow, and led her out of earshot from the others. "What do you think you're doing, Miss Mary Sunshine?"

"Photographing your wedding, as Lynette hired me to do." Claire smiled too big.

"I understand that, but what's with your perky attitude?"

"I thought you liked perky? I'm a friendly, professional photographer. Do you have a problem with that? If not, I have a job to do." She yanked her arm away from him and smiled.

He gritted his teeth. "Fine, then. Have it your way." Jeff walked back to his father and posed. He shook hands and smiled as if he'd just sealed a business deal. Two could play her little game, whatever game that was.

"That's better." Claire clicked a couple of pictures and thanked Jeff's father before he left the room. Claire turned back to Jeff and demanded another pose. "Hug your sister. That's right. Okay, Pam, please straighten his tie now."

"Not again," Jeff complained, tossing up his hand to stop Pam. "She about choked me the last time she touched it."

Claire smirked in a way that only Jeff could translate. She seemed miffed, even if she tried to disguise her agitation.

"Pose or I'll tell your bride that you aren't cooperating."

The thought of Lynette made him cringe. Why was he going through with this awful plan? And why did he want to plant a kiss on Claire's luscious lips right about now? Annoyingly so, he admitted silently that he enjoyed her take-charge attitude.

"Come on, Jeff, smile."

"I'm finished posing. Why don't you busy yourself in another room, Claire?"

"No problem. Thanks, everyone." She spun around, folded her tripod quickly, and zipped out of the room without looking back.

At his growl, Pam chuckled. "I guess she told you, Jeff."

"Don't talk to me." He left the room and occupied himself with talking to friends who had just drifted into the church. All the while, thoughts of the sassy little Claire absorbed his mind.

***

Claire clicked a picture of the bride.

"Lynette, stop moving," Jenni demanded as she fastened the hooks on the back of Lynette's bodice. Lynette, an only child, had lost her mother a few years back, so Jeff's mom had offered to help her dress. When time started to run short and Jeff's mom needed to finish getting ready, Jenni offered to take over.

Claire was grateful to have Jenni in the dressing room. Today was harder than she pretended. Claire bit her lip and snapped another picture.

She had to admit, Lynette's satin dress looked stunning, with its intricate embroidery stitched along the border and up the center of the train. Claire had heard that it took a skillful needle worker almost a month to finish the stitchery.

Claire clicked yet another photograph.

"Stop taking pictures of me," Lynette barked. "I'm getting dressed! Someone, please make her leave."

"Isn't that why you hired me, to take pictures?" Claire asked. "I want to give you your money's worth."

"And I can fire you, too."

Just as Lynette had evicted her? Honestly, Claire hadn't set out to cause trouble. With Jeff, she had wanted to drive home the fact they were now distant friends, and nothing more. With Lynette, she just wanted to do her job. Jeff's fiancée still seemed bothered about everything that had happened between them over the last couple of days, understandably so, and she didn't realize Claire wanted to make peace.

"You'll thank me later, when you look back and think about today." Claire had photographed weddings before, and she considered it part of her job to calm down nervous brides. "I've taken a lot of nice pictures, ones you'll cherish for years."

Lynette looked at her.

"Just relax," Claire encouraged. "You're the epitome of elegance." She looked gorgeous with her blond hair pulled away from her perfectly made-up face. A few loose, long curls fell onto her bare skin, courtesy of the low-cut neckline on the back of her dress.

"Everyone gets nervous before their wedding," Claire reasoned. "You'll be fine."

Jenni looked up from her tedious work and studied Claire, who smiled in return.

"I don't know why you're being so nice, but thanks," Lynette said.

Jeff's mother rushed over to them. "You need to hurry, Lynette. The wedding is about to begin."

# CHAPTER TWENTY-TWO

**Meanwhile, on Pony Island:**

Mario, the newborn colt, nursed peacefully while his mother drank from the marsh pond. He looked much steadier on his legs, and his tiny body had filled out a bit more. It was a sunny day, with the sky a bright neon blue, and a pleasant day to hang out at the watering hole. The horses took turns drinking, and all was peaceful, until a dog's bark pierced the quiet afternoon.

Magic snapped his head up high. He whinnied to his harem, his nose flared to smell the intruder's scent. A German shepherd shot over a thirty-foot sand dune and ran toward the herd.

Whinnying again, the stallion spun on his haunches. The horses splashed through the muddy water to the shore and their escape. Mario's mother tore away and the baby struggled to keep up with her. There was no time to waste.

The older foal, Dante, struggled to stay with the herd, too. The whites of his eyes were large, and fear tightened his muscles. A little older than Mario, he had more strength in his favor and could keep up easier.

A small whinny escaped from Mario's little mouth as he fell behind. Water splashed everywhere, including his eyes, his face, and the herd moved as a unit to flee the marsh pond.

The dog stretched his legs like a galloping thoroughbred.

When the horses reached dry land, the sound of thundering hooves echoed through the air. Mario and his mother were fast losing ground. His shaking legs slashed the deep water, his quivering body tensed, and his nostrils flared from strain.

Mario's mother trotted out of the water, slowing to wait for her newborn. When Mario didn't follow, she cantered a few steps toward him. The stallion screamed for her to leave. She looked back at her baby one last time, and called out. The stallion screamed again, demanding she leave Mario behind.

Mario's small cry was lost under the pounding hooves of the panicked horses. He splashed his way to the wet bank, but his hooves sank into the mud. He called for his mother again, but the weak plea went unacknowledged. Mario pulled with all his might, and used every muscle he had. His chest heaved and he fell onto his knees. Stretching his neck, he tried to climb back to a standing position, but fell again. His small nose landed on the water's edge.

The dog spied Mario and turned toward him, growling fiercely.

Mario pawed the ground faster, and again tried to muster the strength to stand, but his front hoof slid out from underneath his body. His face slammed onto the ground. Sand coated his eyes and caked inside his nose. He gasped for a small, strangled breath, and another. Then, he appeared to give up.

The dog's deep growl reverberated through the gentle breeze. He didn't hesitate before he pounced, and landed just a few feet from the unmoving colt. The dog's owner ran after him from a distance, leash in hand, and a woman screamed.

*** 

"Dearly beloved, we are gathered here today…"

Jeff shifted his glance to Claire, who stood off to the left side of the altar and looked through her camera's viewfinder. He wanted to be with someone like her, someone who understood his passion, someone whom he loved. But more than anything, he had to stop the wedding for himself, even if the disruption upset everyone who'd bothered to attend. It was finally time to let go of his fears, finally time to think about Jeff for once.

A loud shuffling noise from the back of the church demanded everyone's attention.

"Please forgive me for interrupting," a man said loudly, "but there's an emergency."

Lynette gasped.

An older, Native American man stood in the doorway to the sanctuary, wearing a cowboy hat, a checkered shirt, faded jeans, and old cowboy boots.

Jeff recovered first. "Jim, what are you doing here? What's wrong?"

Jim walked quickly down the aisle and talked in a voice loud enough for everyone in the church to hear. "We got a call from a tourist on the island. She said that someone let his dog off its leash and it went after the horses in the marsh pond. The baby wasn't able to keep up with the herd when they took off, and he fell into the water. The woman doesn't know if he's alive."

Several people screeched and one lady started crying. Jeff turned to Paula. "We need to get out there now. Drive to the dock and wait for me. I'll be right behind you."

Jeff noticed Paula's quick glance at Lynette. Even though her best friend was in the middle of her wedding, Jeff knew Paula's loyalty belonged to the horses during an emergency.

Before Jeff could apologize to Lynette, she cried out. "What about the wedding? You're going to leave me at the altar for some dumb pony?"

Jeff glared at her. "I'll pretend you didn't say that." If she had that attitude, it only confirmed she wasn't the woman for him. She clearly didn't understand the severity of the situation. Jeff turned to his father. "I need men. Can you get the volunteer crew together? Most of them are here anyway. And then grab blankets from home and take the Sea Horse Ferry out to the island?"

"I'll go get the ferry ready," Keith offered.

"That'll work," his father said with urgency. "And Jeff, hurry."

"I'm on it." Jeff ran out of the building, opened his truck door, and hopped onto the seat. Claire startled him when she climbed into the passenger side.

"I'm going with you."

"What about meeting Black Eagle? He'll show up at the reception, not knowing it's been canceled."

"I'll see him another time. This is life or death, and the colt needs us."

"Claire, this might be ugly."

"Go! Don't worry about me." Claire fastened her seatbelt and braced herself with one hand on the dashboard. With the other hand, she grabbed the handle above the door.

Jeff flashed Claire a look of approval, pressed the accelerator, and skidded out of the gravel parking lot. His heart thumped so loudly he could hear it pounding in his ears. If anything happened to that colt, he'd personally see that justice was served to the idiot who hadn't obeyed the leash law. He'd also bet the ferry owner hadn't informed the tourist about the law. Mario was paying the price for human negligence.

Anger coursed through him. He needed to get a grip before he saw that foal. He hoped the dog's owner had left long before he arrived at the island. He wasn't sure how he'd react if he came face to face with him.

Jeff made incredible time from the church to the dock. When he shot into the parking lot, he slammed his brakes and parked sideways in the gravel's dust. He launched out of the truck, not bothering to lock the doors. "Run, Claire."

Claire was already running and they reached the boat at the same time. Thank goodness Paula waited onboard with her gear stacked next to her. Jeff jumped into the skiff and had it untied with the motor running in record time.

"Hang on. This might be a wild ride," he said.

The surf flew over the railing and sprayed his black tuxedo, but he didn't care. The salt burned his eyes and his face was wet with cold water.

He jetted through the waterway. Right now the usually relaxing ambience was nothing more than a blurred background. His only focus was to get the boat to the island as quickly as possible, and to save the newborn colt.

As soon as the boat slid into the cove, Paula launched herself into the shallow water. Claire tossed the medical bag over the boat's side. Paula grabbed it and took off running.

Claire kicked off her heels, jumped overboard, and splashed into the water. She ran barefoot toward the marsh pond after Paula, who had now disappeared from sight.

Jeff secured the boat and easily caught up with Claire moments later. He grabbed her hand to encourage her to run faster. He knew how much she cared about the foal, and the faster they got there, the better. It seemed important to do this together.

He hoped she was able to handle the situation if Mario wasn't all right.

# CHAPTER TWENTY-THREE

By the time Claire and Jeff reached the marsh pond, a group of people stood nearby and a woman held Mario's precious head in her lap. The colt was alert but lethargic. Paula was already working on him with a stethoscope.

Jim, the man who had interrupted the wedding, knelt next to Paula. How had he gotten to the island before them? The more Claire studied him the more she realized that he seemed oddly familiar. Could it be?

Paula looked up at Jeff. "I need someone to carry him to the boat."

Jeff moved closer, and the small group parted.

Claire watched Jim closely as he assisted in lifting the limp Mario into Jeff's arms. At the wedding, when Jim had announced the emergency, she hadn't recognized him, but studying him now, the familiar mannerisms spoke loudly. She didn't know why they called him Jim, but his name was Black Eagle.

Once Jeff stood, he struggled to situate the colt in his arms, and with Jim's help, they shifted the baby around so Jeff wouldn't drop him. Then Jeff dodged the small crowd of onlookers who had moved closer to watch.

Just then, Jeff's father, brother, and several other men hurried toward him.

Claire heard a few murmured questions from the observers about why the men were in tuxedos, and whether the emergency had interrupted a wedding. One compassionate woman even questioned where the unlucky bride was. If they only knew the truth about how unsupportive the bride had been, and how devoted and caring the groom was, they wouldn't pass negative judgment on Jeff.

Claire surveyed the area for the dog, or the dog's owner, but nobody stood around with either a leash or a pet. She wondered what the consequences would be for the owner's negligence.

The walk back to the boat proved difficult, and after Jeff almost fell and dropped Mario once, Tom offered to help. "Do you want me to carry Mario the rest of the way?"

"Thanks, bro. I got it." Jeff stopped a moment to reposition the baby.

After he finished, Claire reached out and held Mario's head still on Jeff's shoulder, to prevent it from constantly slipping off. When her arms began to ache, Paula stepped in to help her, and before long, they fell into a rhythm of taking turns holding Mario's head.

When it was Paula's turn, Claire watched Mario, who continued to lie still in Jeff's arms as they walked. The poor baby had sand caked in his small nostrils, and she could tell where Paula had tried to wipe the gunk away. His brown eyes were open, despite the faraway look and the sand speckled in them.

The colt had to live.

To avoid an emotional scene, she diverted her attention from the foal to Black Eagle, who seemed safer for the time being. She studied his backside as long as possible without risking stumbling. Her real father's presence provided a temporary distraction from the foal. A more in-depth scrutiny would have to wait, until they had loaded Mario onto the boat. While she was curious about Black Eagle, and ready to meet him again, she never imagined reuniting with him over Mario's rescue mission.

She doubted Black Eagle recognized her now that she was a grown woman. It seemed strange that no one had mentioned to him that she'd be photographing the wedding. If he did know, he most likely had overlooked her in the church because of the emergency. He also hadn't acknowledged her at the marsh pond, which made her believe he didn't know whom she was. Certainly, the truth would surface soon.

Finally, the boats were within view a hundred feet or so away. Keith had parked the ferryboat next to the skiff, and he waited at the helm to taxi the volunteer crew back to the mainland. The amount of local support for the horses amazed Claire. She realized that somewhere along the line, she had allowed herself to become part of a community where everyone worked together. Small-town living had drawn her in.

At last they reached the skiff. Black Eagle hopped into the boat and Jeff awkwardly handed Mario over to him. Claire let go of the baby's head, and that was when her eyes first met Black Eagle's.

He turned away, obviously focused on the colt, but when he laid Mario on a blanket, and Claire continued to stare at him, he looked back. His eyes held a question. Maybe he wondered why she watched him. Then surprise registered on his weathered face.

He didn't say a word, didn't have to. Everything Claire wanted to know was evident: the love his eyes revealed, the warmth he conveyed, the familiarity he exuded.

Finally, with his voice shaking, he said, "Claire Bear?"

Tears sprung to her eyes and her lips puckered into the sad frown of a child. Her daddy was back—the memories, too. A lifetime of forcing herself to keep people at a distance melted away in seconds.

"Black Eagle." She choked out the words.

Jeff appeared at her side. "Claire, this is Jim, not Black Eagle."

Claire shook her head. "No. He's my father."

"I'm only Jim to locals. That's a nickname, Jeff," Black Eagle explained, his eyes never leaving Claire's. "Bear, I looked for you for years. I've written to you a lot but never mailed the letters."

"I ... know," she said. Still on the outside of the boat, she stepped toward him but hesitated. He reached over the boat's bow and hugged her until she groaned from his strength. "Sorry, Bear, I didn't mean to squeeze you so hard." Tears streaked his weathered cheeks and his voice was thick with emotion.

"It's okay, really." She smiled through her own tears.

Jeff's father called out, "Hey, we need to get going." The boat roared to life and Jeff, now in the boat, reached out a hand to help Claire aboard. She slipped her heels back onto her sore feet and squeezed between Mario and the boat's center console. Jeff, his father, and Paula left Claire alone with Black Eagle. Mario seemed stable and they could do nothing for him right now except comfort him.

Claire alternated between watching the lifeless colt and watching the emotional man who sat across from her. She actually had a father, a real-life man, instead of only a remote memory. And he was within arm's reach.

The ride to the mainland seemed to take forever, even though she suspected they cruised at just a notch below the wild speed of the earlier trip to the island to maintain Mario's stability. When the dock came into view, Claire noticed a horse trailer waiting. A lump formed in her throat as she looked down at Mario, who now slept soundly. She slipped her hand under the blankets and petted his warm coat. Warmth was a good sign.

"You're going to make it, little guy," Claire managed to say. "Islander Ponies are tough."

Black Eagle looked up. "I bet you're tough, too, Claire."

She swallowed hard and managed to smile. "Thanks." Although her emotions had experienced quite an upheaval today, between the nerve-wracking wedding, the upsetting accident with the colt, and the painful but joyous reunion with Black Eagle, she'd gained a remarkable sense of self-acceptance. She felt as though she could take on almost anything. The Lynettes of the world couldn't touch her.

Jeff pulled the boat into the slip and tossed someone a line. Keith pulled into a vacant space next to them, and several men hopped out and jogged toward Jeff's skiff.

"Have Jenni move her trailer closer," Jeff yelled to his sister Pam, who waited at the dock.

She ran toward Jenni's open truck window. They conversed for a moment, and then Jenni backed the trailer some more while Pam walked alongside it. When the trailer stopped moving, Pam lowered the ramp.

Claire stayed out of the way and watched as the team worked together. Another moment of small-town pride welled up inside her. She was grateful for the united effort to save the baby.

Black Eagle gathered Mario and the blankets carefully, and lifted the colt out of the boat. He handed the baby to Jeff, who carried the foal quickly but gently up the ramp and into the well-padded trailer. He lowered the bundle onto the floor as Paula sat down beside Mario.

Jeff walked out of the trailer and joined Claire. "Paula always insists on riding back there with the horses. She likes to be with them," he explained. "She is opinionated, no doubt, but she's a good person and cares about the Islander Ponies."

"I know." After the confrontation with her over Jeff's kiss, and then the uncomfortable conversation about Lynette's refusal to sell the studio to Black Eagle, Claire had started to develop a dislike for her. But Paula had once again revealed a vulnerable, soft side. When Paula settled in next to the foal on an old quilt, and Pam closed the ramp door, Claire choked back tears.

"Come on, let's go," Jeff said. "I want to follow the trailer." Jeff and Claire jogged to his truck. He tore out of the parking lot to catch up with the trailer, now traveling in the direction of Jeff's ranch.

"Do you think Mario will be okay?" She glanced at Jeff but he kept his eyes trained on the road.

"I don't know. He doesn't look that good, Claire. Don't get your hopes up."

She turned and gazed out the side window. Jeff grew silent and neither of them talked for a few minutes.

"I'm sorry your wedding got ruined." She continued to stare out the window.

"Claire," he said, reaching for her hand, "I'm not marrying Lynette."

It took a moment for his words to sink in. "You're not?" She turned toward him and tried to analyze his serious expression. He had stood at the altar earlier, fully prepared to go through with the ceremony, and now he was declaring his intention of canceling the wedding. Something didn't add up.

"I stood up there watching you. I was trying to figure out how to stop the wedding," he said, obviously detecting her confusion. "It never should've gone that far. I barely heard the preacher. I want someone I can love, Claire, someone who understands and supports my passion. You obviously do, because look where you're sitting right now. Where's Lynette? She's probably crying on her father's shoulder because I left her at the altar. Don't get me wrong, that was awful timing, but emergencies aren't planned events. They just happen."

When Claire didn't respond, he continued. "Claire, I was just about to stop the wedding, but Jim beat me to it."

"Jim—" her voice trailed off.

"Yes, Jim. I had no idea he was your father. Somehow I didn't realize Jim was a nickname. I never gave it much thought."

"It's okay."

"I'm sorry you had to meet him like this." He patted her leg briefly, hesitating for a moment before he pulled his hand away.

"Actually, it was perfect," she said. "All my memories of Black Eagle revolve around horses, so it makes sense to reunite with him over Mario. The plan to meet him at the wedding reception had seemed all wrong."

He glanced at her and grinned. "I'm glad you're handling this so well. He's a good man."

"I know. Where did he go? Will he follow us to your house?" Now that she thought about it, she'd lost track of Black Eagle when Jeff carried Mario into the trailer.

"I doubt it. Jim's a quiet guy. He usually helps during the beginning stages, and then he fades into the background."

"So he's decided to hide again, to run away from reality? He seems to do that when things get tough." She was shocked at the bitter edge in her voice. The leftover resentment had bubbled to the surface so fast she hadn't been able to temper the emotion. She felt disappointed, abandoned again. "He didn't even say goodbye."

"Claire, people handle things differently. Just because he prefers to keep a low profile doesn't mean he's a coward. In fact, he's one of the most caring and bravest people I know. I'm sure he was happy to see you today, but it probably took him by surprise. It even surprised you. Give the man a chance."

A chance. She wanted more than anything to let him back into her life, to trust him and have a family again. As Jeff said, he liked to remain in the background. He was there for Mario today, and now that Mario was safe, Black Eagle had stepped aside. That's what he had done with Claire. She reminded herself that he loved her enough to allow her a life free of prejudice, by allowing another man to raise her. It wasn't his fault her mom had taken off with her to Charlotte. That hadn't been part of his plan.

She glanced back at Jeff. He was always there when she needed him. Even now, after the canceled wedding, he'd pushed his problems with Lynette aside and encouraged her to talk about Black Eagle. Jeff was amazing. Today he'd made some important decisions about his future, which had allowed him the strength to disengage from Lynette.

He didn't get married.

"All right. I'll give Black Eagle a chance, but I have to move at my own pace."

"That's understandable," Jeff said.

"By the way, how did Black Eagle get over to the island? He didn't ride on a boat with any of us."

"No one knows how Jim, I mean Black Eagle, does anything," Jeff explained. "He's a man of mystery."

Jeff's cell phone came to life and with each ring, tension filled the truck. He glanced at the display screen and then back at Claire before he answered. "Lynette."

Claire could hear the other woman's frantic voice, although only garbled words managed to seep through the earpiece. Claire's belly tightened in a firm knot.

"I'm sorry about the wedding," he said. "No, we aren't having it."

The high-pitched voice continued to flood the quiet truck.

"We'll talk about it later."

Lynette started yelling.

"Listen," he raised his voice, "I need to go. I promise, we'll talk soon." Finally, when the hysterical woman paused for a moment, he said, "I'm sorry, for everything." He clicked off the phone, pulled into his driveway.

The knot in Claire's belly loosened and she felt the bud of excitement begin to bloom.

Jeff drove up to his house and backed his truck next to the trailer, which Jenni had parked close to the barn. "Let's go," he said, and then hopped out of the truck. Claire jumped out, jogged around the backside, and joined him as they approached the trailer. Jenni opened the ramp and they saw Mario looking out with doe eyes, his head resting on Paula's lap.

"How's he doing?" Jeff asked.

"He's weak, but I think he might make it," Paula said. "He needs to nurse, though. I'll have to look, but I don't think I have any milk replacer in my truck." Someone had driven Paula's truck from the dock to Jeff's ranch. The volunteer crew, which was dispersing now, had obviously perfected its routine from the many times they had worked together as a team.

"Jenni, can you stay with Mario a minute?" Paula asked. When Jenni joined her in the trailer, Paula laid the colt's head onto a blanket and went to her truck. Jeff and Claire followed her. She opened the hatch and searched through several medicine drawers. "Nope, I don't have any with me."

"Tom probably has bottles," Jeff offered. "But what are we going to do about the milk?"

"It would take too long to drive over to the clinic," Paula said, and then frowned. "Mario needs to eat soon."

Jeff bit his lip and appeared to be thinking. "Wait a minute. I think I might have some in the house, from the last foal we rescued." He turned to his approaching sister. "Pam, can you get baby bottles and nipples from Tom?"

When she nodded, he took off at a run, leaving Claire and Paula alone at her truck. Paula managed to ignore her as she slid the medicine drawers closed after her futile search. When Claire started to walk away, Paula spoke. "Listen, you got lucky today. I mean, what are the chances that this would happen right before Jeff got married?"

"Maybe his wedding wasn't meant to be."

Paula glared at her. "Right. You've managed to come between them one too many times. You need to back off and let them work things out together. Why are you here anyway?"

She didn't have to justify her presence to Paula, but at the same time, she didn't want to make a scene when Mario teetered on the edge of life and death. "The horses mean a lot to me." *Jeff does too*, she wanted to add. Before Paula could argue, Claire turned and headed back to Jenni and Mario.

When Jeff returned to the trailer, panting hard from the long sprint, he held up the milk replacer. "I found some." He tossed it to Claire. His grin vanished when he glanced first at her and then at Paula, who now stood near the rear of the trailer with Pam.

"Let's get this foal into a stall," Paula commanded.

Claire understood Paula's reaction, but she didn't need her permission to be on Jeff's farm. It wasn't his cousin's place to dictate Jeff's acquaintances. Of course, Claire only hoped her attraction to Jeff would lead to something more. She had every intention of fighting for the man she loved.

Right now, however, Lynette was more of a concern. She doubted Jeff's ex-fiancée would stand for someone stepping into her shoes without a fight.

Jeff lifted Mario into his arms and carried him out of the trailer and into a stall. He gently laid him in a pile of fresh straw that the volunteer crew must have prepared earlier when everyone else was on the island.

Paula immediately kneeled and started rinsing Mario's eyes with Pam's help.

"Claire, since they're busy, can you make the bottle?" Jeff asked as he covered the damp baby with a blanket.

"Sure." Claire grabbed the bottle from next to Pam's leg, and twisted off the top. She felt Jeff's heated gaze on her as he explained how much powdered milk to mix with the warm water Pam had already put in the bottle. It was an odd but intimate moment. The rest of the group blended into the background and for several long moments, they ceased to exist.

"If you sit down, I'll put Mario's head in your lap," Jeff suggested.

Claire looked down at her expensive business suit, now wet and sandy with a few unidentifiable stains. It made no difference; Mario's life was well worth a destroyed outfit. She could always buy another one.

She lowered herself onto the stall's fresh bedding and wrapped her arm around the baby's soft neck. Jeff rested Mario's head in the crook of her arm. Then she looked up into the gentle man's eyes. Their faces were only inches apart, and for an instant she held her breath. There was something raw and sexual about their closeness, something special about working together to save one of the Islander Ponies.

"Horses are more difficult than other animals to bottle feed, especially since he's nursed from his mother before." Paula's voice broke the intense silence.

As Paula predicted, Mario didn't seem interested in the bottle at first. Jeff leaned in even closer and glanced down at Claire's chest, exposed by her low-cut blouse. "He has a natural reflex," he explained, "so if you tease his lips with the bottle's nipple, he'll start to suck." He cleared his throat, and in a deep, masculine voice, he said, "Or let him suck on your finger first and then try the nipple."

Claire's pulse pounded and she was sure sweat had beaded her forehead. She commanded her mind to work and touched the bottle's nipple to the baby's mouth. Mario licked his lips and began to suck on his upper lip before he found the nipple.

"Yeah! He's drinking," Claire exclaimed.

Claire and Jeff's eyes met again over the colt's head and lingered. He was a free man now, available, and therefore none of the rules and limitations from before remained.

"Success. We did it," Jeff said. He broke eye contact, but was still close enough for her to reach out and touch his face if she wanted.

Paula stepped back, analyzing Claire and Jeff. From the expression on her face, she guessed that Jeff had changed his mind about marrying Lynette.

Paula's face turned cold as she spoke to him. "You'll have to bottle feed Mario every couple of hours, but once he can stand again, you can train him to bucket feed. Call me if you have any problems." With that, she left.

Claire actually empathized with her. She was sure Paula wasn't ready to acknowledge that Jeff's relationship with Lynette was over. It must have been difficult to choose between her friend's happiness on her wedding day and the Islander Ponies during an emergency, but true horse people would choose the foal over almost anything in the world. And Paula, like the rest of them who helped today, was a true horse person. She shared that bond with Claire, whether Paula liked it or not. At some point, especially if Jeff ended up with Claire, she'd have to come to terms with Jeff's decision.

"What will happen with Mario now?" Claire asked.

"If he survives, he'll be put up for adoption."

"Adoption?" Claire couldn't imagine the baby going elsewhere. "Can't you adopt him?"

"Sorry, but I already own too many horses. I can't keep them all. My mission is to find good homes for the rescue horses."

Claire made a rare and impulsive decision. "I'll adopt him. I've always wanted a horse." She had no idea where she'd keep him or how she'd pay for him, but he couldn't be that expensive.

As if he read her mind, Jeff offered a solution. "You can keep him here if you want. If you want to exchange board for feeding all the horses once a week, I'll take that."

She studied him to make sure he was serious. "All right. It's a deal."

When they finally went inside, Jeff, still in his dirty, damp tuxedo, collapsed on his leather couch, and Claire dropped onto the loveseat. He glanced over at her and said, "Jenni told me that she packed up your cameras and equipment at the church after we left. She had plenty of time to get the horse trailer before we showed up with Mario."

"Oh, I forgot my cameras! That's a first."

Jeff stared at her in amazement. "You are as committed to the horses as I am. That's incredible. The fact that you forgot your equipment says a lot."

She didn't answer, but smiled.

"Would you help me with Mario tonight?" He hesitated and then forged on. "I can always call Pam and have her bring some clothes over later for you. I bet one of my shirts would fit you as a nightshirt, and I have extra toiletries in the spare bathroom upstairs, next to the guest room. If you spend the night, I promise to behave."

"Of course I'll stay, if you leave out the behaving part." She stared directly into his blue eyes and couldn't believe her good luck. This time last night, at the rehearsal dinner, the situation had looked dismal. She had thought for sure that she'd spend tonight alone, crying in her small apartment until her eyes had no tears left. It had seemed inevitable that by tomorrow she'd have built a tall, protective wall around herself.

He stood and walked over to the loveseat and bent down. He kissed her softly at first, and then with yearning. "Come on."

She didn't ask where they were going, but took his outstretched hand and followed him into his bedroom. He took off one piece of her clothing at a time, and left a hot streak wherever his fingers touched.

"I've waited for this moment for a long time," he confessed as he whispered in her ear.

She suspected he hadn't waited nearly as long as she had waited. Claire had held onto her broken heart for a lifetime, and when he touched her with gentle caresses, her heart felt whole. They made love often throughout the night, in between the times they went out to feed Mario.

Life seemed great right now, except for one niggling concern. How would Lynette react once she found out Claire spent the night with Jeff?

# CHAPTER TWENTY-FOUR

The following morning, Jeff kissed Claire goodbye despite her protests. He had an urgent errand to run.

He climbed into his truck and drove to town. Before long, he parked his truck haphazardly in a space near the ticket booth of *Pony Island Excursions*. The ferry's weathered sign hung from its rusted hinges. The breeze blew the plank and caused it to squeak ominously. The atmosphere, intensely foreboding, enveloped him, like the moments before an old western gunfight.

Jeff approached the shack just as the disheveled ferry owner made his way out of the enclosed storage area and into the booth. The man stopped dead in his tracks when their eyes met.

"What do you want?" the man growled.

"You. I want you." Jeff's words swirled in the air. "You messed up yesterday."

"Since when are you the ferry police? I don't need to answer to you."

"I'm the ranger on Pony Island and you are wreaking havoc over there." Jeff paused for a moment to keep control of his anger. He felt his jaw clench and forced himself to relax before he spoke again. "It's your job to inform people about the leash law."

"And it's none of your business what I do." The owner walked out of the booth and took a threatening step toward Jeff.

Jeff forced a smile. "You have a responsibility to the people you drop off, and to the horses that live there."

The owner swung his right fist at him, but Jeff caught it in the palm of his hand with ease. He held onto it for emphasis as he said, "Violence will land you in a bad place. I suggest you pack up your things and move on out of here. You've made the locals mad about that little colt. Mario almost died yesterday. Save face and quit while you can."

"I ain't goin' nowhere."

"Suit yourself." Jeff dropped the man's cold hand and pointed his index finger at him. "That was your last mistake. If you don't voluntarily close down your ferry service, I'll make sure the Park Service revokes your license."

The man spat, but the tobacco stream hit the ground a few feet from Jeff's foot. Jeff recognized the misfire as an act of submission. The battle was almost over, even if the man refused to admit his loss.

Jeff stood his ground and didn't move. Under no circumstances would he allow the ferry to continue to operate and to put the horses at risk again. When the ferry owner finally turned his back and retreated to his storage shed, Jeff grinned and walked away. Before he reached his truck, his cell phone rang.

"What's up, Claire?"

"Where are you?" Her voice sounded urgent.

"I just finished my errand. How's Mario this morning?"

"That's why I'm calling. He's not doing well. You need to get back here right away."

***

Mario squinted with both eyes and tears streaked his cheeks. When Jeff pried one eye open, it revealed a small cloudy spot. He checked the other eye and it looked the same. The situation didn't seem good.

"Do you think they're infected?" Claire asked. She was now dressed in an old pair of jeans and a shirt Pam had loaned her.

"It's likely. It could be an allergy of some sort, since both eyes are affected, but it's doubtful." He pulled his cell phone from his pocket and dialed. "Paula, this is Jeff."

He used his shoulder to hold the phone against his ear in order to free his hands, and turned Mario's head so he could look into the colt's eyes again. "Can you come out here to look at Mario? We think his eyes are infected."

The word "we" hung in the silence between Jeff and Claire. That one simple word made them a team.

"I can be there in about an hour," Paula said. "I rinsed Mario's eyes after the accident, but apparently it wasn't enough. He did have a significant amount of sand in them." She grew silent and made a crinkly noise in the phone, as though she was thumbing through a day planner. "I'll see if my next client, whose appointment is just for routine vaccinations, can switch times with you. If it is an eye infection, I'm concerned Mario might lose his eyesight if we don't act fast."

"Thanks, Paula."

"Love ya, Jeff. I'll be there soon; I'm nearby."

"Okay. Love you, too."

When he disconnected his cell phone, he glanced at Claire. Oh, crap. He'd just told Paula he loved her. "You know she's my cousin, don't you?" Before now, it never occurred to him that Claire might misperceive his relationship with Paula, especially if she didn't realize the family dynamics involved. The last thing he wanted was more friction between the two women.

Claire nodded. "Shirley explained she's your cousin. Everything's fine, Jeff. More than fine."

He pulled her close. "I guess you figured out that Paula and Lynette are best friends, but Paula will come around." At least he hoped so. "As far as Lynette's concerned, I need to talk to her and explain everything. She deserves to know the truth, about how I had planned to stop the wedding even before the emergency."

Claire remained quiet.

"She might pitch one heck of a fit, but she'll eventually get over it," he continued. "You'll probably get the brunt of the backlash, so you might want to move out of her rental unit as soon as possible. I'm sure she'll willingly release you from your lease. Then you can move into my building."

"I appreciate your offer." She frowned and didn't appear too thrilled by his suggestion.

"Then what's wrong?" Jeff asked, disturbed by her cautious reaction.

She sighed. "It's just that when I moved to Big Cat, I wanted to be independent. If I move into your building, I'll be dependent on you."

He set his jaw. "Is that such a bad thing?" He pulled away from her to put distance between them. His fear of her running back to the city ran rampant through his mind.

"I don't know. All my life I've mistrusted men, and for good reason." She stopped talking for a moment. "When you combine a business relationship with friendship, things get complicated. Just because Lynette might make life a little miserable doesn't seem reason enough to move."

"The decision is yours, no pressure of course. If it makes you feel better, we can always sign a lease. My rent is usually higher than what you pay now, so I'll give you a break on it for the first year. You can pay me more after you make a consistent profit." If any part of her hesitation had to do with affordability, then he'd just solved her dilemma. He usually got almost double the rent that Claire would pay, but he wasn't interested in the money. "Besides, the building is bigger and in a better location."

"I appreciate it, but I don't want favors. Why don't you lease to someone who can pay full price?"

He sighed in frustration. He wanted her in his life. "If we're going to make a go of our relationship, Claire, then you need to trust me. I'm not trying to control you or your business. I offered you a better location at an affordable price, and without strings attached. If things don't work out between us, though I suspect they will, then you'll still have a signed lease to protect yourself. I own that building free and clear, without a loan, so it's nothing for me to charge you less rent. I'd rather lease to someone who'll take good care of it."

She looked up at him with apprehension. "I need to think about it."

He pulled her back into his arms. "That's fine." Maybe he had applied too much pressure and needed to back off a bit. "I'm glad I met you when I did. I almost made the worst mistake of my life." He bent down and kissed her gently.

Just then, Paula pulled into the drive. After she examined Mario, she pulled back and frowned. "He has an infection in both eyes. His condition can go from bad to worse fast. I recommend you drive to the veterinary school at NC State in Raleigh, and have his eyes treated immediately. I'll call and let them know this is an emergency and that you're coming."

"Will he be okay?" Claire asked, her voice barely audible. She repeatedly stroked Mario's neck.

"To be honest, he might lose sight in both eyes unless they're treated aggressively. Time is of the essence."

Jeff walked out of the stall to get his truck. He slowed when he heard Paula say, "Claire, I want you to know that I hold no grudge against you. There's a lot of speculation flying around town about you and Jeff, but I knew from the beginning that you two were right for each other. I just didn't want to admit it at the time. Don't let other people get in the way of what you want."

"Thanks for saying that," Claire said.

"I have to warn you, though. Lynette will be out for blood, your blood."

***

Within fifteen minutes, Jeff and Claire were driving down his long driveway. Claire didn't want Mario to ride alone in a big, scary trailer, so she had lined the truck's backseat with blankets, put a large baby diaper on Mario–left over from Jeff's nephew—and put him on her lap.

"If I ever doubted your commitment to the horses before, I never will again." Jeff looked back at Claire as she held Mario.

"I'm just as committed to them as you are, and don't worry, I'll never up and leave Big Cat to return to the city."

"Really?" Dana had said the same thing.

Before they reached the main road, Lynette's flashy sports car raced into the driveway and blocked their exit. She stomped over to the truck and Jeff reluctantly lowered his window.

"We need to talk," Lynette said. She glared at Claire in the backseat.

"Yes, we do, but not right now. We have an emergency," Jeff explained.

"You pushed me aside for that pony once before, at the altar of all places, and you won't do it again." Lynette poked her head into the window and Jeff leaned away.

"Why won't you kiss me?" Lynette whined. "Is it because of *her?* You mean to tell me you're dumping me for Nature Woman?"

"Lynette, get a grip—" Jeff started to say.

"Thanks for the compliment," Claire interrupted.

Jeff snickered. "Okay, that's enough. Lynette, we need to get to Raleigh. I'll talk with you when I get back. Now kindly move your car before I drive over it."

Lynette's mouth dropped open. "Fine, you two deserve each other. Claire, I want you out of my building tomorrow."

"I'm not ready to move yet." Claire's voice sounded strong and confident. "If that's a problem then you can call a lawyer, but since we have a lease, there isn't much point."

Lynette huffed, stomped off, and sent up dust as she drove away.

Jeff looked back at Claire. "I'm sorry you had to hear that. I never realized how self-centered she was, although I had a hint on our wedding day, when she expected me to go on with the ceremony and ignore a dying horse."

"Some women hide their true personality until they are declined something they really want."

Jeff glanced in the rearview mirror. "That's right, and some women are down-to-earth to their core."

She smiled.

Claire became quiet for the next couple of hours, which gave him a chance to think, to process all that had happened in the last twenty-four hours. One thing was for sure, Claire was perfect for him. He had to believe her promise that she wouldn't move back to the city.

Even though he hadn't known her for long, she seemed to be everything he dreamed of in a woman. He just needed to convince her to take a chance on him. Her willingness to rent his building was an important step.

When they arrived at the vet school, a small group of people met them outside. Jeff climbed from the truck and joined them in the parking lot. "We have Mario, the foal from Pony Island."

A young woman looked around. "Where is he? Where's your trailer?"

Jeff pointed to the truck. "You have to see this."

They moved toward the truck and peered through the window. Claire looked up and waved.

"I've never seen anyone transport a horse in their vehicle before," the woman said in disbelief.

"Claire defies all norms, in the best way possible," Jeff said with pride in his voice.

"I love it. Let's bring him inside then," the woman said.

Mario was an instant hit among the staff. He behaved well and seemed to enjoy all the attention showered on him. They even nicknamed him "Mario the wonder horse."

After hours of examinations and consultations, Jeff and Claire were finally back in the truck with a full course of antibiotic eye ointment. Luckily, they had caught the infection early.

"I'm glad Paula suggested we bring Mario up here today," Jeff said. "We saved his eyesight, or at least he has a fighting chance now."

"No kidding. Paula is a remarkable vet, or excuse me, veterinarian." Claire laughed good-naturedly and Jeff joined her.

The ride home was long, and became longer when Mario's urine seeped through onto Claire's lap. Unfortunately, they hadn't brought enough diapers along, and the last one was soaked through. She fed Mario the last remaining bottle to keep him hydrated despite the fact more urine was inevitable.

Jeff, thankful for Claire's good spirit, realized Lynette couldn't have come close to tolerating even a fraction of their endeavor, or have understood the reason behind the emergency trip to Raleigh.

He glanced in the rearview mirror. Looking at Claire, with Mario on her lap, made him realize that his fear—the fear of falling in love again with someone who wasn't born in Big Cat—had vanished. Surprisingly, if Claire wanted to move back to the city, he'd be willing to go with her. Considering he had known her for only a few weeks, that was a startling discovery.

He wished, however, she proved as committed to him as he was to her. It almost crushed him when she refused his offer to move her studio into his building.

Jeff turned into his driveway and parked close to the barn. He reached inside the truck and carefully lifted Mario into his arms. Then he carried the colt into the stall, and Claire helped him lower the baby onto the straw. The second they were finished, she kissed him and ran for the house, most likely for the shower.

Jeff made his way to the side door, which led into the mudroom and kitchen. He picked up his cell phone and dialed Pam. "Sis, can Claire borrow some more clothes?"

She clicked her tongue. "You move fast, brother. Will she spend another night with you?"

"Actually, the colt peed on her and she's soaked. She never even complained. She's one of us for sure." He paced the kitchen floor as he talked.

"Really? I knew she loved horses, but that's beyond what I thought. I assume the wedding is off?"

"Um, yeah. I was just about to stop the minister myself when Jim ran in." He hoped she believed him.

"I'm glad you didn't marry Lynette out of convenience." Her voice held definite approval and perhaps relief.

"Me, too."

"How's the colt?" She sounded concerned.

"We caught the eye infection early, so he should be fine," Jeff explained. He wanted to hang up before she asked any pointed questions about Claire. He wasn't much of a phone talker anyway.

"I'll bring the clothes over right away, and Jeff ... even though you sound tired, you sound happy." Her voice softened and took on a dreamy tone.

"I am. I'm not going to let this one get away. Listen, I need to get off the phone." He wanted to start dinner before Claire got out of the shower, and wanted time to prepare mentally for his conversation with her about renting his building. He needed to know that she was willing to take that small chance on him, needed to know they had a future.

"I'm thrilled for you. See you in a few," Pam said, and then disconnected.

Jeff pulled out the ingredients to make his famous oven-baked spaghetti, at least famous within his family. He often brought it to the frequent family get-togethers, and in all honesty, it was about the only dish he knew how to make well.

Just as he shoved their dinner into the oven, his cell phone rang. "Jeff, I'm standing outside your door. Let me in," Lynette demanded.

He groaned. He wanted to talk with her, but not now, with Claire in his shower, his sister on her way over, and after the long day he'd had. But he had to address the situation at some point, so he figured he might as well do it now. He reluctantly opened the front door.

"Lynette, why don't we meet tomorrow for dinner at the Salty Mug? My treat of course," he said.

"I want to talk now."

Pam walked up behind her. "Here are the clothes you wanted. Hi, Lynette."

***

Claire walked into the living room with Jeff's robe tied snugly around her. She stopped short when she spied Lynette, and turned back in the opposite direction.

Pam pushed around Lynette, who blocked the doorway, and scurried toward Claire. "Here are the clothes." Then she whispered, "Don't let Lynette's bad temper scare you off. They need to talk about a few things, but it'll be okay. Just remember to be patient."

"I will. Thanks for the clothes." Claire took them and retreated to the safety of the nearest bathroom. She wasn't a person that thrived on conflict, though she held her own when needed, and she definitely didn't want to get involved in Jeff and Lynette's conversation.

She had to trust him, as he stated earlier. She mostly did, at least when it came to the conversation with Lynette. Claire considered that progress.

Men in her past hadn't been honorable, but she realized now that was her own fault. She had dated the wrong type of man. But there was still an underlying mistrust that went beyond her feelings for Jeff.

She had succeeded in her quest for independence all right. She didn't need to find someone to replace her father anymore, didn't need to lean on a man because she wanted some semblance of family. Jenni, Shirley, Pam, and even Paula were fast becoming her substitute relatives. But she needed more, deserved more.

So why did she fear moving into Jeff's building? The answer was actually easier than she cared to admit, even to herself. The mere thought of being vulnerable scared her. However, Jeff seemed to understand her hesitance. Grateful he'd suggested they sign a lease as a precaution, she had a hunch she'd be fine if she rented from him. So why hadn't she agreed to the offer?

Lynette's voice drifted under the bathroom door and it sounded as if they'd moved into the kitchen now. Claire didn't want to hide out in the lavatory, but she didn't want Lynette to drag her into the argument, either. They had to work out their own issues.

It soon became obvious that the conversation was going to take a while, so Claire meandered out of the bathroom and into the living room. She snuggled into the comfortable couch and began to thumb through a magazine when Frank joined her, shaking and panting. Claire patted his head and tried to calm him.

"It's okay, boy. I don't like hearing them fight, either." As if on cue, Lynette's voice rose and she started to cry.

Claire empathized with the woman; her wedding and dreams had been shattered. Lynette's motivation seemed more about status and Jeff's money than about his love.

"Why don't you want to get married?" Lynette asked loudly. Their voices echoed from the large kitchen.

"Because I was marrying you for the wrong reasons," Jeff said. "You deserve to have someone who loves you, I mean really loves you. And I know you wanted to marry me for the wrong reasons, too. Lynette, you have a lot going for you. You'll find someone else."

The doorbell rang. Now who was about to join the party? Claire waited for Jeff to answer, but when he didn't make a move toward the living room, she got up and padded to the foyer. When she opened the door, she gasped. Black Eagle stood there, ramrod straight, with his cowboy hat tilted.

How had he known where she was? Claire pushed her feet into Pam's too large boots and walked outside with Frank glued to her leg. "It's not a good time to come inside. Lynette's over here and things are rather loud."

"I saw her car. You want to go for a walk?" he asked. When she nodded, he stepped aside to allow room for Claire to pass him.

"Let's go to the stable," she suggested. "I'm sure you want to see Mario."

"I do," he said. They walked toward the horses and Frank followed. "How's he doing?"

"Getting better. He had an eye infection in both eyes. We have to bring him back to Raleigh for a follow-up appointment, but I feel certain that he'll keep his eyesight. He's a lucky colt. Someone must have been watching over him at the marsh pond." A thought occurred to her. "Do you think it was my father—I mean Robert?"

"It's okay if you still call him your father. You always called him that. Yes, I think he looked out for Mario. He looks after all the horses on Pony Island."

"I felt his presence the first time I was on the island, the night I stayed out there. I bet he looked after me, too."

"I'm sure he did."

"I'm glad he's buried out there and not in a regular graveyard." She smiled awkwardly. "He'd hate that." She wanted to allow Black Eagle back into her life, but some unwanted, leftover resistance prevented that from happening.

"I'm sorry about how things turned out with your mom leaving." He turned away for a moment. "I missed you." When he turned back, Claire noticed his eyes were wet. "I have something that belongs to you." He pulled Claire's pewter mustang necklace from his pocket.

"My necklace! Where did you find it?" She held out her hand, but he smiled gravely and motioned for her to lift her hair. He latched the necklace behind her neck.

"I found it on the island. I looked down and there it was. I knew it was yours because I gave it to you."

She looked puzzled. "My father gave it to me. I remember."

Black Eagle shook his head. "No, Claire. I gave it to you. I brought it home one day after a trip into town. I had carved a horse's head and traded it so I could give you the necklace as a birthday gift. I had no money, and I wanted you to have something special from me. I had an odd feeling your mother might take off with you."

The distant memory cleared like dissipating fog. He was right. She had always assumed Robert Kincaid had given her the necklace, but only because she barely remembered a man latching it around her neck. She had automatically assumed it was Robert.

"Thank you." She reached forward and hugged him, and then kissed him on his wrinkled cheek.

"Why don't you come to the house Tuesday night and meet the rest of your family? Robin wants to see you."

Claire thought about that and decided she was finally ready. "Thanks, I'd like that."

They meandered back to Black Eagle's truck and Claire hugged him goodbye. After he'd driven away, she reluctantly walked up the sidewalk to the front porch, in no hurry to return to the tension in the house. When she reached the front porch, she didn't expect to run smack into Lynette, who had thrown the door open to leave.

"You're a selfish jerk, Jeff," Lynette yelled as they collided. She turned on Claire like a cornered dog. "As I said, I want you out of my rental unit tomorrow." Her voice quavered with anger.

"And like I said earlier, I'm not relocating. Call a lawyer if you need to." Claire refused to back down to Lynette's demands. She'd had enough of her temperamental way. What she hadn't expected was the hurt that shot across Jeff's face.

He turned and walked inside.

"Jeff, wait," Claire called after him.

When he didn't respond and shut the door with a quiet but deafening click, Claire stood rooted on the porch.

"That's some way to treat a man who offered you his building for next to nothing." Lynette chuckled. "Yes, he told me all about it. Your relationship with him is already doomed." She climbed into her car, and as she peeled off, the tires kicked up gravel.

Claire glanced at the closed front door. She refused to let him walk away like that. They had come too far for him to give up on her that easily. She ignored Lynette's stare and tried the doorknob. Locked. She knocked on the door. When he didn't open it, she rang the bell. Still no response.

She dialed Jeff's number with her cell phone. No answer. She left him the first of many voice-mail messages.

Her stomach clenched and she felt like someone had used it for a punching bag. Reluctantly, she called Pam and asked if she'd take her home. Jeff's sister was eager to comply. In the meantime, until Pam got there, Claire sat on the ground, wrapped her arms around her knees, and gasped for breath. This couldn't be happening. Perhaps Lynette was right and they were doomed. His stubborn pride could very possibly be the end of them.

# CHAPTER TWENTY-FIVE

"Pass me a beer, Donovan," Jeff commanded. The past few days without Claire had been miserable.

With a questioning glance, the bartender opened a bottle and slid it to Jeff. Steve Jones, one of Jeff's rangers, walked up and sat alongside him.

"What are you doin' here, Jeff? Aren't you supposed to be home taking care of Mario?"

"He's on my sister's watch tonight." Jeff took a long gulp and then turned toward his friend.

"So I guess the dog owner gets away with a measly fine for breaking the leash law, huh?" Steve asked.

"Unfortunately, that's all we can do." Jeff didn't like it anymore than Steve did. "Mario almost lost his life because of him, and then his eyesight." Jeff shook his head.

"I'm sorry," Steve said. "It was dumb luck."

"Dumb luck. There's justice for you." Jeff took another long pull from his bottle.

"Well, there's good news." Steve flagged the bartender and ordered a club sandwich and fries for dinner. "Bob called it quits.

He took down his ferry sign today. Seems he couldn't handle the pressure from the bad write-ups in the newspaper."

Jeff made an effort not to reveal any emotion on his face. "Paper? I never saw the articles. Guess I was too busy trying to save Mario's eyesight to notice." Jeff rubbed his tired eyes. He was suffering from a severe case of sleep deprivation. Claire hadn't been there lately to help him with the colt. He had also worked on the island all day today, playing catch-up. Springtime, with all the birth control administration, was always busy.

"Sorry for complaining," Jeff said. "It's been a rough couple of days."

"No problem. So how did the talk with Lynette go?" He pointed at Jeff's beer. "You never drink alcohol. This must be bad."

Jeff didn't bother to ask how Steve knew about the conversation with Lynette. "She didn't handle it all that well. Do you want to hear the worst part? I'm not upset about her, I'm disappointed in Claire."

"How so?" Steve thanked the bartender as he set the plate of food in front of him. He picked up his sandwich and took a large bite.

Jeff grabbed a French fry off his plate. Paybacks were great. "I thought she was interested in me. For the first time ever, I thought I'd finally met the right one. Heck, I left my bride at the altar because of her."

"Correction, you didn't leave your bride anywhere. Jim ended the wedding with his announcement."

"I swear I was standing up there trying to figure out how to stop the ceremony. I wasn't going to go through with it." Jeff grabbed another fry and Steve didn't stop him.

"You still haven't answered my question. What did Claire do? Why are you in here drinking a beer instead of talking to her?"

Jeff gulped another swallow of beer to postpone the conversation, even if it were only a few seconds longer. "I offered to rent my building to her because Lynette wants her out. Claire refuses to move. If she doesn't believe in me enough to rent my building, how well does that bode for our relationship?"

"Why do you care if she moves into your building, or where her studio is?" Steve frowned. "So what if she declined your offer? You need to ask yourself why that matters." Steve took another mouthful of his sandwich and continued talking with his mouth full. "It sounds like your pride talking. The issue here isn't her, it's you."

Jeff stared at him. "What do you mean? Of course I care where she rents. She's indirectly admitting she doesn't have the confidence that we'll make it as a couple. She thinks when we break up she'll be in the same position she's in now, renting from somebody who doesn't want her there."

Steve shook his head. "First of all, you don't know what she's thinking until you ask her. Second, let her ponder your offer, and then leave it up to her. Be satisfied with her decision, whatever that might be."

"That's not as easy as it sounds." Jeff folded his arms across his chest in frustration.

"She's an independent one, and you best remember that she likes things to be her idea. My wife is the same way."

"Independent. What does that have to do with renting my building?"

"Because you got mad when she said no. That's controlling, Jeff. It's none of your business who she rents from. Sure, your offer was a nice gesture, but you set your mind on a certain idea and you don't budge. Again, this is about you, not her." Steve slid his almost empty plate away. Jeff grabbed the remainder of the fries and shoved them three at a time into his mouth.

"Haven't you eaten?" Steve asked.

Jeff shook his head. "Nope. I was too busy feeling sorry for myself. Thanks, Steve, for showing up and proving I've been a real jerk."

"My pleasure." Steve stood and punched Jeff lightly on his upper arm. "Anytime you need a reminder, just ask."

Jeff fervently hoped Claire would be forgiving. With all the phone calls he'd ignored from her, he wouldn't be surprised if she'd given up on him. He wouldn't blame her a bit if she had.

*** 

The next morning, Claire walked downstairs to the studio. Shirley had taken a few days off, so they hadn't had a chance to talk since the canceled wedding. She couldn't say she looked forward to the exchange. Although Shirley was wise and Claire usually welcomed their conversations, right now she wanted to be alone. She wondered how much the older woman had heard from the gossip hotline, and prepared herself mentally for the usually welcomed advice.

When Claire walked through the studio door, Shirley handed her a mug of seeping green tea.

"So, sweetheart, is everything all right between you and Jeff?"

Claire swirled the teabag around the perimeter of the mug before she answered. She wasn't surprised if Shirley knew exactly where she had stayed Saturday night, and how quickly that had ended. "No, I spent the last couple of nights at home." She sniffed the air in search of her mother's always reassuring perfume. But even her mother didn't want to be present for this conversation.

"At least he ended up not marrying Lynette. That means there's hope for the two of you."

Claire nodded. "True. I never imagined this scenario. I thought for sure he would get married."

Shirley reached out and touched Claire's hand. "I know, sweetie. I'm glad he came to his senses. Jeff and Lynette were so wrong for each other, and most everyone saw it but him."

"Lynette has shown up twice now and created a scene both times," Claire explained, thinking about Lynette blocking the driveway with her car, and the horrible argument that unfolded in Jeff's house. She might as well tell Shirley the details because she was bound to find out eventually anyway. Maybe Claire would feel better if she talked to someone she trusted. "Jeff and Lynette argued for two hours Sunday night. I don't believe she really wants him, but her pride is wounded."

"I bet you're right," Shirley empathized. "Nobody likes rejection, and I bet that's exactly how she sees it. And bless her heart, she's rather spoiled. She's used to getting everything she wants." Shirley took a sip of tea. "She'll get over it. Keep your eye on the reward."

"That's good advice, but something else happened." Claire's throat thickened. She pretended to drink from her mug but the tea was unusually hot. At least the mug provided a great prop to hide behind until she felt able to talk again.

Claire cleared her throat. "Lynette stormed out of the house and bumped into me, and we had a scene outside Jeff's front door. She demanded I move out of the studio the following day, and I refused. I reacted without thinking about how Jeff would take that."

"Wait a minute. I'm missing something here." Shirley leaned forward with obvious interest. "Why would Jeff be upset about that? He doesn't want you to leave town, and if you vacated this building, that's what would happen."

"You mean the gossip mill left out a juicy piece?" Claire managed a weak smile to soften her words. "One of Jeff's tenants is moving out today. He offered to lease his place to me, the big yellow and white building on Front Street. He got upset when Lynette demanded I move and I refused to clear out of this building. He thinks I don't trust him, and that I rejected him personally."

Shirley's face brightened. "Have you seen the inside of Jeff's building? The view is remarkable. It's also in the middle section of Front Street instead of at the end, like this one is. That would be a good move."

"Didn't you hear what I said? We aren't moving. I declined his offer."

"Why did you do that?"

"Because I don't want to rely on a man, even if it means I have to fight Lynette to stay here." Without thinking, Claire drank from the mug and burnt her tongue. "Ouch!" Shirley always made tea the perfect temperature, so Claire had forgotten it was hot.

Shirley grinned as if Claire had gotten what she deserved. "So you think you'll lose your independence. I see," the older woman said in her grandmotherly tone. "Relying on good people doesn't mean you have to give up your independence, sweet child. True independence is when you select who your friends are, who you allow to help you, and who brings positive experiences into your life. You have to build a team. You can't do everything yourself. In fact, you'll be much happier and more successful if you allow others to help and guide you."

"I guess, but people aren't always trustworthy," Claire said. "I mean, look at my mom. She never told me the truth about my father. All my life I believed he didn't love me, and maybe that's why he'd never found me. Then, add my cheating ex-boyfriends to the mix, and that further proves my point about people."

"Not really. Look around and you'll realize you already have some good friends in this town."

Claire glanced up at Shirley. "I know; I guess I need to be reminded from time to time. You're one of the best teammates I have."

"I feel the same way about you. This is a new journey, sweetie. Don't use an old road map to get where you want to go, because circumstances change."

For a moment there, Shirley reminded her of her mother, except her mother's lessons tried to prove men weren't worthy. Like the time when her mother stated Claire was wasting her time trying to find her father. Boy had she been wrong. Right now, Shirley's wisdom was exactly what Claire needed to hear.

"You're a smart woman." Claire leaned forward and gave her a hug. "I'm glad I have you as a friend."

The bell above the door tinkled and in walked Lynette. "I see you haven't started to pack yet." She headed straight for their table. Her body language screamed that she was a woman bent on causing trouble.

Claire winked at Shirley and turned back to Lynette. "Actually, we plan to start packing today. I'll be out by the end of the week."

"Where do you plan to move?" Lynette flashed a cocky smile. "I just spoke to a client of mine, and he wants to rent Jeff's building for the full amount."

Claire's breath caught. With great difficulty, she kept the shocked expression off her face and refused to reward Lynette's malicious attempt to disrupt her morning.

"Thanks for the information, Lynette," Claire said calmly.

"Oh, just so you know, I stayed at Jeff's house last night." Lynette giggled like a schoolgirl. She whirled around and left the studio.

"Well, I'll be."

"Shirley," Claire said, "I'm sure there's a logical explanation." She only wished she believed it herself. Despite her confident tone, her heart hammered double-time in her chest.

*＊*

Claire decided not to risk the possibility of Jeff ignoring her call this time. She was unsure how to find him on the island, if he was even there, but then she reasoned springtime was his busy time. He'd be out there, somewhere. She headed straight to Jenni's ferryboat.

"Oh, so you do still exist," Jenni teased.

"Very funny. I need a ride over to Pony Island right away. When's your next trip?"

"For you, we can make a trip right now. What's up?" Jenni asked as her brother walked off to ready the boat.

"I need to talk with Jeff before he signs a lease for his building. According to Lynette, she's found someone interested in renting from him."

Claire wanted to rent that building. And she was ready for a relationship with him, one based on trust as Shirley had suggested earlier.

"Let me guess, Lynette evicted you again."

"She did, although she can't legally enforce it. I've decided I'd rather move the studio. Jeff's building is a better location."

Jenni shot her a knowing grin. "And in a way, you're making a commitment to Jeff. Good for you."

A commitment. "That's right. That also means Lynette's building will be free for you to rent." Claire grinned at her perfectly executed plan to change the subject. "It's an ideal location for the coffee shop you wanted to open."

Jenni blanched. "I don't know if I'm ready to do that."

"I've been through starting a business, so I can help you." It was her turn to assist a friend in need. She felt happy knowing she had friends to help.

"You'd do that?" Jenni seemed surprised.

"Of course. We can start by talking to my banker in Morrisboro." Claire was determined to help her friend's dream come true.

"Thanks, Claire. I mean it."

"No problem." Her offer to help to Jenni was the easy part. She still had to admit to Jeff that she wanted to accept his help, despite Lynette's confession to having spent the night with him.

# CHAPTER TWENTY-SIX

Jeff had to be on Pony Island somewhere. The place was only so big. Unfortunately, he wasn't at the dock, the nearby dunes, or the marsh pond. That left the area by the graveyard, where Black Eagle had secretly buried Robert Kincaid.

Sure enough, as soon as Claire crossed the water and walked around a dune, she saw Jeff standing about a hundred feet away, frowning. She silently watched as he picked up his cell phone and started to dial, and then he hung up. He repeated his behavior two more times before he shoved the phone into his pocket.

Claire stepped closer, unsure if he'd be receptive to seeing her again.

As she approached, he looked up. "Claire! What are you doing here?" It seemed to take a moment for him to collect his wits, and then he covered the distance between them with surprising speed. "I'm so glad to see you." He picked her up and hugged her close to his chest.

When he set her down, Claire stepped away. While she was glad to see him, she felt betrayed at the thought of Lynette spending the night at his house. The vision of him holding the woman, consoling her, made her guarded. Sure, she wanted to make amends with him, but before she could be receptive to his affection, he needed to do some explaining.

He backed off, obviously in reaction to her wariness. "Why are you out here?" he asked with concern.

"I wanted to talk with you. Lynette paid me a visit at the studio today."

At the mention of Jeff's ex-fiancée, he visibly stiffened. Did his reaction mean Lynette had told the truth? Had she spent the night with him?

"What did she say?" He backed farther away and put some space between them.

"She said a lot of things. For one, she took delight in informing me that one of her clients is interested in renting your building." She held her breath for a moment in anticipation of his response.

"That's true. She left me a voice mail."

Claire waited a moment for him to continue, to enlighten her with the details. She hoped he said something to break the unbearable silence, but he didn't.

"Are you going to rent to someone else?" she asked. When he scowled, she cringed.

"That's all you care about? And I thought you came here to make things right between us." His clenched jaw started to pulsate.

Claire inhaled a deep breath. "Of course I came out here for that reason. I wanted to get the easy part out of the way first, the part that doesn't matter as much." She stepped toward him. "But Lynette also said something else."

His face hardened. "Don't believe anything that woman says."

"Did she spend the night at your house?"

He didn't answer for what seemed forever. "Yes, she did." Before he could elaborate, she backed away. "Claire—"

"I've heard enough." She wouldn't cry, wouldn't shed a tear in front of Jeff. No way. She spun around and fled. Her eyes burned and her heart hurt with a deep, stabbing ache. A memory flashed before her, a painful recollection of a man who had disappointed a little girl, one who cried herself to sleep night after night, waiting for her daddy to comfort her. Why was she so unfit for men to love?

Someone grabbed her arm and pulled her around. Through her tears and anger, she saw a gentle man reaching out to hold her. "Claire." When she didn't respond, he said again, "Claire. It's okay."

The man hugged her so tightly she could barely breathe. His warmth permeated her frozen being and thawed her fears. He felt so comforting, so loving, that she was unable to resist his embrace.

Eventually, after she'd calmed down enough to recognize Jeff again, he pulled her down onto the sand. "I didn't get a chance to explain what happened."

"I … I don't want to know."

"Sweetheart, everything's fine. Lynette let herself into my house and refused to leave. She threw a king-sized tantrum, so I left. I spent the night at my sister's house. And my locks will be changed today."

Claire looked up into his aqua eyes. "You were at Pam's house?"

"Have faith in me. I'm finished with Lynette. I repeat, finished. I'm holding the person I want. I love you."

"I …" She hiccupped. "I love you, too."

Jeff bent down and gave her the most tender kiss she'd ever experienced. He tasted like a tangy blend of salt and spearmint. Claire laughed. "I caught you with gum in your mouth."

He kissed her again. "So you did," he whispered. Eventually, he pulled back a few inches from her face and said, "As far as my rental building, are you suggesting that you're interested?"

"Yes. I'm ready to make a commitment."

He smiled. "A commitment sounds serious. Does that mean what I think it does?"

She nodded. "I'm ready to stop hiding behind my past, ready to confront the uncertainty of the future, and ready to handle you." She giggled.

"I like the way that sounds. Are you able to trust me?"

"Yes," she said without hesitation.

"Then my building is yours."

What a relief. But she still had one more issue from the past to deal with, and it was a big one. She had agreed to meet her new family tonight, at the risk of their rejection.

***

Claire stopped her car a mile from Black Eagle's house.

"What's the matter?" Jeff asked.

"I don't know. I can't go through with it." She ran her hands continuously over the steering wheel.

"It's okay. You don't have to go if you don't want."

Good move on Jeff's part. "You're a smart man. Letting me off the hook makes me determined to follow through with this. But I'm afraid."

"Of what?" He reached across and took her hands in his.

"I don't know. Maybe of being vulnerable. What if he abandons me again?" Her throat constricted and it suddenly became difficult to swallow.

"Claire, he didn't abandon you the first time. Your mother took you away." Jeff pulled her into his arms. "She never told him where you were. I'm sure Black Eagle has been troubled by that all this time. The man loves you."

She stared at him. "You're probably right." She paused to allow Jeff's words to absorb into her brain. "He didn't abandon me," she repeated. "I just thought he did. I have to find a way to let that go, so I can enjoy him now."

"That's right. If you don't go over there, you'll be hiding from your dream, your family. Face your demon, Claire. It's scary to feel vulnerable, but it's lonely when you hide from reality. I'm here with you."

Grateful she had brought Jeff, Claire gave him a lingering kiss before she turned back to grab the steering wheel. Tonight was a pivotal point in their relationship. She believed in Jeff enough to share her family reunion with him, and to share her fear. She pulled back onto the road and drove to Black Eagle's.

As Claire parked her car in the driveway, Black Eagle walked outside the house. An older woman followed closely behind him, and then a younger one who looked a lot like Claire. When Claire and Jeff climbed from the car, Black Eagle gave her a welcoming hug and warmly shook Jeff's hand.

"This is my wife, Judy, and my daughter, Robin," Black Eagle said. "This is my other daughter, Claire."

Judy reached out warmly and shook hands with Claire. Robin leaned forward and hugged her.

The level of love and acceptance Claire felt surprised her. "It's … it's nice to meet you both," Claire said, her voice quivering. Jeff put his arm around her and drew her in close. The heat of his embrace compounded her feeling of security.

"My father told me so many stories about you while I was growing up," Robin said. "You're almost famous."

Claire looked at Black Eagle and noticed the pride on his face. "He's a great man. I have plenty of stories about him, too."

"I'd love to exchange memories with you sometime," Robin whispered, clearly emotional.

"Please come in the house," Judy said in a welcoming and motherly tone. When a breeze kicked up and exposed her knees, she smoothed her dress before leading the way into a small but tidy home. "Make yourself comfortable. Can I get you something to drink? Iced tea or lemonade?"

"Tea sounds great, thanks." Claire stepped into the earthy-looking living room with its walls covered in handmade baskets and Native American blankets. Black Eagle followed Judy out of the room to fetch the drinks and left Robin behind to talk with Claire and Jeff.

"I can't believe I finally get to meet my sister," Robin said.

*My sister.*

"I've always wanted a brother or sister, but Dad said he didn't deserve another child, because he lost you."

"I'm sorry," Claire offered. She was amazed the woman didn't resent her. Was guilt the reason her own mother never remarried or had more children? Maybe she had punished herself for not telling Claire the truth about Black Eagle.

"It wasn't your fault. Have a seat." Robin pointed to a loveseat and sat down in an old rocker that looked oddly familiar.

Jeff and Claire nestled close together and she was again grateful that he had agreed to come with her. "I've always wanted a brother or sister too," Claire said, now able to talk in a full sentence without her voice quavering. To her, happiness equaled family and friends. "It was always just my mother and me, and our holidays were lonely. I dreamt of big get-togethers, food everywhere, and kids running all around. When my mom died, I thought I was alone." She studied Robin's black hair and young, healthy skin.

"You have a family now." Robin truly seemed happy about that. "I'm not married and I don't have tons of kids running around, but we do get together once in awhile, and always on holidays." She studied Jeff and Claire for a moment, as if she hadn't heard the most recent gossip and wondered why they were together.

"I have a bunch of relatives that I'm willing to share," Jeff offered. "Between your new family and mine, you'll have more get-togethers than you ever thought possible."

He seemed so sure about their future. It surprised her, but she felt just as confident about him.

"Even in my dreams, I never dared to wish for all this," Claire said, reflecting back on the day the ferry had left her stranded on Pony Island. She'd wanted to find her father so he could fill that empty place in her heart marked "family." She looked around at the people who sat in the room, and the ones who carried drinks in and placed them on the coffee table in front of her. Shirley had been right. Once Claire had allowed safe and trustworthy people into the small circle she'd drawn around herself, she felt much happier.

The visit went by too quickly. When Claire got home late that night, after dropping Jeff off at his house, happiness overflowed from places she didn't know existed. Not only had she found independence and its true meaning, she had found a sense of family. She'd also found a man she loved, a man who had willingly led her into the scary depths of her fears and taught her how to overcome them.

She walked to the pantry, opened the door, and admired her progress. She moved another few cans out of place, which made over half of them now. Before long, nothing would remain in alphabetical order. "I'd say I've come a long way."

Then she noticed a disturbing new trend. All the vegetables were grouped together, all the soup cans together, and the same with the tomato sauce. She quickly interspersed them.

The doorbell rang as she finished. When Claire opened her apartment door, the man who refused to leave her mind stood there with an armful of fresh-cut flowers, most likely picked from his sister's yard. Her future included Jeff and it looked bright indeed.

# *EPILOGUE*

**Six Months Later**

The sky held puffy white clouds, the air stirred with a gentle breeze, and the water sparkled with sun diamonds strewn across its surface. Claire couldn't have wished for a more perfect day to have her wedding.

Kayla, Jeff's niece, led Mario down a sandy aisle, defined only by the folding chairs filled with wedding guests. Jeff's nephew, Will, gripped Frank's leash and followed a good distance behind his sister.

With her hair pulled back in a chignon, Claire looked pure and virtuous, her innocence accented by the simple but elegant satin gown. With spaghetti straps that exposed her olive skin, delicate beadwork that complemented her femininity, and a slender cut that flattered her petite curves, the gown looked as though it had been custom-made just for her. She focused on the wedding even as she remembered another wedding not too long ago.

Uplifting classical music, a lovely piano solo with a hint of cello as accompaniment, wafted through the air from a nearby boom box. Not a typical wedding march, but one she and Jeff had picked out together.

Claire stood at the head of the aisle as the warm, salty breeze blew against her face and upper body. She held onto Black Eagle's arm with the grace of an angel. Her dream wedding had finally come, and with the added bonus of her real father to give her away. Black Eagle, with his long salt-and-pepper hair braided neatly behind, had tears in his eyes. Claire found the vulnerable side of his personality appealing, and understood her mother's attraction to the man and the dilemma she had once faced.

As if the act of thinking about her mother had conjured her up, Claire smelled a blend of her familiar perfume mixed with Robert Kincaid's spicy cologne. Black Eagle seemed to notice it too, because he winked at Claire.

She almost floated toward the altar. Guests stood to watch, smiling, so happy that she and Jeff were about to marry. Seagulls squealed their approval as they circled above.

Her eyes wandered over peoples' faces, not registering who half of them were, until her gaze rested on Lynette. *What is she doing here? Please don't make a scene*, Claire silently pleaded.

Black Eagle led her to Jeff, whose aqua eyes glittered with unshed tears, and his smile revealed his happiness. He wore his love openly, clearly not caring who saw his feelings for his bride-to-be. She felt as if she were finally awakening from a long slumber.

Her half-sister Robin stood nearby as her maid of honor, and as bridesmaids, her new friend Jenni, Jeff's sister Pam, and his cousin Paula stood together. Shirley sat in the front row. By letting these people into her life, along with Jeff's family and Black Eagle's family, she'd found a true sense of belonging.

Then the music quieted. The minister began to talk. Claire tried to focus on the man who stood beside her, but her thoughts returned to the woman watching. Lynette had badmouthed her to most of the town, but fortunately Claire's photography business remained strong. So why had she come today? Did she plan some sort of revenge?

Jeff took Claire's hand and held her eyes with his. He seemed to sense her nervousness. Marrying him was the last step in allowing the old wounds to heal. Those wounds would never go away entirely, but she could live with the scars. She reminded herself that Jeff was safe. He wouldn't abandon her.

The minister continued with the vows, and when it was time for Claire to say, "I do," Mario whinnied. Everyone chuckled, and Jeff leaned forward and whispered, "Trust the horses, Claire. They're always right."

She stared deep into his eyes and saw the stability, warmth, and love that glistened in them. Before she knew it, they kissed. She was his wife; she had done it. She had given up what she had originally thought of as independence, for what she now understood to be freedom and love.

After the ceremony, Jeff's mother walked up to Claire and squeezed her in a tight hug. "Welcome to our family. I can't wait to have more grandchildren." Jeff's mother was overbearing at times, but her biggest fault, if you could call it that, was she wanted her son to be happy. Claire intended to make his mother's wish come true.

"I'm glad to be included," Claire said. "I've always wanted a big family." She looked around at all the people making their way toward them.

Her new mother-in-law kindly pulled away. "It's time to greet everyone."

Everyone. That included Lynette.

As the wedding party stood in the receiving line, Jeff's ex-fiancée approached, actually smiling. Claire tried to hide her discomfort until she reminded herself that the wedding was over and Lynette had behaved. And she appeared friendly.

Claire returned the smile to welcome her. "Lynette."

"I owe you an apology." Lynette reached forward and took Claire's hand. "On some level, I've always known Jeff and I weren't meant to be, but I guess I didn't want to accept the truth. I blamed you for interfering." She glanced at Jeff, who stood next to Claire with an obvious mixture of confusion about Lynette and protectiveness toward Claire. "Actually, I owe you both an apology. Jeff, I thought we loved each other, but I now realize I didn't have a clue about love. I'm sorry about that. I just wanted to get married; I'm tired of being alone. And Claire, I'm sorry for saying bad things about you."

"It's okay, Lynette. Thanks." Claire let go of Jeff's hand and leaned forward to hug her. She was receptive and hugged Claire back.

"I'm truly sorry," Lynette said again. She let go of Claire and looked at them both. "Congratulations."

"We appreciate the apology," Jeff said. He put his hand on her shoulder. "I'm sorry, too. I wish you the best of luck. Thanks for coming today." Wedding guests pressed closer, obviously wanting to overhear the exchange.

"I wouldn't have missed it," Lynette said. "We've known each other for a long time." She backed up a couple of steps. "Listen, I'm holding up the line. No hard feelings?"

"No," Claire and Jeff said at the same time. What a nice gesture, apologizing, and Lynette seemed to mean what she'd said.

"You two make a great couple." Lynette walked off with a spring in her step. Maybe she'd felt pressure to marry Jeff, too.

When everyone finished their congratulations, Jeff leaned forward and whispered in Claire's ear. "Now that we're married, can we try to make a baby tonight?"

Claire beamed. "Of course. We can practice as often as you want."

"Practice what?" Black Eagle approached. The man was not only a horse whisperer but could read people as well.

"Nothing, Dad." Claire winked at Jeff and then turned back to Black Eagle. "You stick with the horses and leave the rest to me."

~~The End~~

## *ABOUT THE AUTHOR*

Lori Hayes lives in North Carolina with her family, horse, and two overly affectionate cats. She grew up in St. Louis, Missouri, which she loved, but moved to the coast because she treasures being close to the beach and mountains. If she had to pick one as a favorite, she'd choose the beach without a doubt. Family, photography, writing and horses are her passions. Please sign up for her newsletter by visiting her website at LoriHayesAuthor.com.

Made in the USA
Middletown, DE
17 August 2023

36850547R00168